To Love a Lady

Dollar Princess Book One

Gabrielle Meyer

Belle May Press

For Maud Hart Lovelace

My favorite author and kindred spirit

1

October 22, 1882
New York City

I knew how to blend into the dangerous tenement neighborhood of Five Points to stay safe. But here, just outside the Metropolitan Opera House on opening night, among the city's wealthiest citizens, I stood out like a thistle among the roses—except no one really saw me.

"Buy a flower?" I asked a fashionable lady as she walked past me in a fine gown. The bustle was draped with yards of purple silk, which trailed along the dusty street behind her, bouncing with each step.

The woman didn't bother to acknowledge me as she stepped closer to the man escorting her down the street.

A sharp wind sliced along Broadway, and I wrapped my thin shawl a little closer, pretending I was cold, when the truth was, I didn't want anyone to see the state of my gown. The only one I owned. Stained, worn, and drab.

"Buy a flower?" I asked a distinguished gentleman in a silk top hat, offering the same fabric flower. Though I had scrubbed my hands before leaving Mulberry Street, my fingernails were stained with dirt. I tried to hide them beneath the petals of the flower.

"No, thank you," the man said, without glancing in my direction.

I tried not to feel discouraged, though I had been outside the opera house for two hours and had only sold two flowers.

Darkness had fallen upon the city, though the streetlamps offered a soft glow for me to see the beautiful people passing by. Dozens of gleaming carriages lined West 39th and 40th Streets and a trolley drove down Broadway. Even at this time of night, the streets were busy with traffic. I should be on Mulberry Street, piecing together shirtwaists, but I could not pass up opening night of the newly built opera house and the opportunity to make a little extra money.

Ushers in black tuxedos opened the doors of the opera house, and people began to stream out onto the sidewalk.

There were hundreds of men in black evening suits and top hats, with capes and walking sticks. And just as many beautiful women in gowns of every imaginable color with jewelry that sparkled under the lamps. My eyes feasted upon the ornate stitchwork and expensive fabrics.

The conversation hummed with excitement, talk of the opera, and the dinner parties being hosted throughout the city that night.

This was the moment I'd been waiting for, though I wasn't the only hawker on the street. I held up my satin rose, one of dozens I had made in secret these past few months, and competed for attention.

"Buy a flower?" I asked, holding it up from one person to the next. "Buy a flower?"

People pushed and prodded as if I was not there.

"Buy a flower, ma'am?"

"Yes, of course," a lady finally said, without even looking at me or the flower. She wore a stunning mauve evening gown with a thick bustle, long train, and a sparkling diamond tiara on her dark hair. She was easily in her upper forties but carried herself with a youthful elegance. "Give her a dollar, Alec, and then we must find our carriage. What a crush this is. I can scarcely breathe."

My lips parted in surprise. A dollar? I had been selling my flowers for a nickel apiece.

"That's too much, ma'am," I told her, conscious of my course Irish accent beside her refined American one. "A nickel will do."

She didn't seem to hear me as she turned to a woman beside her. "What a stunning rendition of *Faust*, don't you think, Mrs. Vanderbilt?" she said. "Signor Italo Campanini was brilliant. And to finally have a box at the opera! What a coup. Mrs. Astor must be steaming mad tonight."

People bumped into me from all sides, pushing me closer to the gentleman instructed to pay me.

He pulled a wallet from inside his suitcoat, though it wasn't easy for him to move his arm, as he, too, was being pushed. "A dollar, did she say?"

"'Tis too much," I said as our gazes met. "I'm askin' only for a nickel."

"What did you say?" He half-smiled as he frowned and leaned closer. He was at least twenty years younger than the woman—perhaps her son?

It was loud but surely he heard me. "A nickel, sir."

His frown disappeared, but his smile remained. There was kindness in his blue eyes—a kindness I didn't often see from gentlemen of his ilk.

"I don't have a nickel." His voice was cultured and sophisticated. "So a dollar will have to do."

"I'll make you some change." I started to dig into my pocket, but he put up his hand to stop me.

"Keep the change."

"Have you found our carriage, Alec?" The lady turned back to us. She paused as she seemed to see me for the first time. Her gray eyes penetrated mine as she looked at me from head to foot and then back up again. "She's beautiful. Look at her, Alec, isn't she beautiful?"

The man glanced away, as if embarrassed by her statement.

"Look, Alec," the woman insisted as she moved her head to try to get a better view of me. "She's exactly what I've been looking for."

"Aunt Maude," the man said to her, "this is neither the time nor the place."

"But look at her," she said again as she touched his arm.

He finally returned his gaze to me. His eyes were the bluest I'd ever seen, and his dark brown hair curled out from underneath his silk top hat in a playful manner, though it did nothing to make him appear childish.

Men like him didn't look at me the way he did—and I felt ashamed of my old dress, my lack of a hat, my unwashed hair, and the dirt smudges on my skin.

I turned my gaze to the ground.

"Isn't she beautiful?" the lady asked. "Under all that filth, of course. Just think what we could do with her."

My cheeks burned with humiliation. What did she think she could do with me?

I no longer wanted their money or their attention.

Clutching the satin rose, I tried to turn away, but there was nowhere to go. I was trapped by the crowd.

"Aunt Maude," he said with admonishment in his voice, "you've embarrassed her. And what if someone hears you?"

The lady glanced over her shoulder, as if remembering where she was. "Of course." She moved a little closer to me.

I tried to back up.

"What is your name?" she asked me, her gaze intent upon my face. She did not look unkind—but she did not look welcoming, either.

I shook my head.

"Don't worry," the man said to me, "she means no harm."

The lady was attractive, though age had begun to erase her youthful complexion. Wrinkles had set in around her eyes, but what she lacked in beauty she made up for in style.

"I don't mean to scare you," she said, clearly trying to control her voice. "I have been looking for someone exactly like you for months."

Again, the man looked away.

"Will you call on me?" the lady asked, handing me a card. "Tomorrow morning at ten?"

Call on her?

I finally found my voice. "For a job, ma'am?"

"Something like that." She smiled, as if to reassure me. "How old are you?"

I swallowed, hoping my voice worked. "One and twenty in June, ma'am."

"Twenty-one?" she lifted her sculpted eyebrows. "I would not guess a day over eighteen. You're so delicate and youthful-looking."

I had never spoken more than a few words to a lady like her before, except for once, a very long time ago, and that seemed like a dream now.

But I had to tell this lady the truth. "I'm a pieceworker, ma'am, not a maid."

"I don't require either one." She lifted her chin and glanced around to see if anyone was watching us.

Thankfully, everyone seemed preoccupied with finding their carriages.

"You'll see on the card that I live at 800 Fifth Avenue. Don't be late." She nodded at the man—her nephew. "Give her enough fare for a cab tomorrow."

A cab? I'd never dreamed of riding in a cab.

Someone tore the lady's attention away again, and the nephew took a step closer to me. He still had his wallet out, so he removed a five-dollar bill and offered it to me, an apologetic look on his face. "You don't need to come, if you don't like," he said quietly. "Though you have nothing to worry about, if you do. Aunt Maude might be a little eccentric, but she's kind."

I swallowed hard as I stared at the money. It would take me almost three weeks, working ten to twelve hours a day, to earn five dollars. Even now, I would have to make an excuse as to why I wasn't at the kitchen table helping piece together shirtwaists.

"I-I can't take your money," I said.

He nudged it closer. "For your trouble."

I looked up into his blue-eyed gaze and found he was serious.

No one handed out free money. Everyone wanted something. Unless he felt pity for me—something I couldn't abide.

"If you come," he said, "use the money for a cab. If you don't come, consider it payment for the flower." He gently plucked the satin rose from my clenched hand and tucked the five-dollar bill in its place. "Her name is Mrs. Hill, by the way. Maude Hamilton Hill." He tipped his hat toward me, his white gloves gleaming. "And I'm Alexander Paxton-Hill, at your service."

No gentleman had ever introduced himself to me. I was both breathless and speechless at the weight of money in my hand and his handsome gaze upon me. "Keira O'Day," I finally managed to say.

"Kee-ra." He rolled my name slowly, with a smile, trying it out for the first time. "It's a pleasure to meet you, Miss O'Day."

I nodded, unsure what to say. I had no experience being introduced to a gentleman.

"If you'll excuse me," he said, "I must get Aunt Maude's carriage before she starts badgering you again. Perhaps you should sneak off while she's preoccupied with Mrs. Wilson."

He was teasing, but I sensed there was some truth in his words. What did Mrs. Hill want from me? If she didn't need a seamstress or a maid, what else did she require?

I moved away from the crowd of people, slipping the five dollars into the hidden pocket in my dress.

What would happen if I went to 800 Fifth Avenue tomorrow? Would I regret it for the rest of my life?

Or worse, would I regret *not* going?

I walked away from Chatham Square Station, where the elevated railway had carried me from Grand Central which was not far from the new Metropolitan Opera House. I was soon in the dilapidated Five Points neighborhood, on my way to Mulberry Street. The temperature had dropped, and the wind had picked up, carrying with it the stench of the tenements. Heaps of garbage, or homeless urchins, piled up in corners and between buildings. Rotten timbers bowed over doorways and buildings slanted at precarious angles.

I kept my gaze down with my shawl lifted over my head, trying to block out the sights and sounds of the only home I'd ever known—at least, within my memory. I hadn't always lived in Five Points. I had been born in London, though I suspected my surroundings there hadn't been much different. As a baby, I'd been handed over to Uncle Charlie and Aunt Orla, who had come by way of Ireland, and we'd left for America. They claimed me as their own, though they reminded me every day that I was simply one more mouth to feed. An unwanted burden, abandoned by a mother I only knew by name.

Nellie O'Day.

I tried to avoid the worst of Five Points at all costs, but our tenement was on Mulberry Street, in the heart of the neighborhood. Men smoked outside gambling dens, prostitutes stood in open doorways at brothels, and gang members lurked in alleyways. If it hadn't been for my cousin, Sean, a member of the Five Points Gang, I could not walk alone on this street at night.

I hurried to 36 Mulberry Street, one of many tenement buildings along this stretch of road and climbed up the two flights of stairs to our small apartment. Six of us lived in the two-room dwelling, consisting of a living space and a bedroom.

I opened the door into the main room and found Aunt Orla at the cutting table. She looked up, her wiry hair, once red, was now gray with age and exhaustion. "Where 'ave you been?"

No one knew I made fabric flowers and sold them outside fine establishments such as the Metropolitan Opera House. If they did, I would be forced to hand over the few nickels I made, the nickels that I hoped would one day get me out of Five Points.

"Out," I said to Aunt Orla, knowing she didn't care what I was doing or who I was with. The only thing she cared about was me piecing together my quota of shirtwaists for the day.

"You 'ave a pile tonight," she said, nodding at my worktable, where at least a dozen shirtwaists were waiting for me.

There were snores coming from the bedroom where the family took turns sleeping. I wouldn't be able to lay my head on the pallet until the shirtwaists were complete, which might not be until the sun rose in the morning. But that would be the time Uncle Charlie and my young cousins Patrick and Imogen woke up and took over the piecework.

One of my other cousins, Polly, sat at her table, staring at me with a scowl. She had hours of work ahead of her, too.

Sean had moved out two years ago, joining the Five Points Gang, and another of my cousins, Fiona, had married and moved to Orchard Street, in another tenement, less than a mile away. Though it could be a world away for the differences. Uncle Charlie had no wish to spend more money on rent to move us half a mile away. Fiona's apartment cost eight dollars a month—more money than I made with piecework.

The smell of boiled cabbage and ham clung to the air. It was a perpetual smell that never seemed to dissipate and, despite how tired I was of the food, it made my stomach growl because I had missed my supper. I'd have to go without food until breakfast tomorrow—which would be cabbage and potatoes.

Aunt Orla, Polly, and I were silent as we sat, long into the night, sewing.

My mind easily slipped to my encounter outside the Metropolitan Opera House and the kind blue eyes of Mr. Alexander Paxton-Hill.

His five-dollar bill sat heavy in my pocket, and I wondered what Aunt Orla would do if she knew it was there. I didn't even dare to touch it, for fear it would make a noise and draw unwanted attention.

I now had nine dollars and fifty cents to call my own. The rest was hidden under a loose floorboard in the back of the bedroom with my only other possession—a locket my mother had given to me and made my aunt and uncle promise to never sell.

Someday, I would take my money, and my locket, and I would leave New York City as far behind as possible. I would board a train and travel west, beyond the Mississippi River, to a place that was wide open and green. As I sewed, it was all I ever thought about. I painted colorful pictures in my mind of the little cabin I would live in by myself, the clear stream I would drink from, and the clean air I would breathe. To provide for myself, I would become a fashionable seamstress and sew clothing that would make people proud to wear it. My mind filled with the designs I would create. It was the only way to survive the grueling life in Five Points.

As the night progressed, I kept watch of the time. The minute hand moved slowly toward ten o'clock, the invitation burning in my mind. Whatever Mrs. Hill offered had to be better than what I currently had—yet, what if it wasn't decent? What if she had a proposition that would shame me?

But what was the worst that could happen? I would be embarrassed and leave, and I would never need to see her again.

The best that could happen—I didn't even want to imagine the possibilities. What if she offered me a job and a place to live in her home on Fifth Avenue? I rarely had reason to go to Fifth Avenue, but when I did, I was left speechless. The homes were so grand, the shops were opulent, and the streets were clean.

What if this was the opportunity I'd been hoping for my whole life?

But what if I was disappointed yet again?

"Keira?" Polly stood above me and tapped my shoulder. "You're daydreaming again. Breakfast."

I looked up and saw a hint of light in the eastern sky outside the single, cracked window in our apartment. It was nearly seven. Aunt Orla was setting plates at the table, which had been cleared of cuttings, and Uncle Charlie was just stepping out of the bedroom, yawning as he pulled his suspenders over his dingy white undershirt.

I quickly finished the last of my shirtwaists and folded the snowy white fabric to set it upon my pile. I stood and stretched. My neck and back were sore, and my stomach growled, but the nervous energy I felt banished my exhaustion.

My hand brushed against my hidden pocket, reminding me that I needed to find time to hide the money. I would have to wait until Aunt Orla and Polly were asleep, and the others were distracted with their work. Then I would slip it in with the other money I had saved.

"Where were you last night, duchess?" Uncle Charlie asked as he turned his bleary-eyed gaze on me and scratched his whiskered face.

My cheeks warmed at the nickname I'd been given as a little girl, when I'd vocalized my daydreams and begged for a pink ribbon for my fifth birthday.

"She won't say," Aunt Orla mumbled as she dished up plates of cabbage and potato, setting them down on the table with a clunk.

"'Ave you taken up with a man?" he asked me, frowning. "You know how I feel 'bout that."

I did know. I was too valuable for them to lose—though they complained that I ate their food and took up space in their apartment.

"Who is he?" Aunt Orla asked. "Not one o' Sean's friends, I hope."

"I haven't taken up with anyone," I said as I took a seat at the table.

"She probably went uptown to gawk at the swells," Polly said as she sashayed across the room with a mocking voice. At the age of sixteen, she was turning into a young lady, but just like her mother, she had little patience for me. "She likes to pretend she's one o' them, don't you know."

Patrick laughed, and Aunt Orla scowled, but little Imogen, just nine-years-old, looked at me with understanding in her pretty green eyes. Imogen liked beautiful things as much as I did but had learned early on not to voice them as I had.

"Always putting on airs," Aunt Orla said to me, "ever since you could talk. Acting like you were too good for the likes o' us. We should 'ave left you in the gutter with your mother, where you belong."

"There's no need for that," Uncle Charlie said as he scolded his wife. Though he teased me, he was the only one who stood up to his wife's insults.

I lowered my gaze, shame and embarrassment heavy upon my shoulders. No one had ever said as much, but I had long suspected my mother had been a woman of the night—and I was an unwanted byproduct. A mistake. Tainted from birth.

And, until today, I'd never had anywhere else to go. I'd been stuck living this life, hoping and praying for a miracle—one that had been handed to me outside the opera house.

I had to go to Mrs. Hill. If I didn't, I would regret it for the rest of my life.

Even if she offered me a job emptying her chamber pot, if it meant leaving Five Points, I would do almost anything.

Almost.

I would never end up like my mother.

2

I took the elevated train from Lower Manhattan to Grand Central Station for the second time in two days and then walked the half mile to 800 Fifth Avenue. Tall, gothic church spires rose toward the heavens, large, plate-glass windows sparkled in the sunshine, and intricate details on the brownstone mansions drew my eye. The wide avenue was clean and free of debris. There was no one loitering and no stench. Everyone had a purpose in their steps. Fashionable women paraded down the street with parasols and plumed hats, servants carrying packages. While men in suitcoats and top hats spoke quickly to one another, tipping their hat when passing a lady.

A police officer stood on one corner, nodding congenially to pedestrians, while a lady in a pink gown strolled past with a large poodle on a leash.

The difference between Mulberry Street and Fifth Avenue was like night and day. I still couldn't believe I would be welcomed into one of the fine mansions lining this street. I'd heard stories of people leaving the tenements and finding respectable work as servants in one of the homes on Fifth, Park, or Madison Avenues—but I had never known anyone who accomplished it. Most tenement workers had sweatshops in their apartments, like ours, or worked in one of the factories. Servants were usually trained in Ireland or England and came to America with the purpose of finding domestic work.

What would Mrs. Hill have in mind for me? I crossed Fifth Avenue to avoid walking past the policeman, who was eyeing me suspiciously, and wouldn't let myself imagine the possibilities, for fear of being disappointed. Even if she had work for me, I probably wouldn't be qualified for it. I had basic cooking and cleaning skills, but I could never help in a kitchen or as a chamber or parlor maid. Maybe I could assist a washerwoman or be a scullery maid. But even then, I'd have a lot to learn.

I looked at the addresses on the houses as I moved along Fifth Avenue. One brownstone mansion after another—until I came to 800 and stopped in my tracks.

This wasn't a brownstone mansion, with its boxed look and dark exterior. This home was tall and gothic, like the church spires, and the stone exterior was much lighter. The intricate carvings and details were a marvel to see. I could have stared at it for days. But it was nearing ten and I didn't want to be late.

I turned down West 52nd Street and walked almost the entire length of the block before I came to the back entrance of the mansion. A low stone fence ran along the perimeter of the house with one opening at the back.

Trailing my hand down the front of my dress, I tried to take a steady breath. I had spot-cleaned the dress before I came, washed my hands and face, and combed my dark brown hair before braiding it and twisting it into a crown on top of my head. There had been no time for a sponge bath—and even if there had been, Aunt Orla would have questioned such behavior. Water was hauled up to the apartment for cooking and drinking, and to keep our hands clean while we sewed. Baths were reserved for the warmer months when we could pay five cents and swim for twenty minutes at the public bath house on the East River.

I was trembling as I walked down a set of stone steps and approached the back entrance to the massive home. It was chilly today, though the sun was shining. The leaves had changed, and most had fallen from the trees, their branches offering a stark contrast to the blue sky.

It took all my willpower to knock on that massive wood door and then step back to wait for a servant to answer. Looking up, I felt dizzy at the height of the four-story structure. I focused, instead, on the beautiful stonework. Even the archway over the door to the servants' entrance had beautiful carvings.

The door opened and a young woman in a black dress, white apron, and mobcap answered. She looked me up and down, her blue eyes disapproving. "What are the likes o' you doin' here?" she asked in an Irish accent, not too different from my own. "We're not buyin' whatever it is you're sellin'."

What *was* I doing here? I lowered my gaze and said, "I've come to see Mrs. Hill."

The maid scoffed. "As if the lady o' the house would see you. Mrs. Walker is the housekeeper. She does all the hirin' and firin'. And she's not lookin' to hire street trash."

She started to close the door, but I showed her the card Mrs. Hill had given me. "Mrs. Hill asked me to come."

"Mrs. Hill herself?" The maid didn't look like she believed me—yet if Mrs. Hill had asked me to come and the maid turned me away, she'd be in trouble.

"Aye," I said. "Outside the opera house last night." Should I mention that she'd paid for me to come? Just thinking about Mr. Alexander Paxton-Hill putting that five-dollar bill in my hand made my heart beat faster. It all seemed like a dream—one I'd soon wake up from.

"Outside the opera house?" she asked. "We'll just see about that. You might as well come in out o' the cold and wait to speak to Mrs. Walker. She'll know what to do with you."

The maid opened the door a little wider, revealing a servants' hall. It was long and wide, with doorways leading off on both sides. There was a lot of activity as people came and went. A tall man in a black tailcoat, a young woman in a gray dress with a white cap, and several others dressed like the maid who had opened the door for me.

"Wait in Mrs. Walker's sittin' room," the maid said as she opened a door into a small, comfortable-looking room. "But don't touch anythin'."

I entered the room, and the maid kept the door open as she left to find the housekeeper.

Glancing at the clock, I saw it was already ten. Would Mrs. Hill be upset that I was late?

Thankfully, Mrs. Walker didn't make me wait long.

She entered the sitting room as if she was in a hurry, but she didn't look at me with the same disdain as the maid. Mrs. Walker had a pleasant face with kind brown eyes. Her gray hair was in a low chignon. "Hello," she said with a smile and a British accent. "Mari tells me you've come to see Mrs. Hill."

"Aye, ma'am," I said, showing her the calling card. "I'm Keira O'Day."

"Ah, yes. I was told to expect you." She looked me up and down, like the maid had, but with curiosity and not condescension. "I'm Mrs. Walker, the housekeeper."

"'Tis a pleasure to meet you, ma'am." I stood under her scrutinizing eye. She surveyed me much like Mrs. Hill and Mr. Paxton-Hill had yesterday.

Would Mrs. Walker be my boss? I wished I had a nicer dress or a stylish hat to wear for her approval.

"Come with me, Miss O'Day," she said.

I wanted to ask her what the job might be, but I held my tongue. If she wanted to tell me, she would.

I followed Mrs. Walker back into the servants' hall, which was covered in white tile on the walls and the ceiling—pristinely clean and clutter-free. Then we walked up a winding staircase to the main floor. Everything was darker here. The walls were paneled, and the floors were polished wood. There was another hallway, this one narrower, and then we went up another set of stairs. People passed us along the way, tossing curious glances at me, but no one said a word to us.

On the second floor, we left the back hallway and entered a large gallery. Huge paintings with gold frames hung around the room. In the center was a stained-glass ceiling and a stone railing, looking down at the black-and-white-checkered floor and grand staircase in the main entrance below.

What was this place? I'd been in a museum once and it looked just like this. But we were in a house, weren't we? Mrs. Hill's house?

I tried to keep my mouth closed as we walked past the paintings. Some were of people, others were of outdoor scenes, and all were vibrant and beautiful and old.

Mrs. Walker didn't say a word as we walked down the long gallery to a door on the other side of the grand staircase. She tapped on the door and waited.

Was Mrs. Hill on the other side of that door?

"Come in," said a lady.

Mrs. Walker opened the door and entered. "Miss O'Day has arrived."

The room was just as lavish and grand as the gallery, with thick trim, walls covered in pink silk, and delicate, cream-colored furniture. Mrs. Hill sat at a desk, wearing a soft pink day gown that matched the color of the walls. Her hair was in a simple knot at the top of her head, and she wore a single-diamond ring—though it was the largest diamond I'd ever seen.

She looked up at me, her gray eyes filling with excitement. "You came!"

I nodded, clasping my hands together as I stood perfectly still, afraid if I touched something it would be stained or ruined.

"Mrs. Walker, tell Alec I want to see him. He hasn't left for the office yet, has he?"

"No, ma'am."

"Good. Have him come as soon as possible."

"Yes, ma'am." Mrs. Walker nodded and then left the room.

I would see Mr. Paxton-Hill again? What did he have to do with hiring servants?

Mrs. Hill stood and moved aside her flowing gown, never taking her eyes off me, as she left her desk.

"I'm so pleased you're here, Miss O'Day. Alec told me your name last night. I was determined to go looking for you if you hadn't come."

I couldn't help but lift my eyebrows at that statement. Irish working girls were a dime a dozen in New York City. Surely she could have found someone else.

"Are you hungry?" she asked, almost anxious, as she went to a cord and pulled. "I should have told Mrs. Walker to bring tea. You're so pale and fragile, we'll need to strengthen your constitution."

She motioned to a chair near a massive fireplace. The heat was warm and comforting—though I was too anxious to enjoy it.

"Please have a seat, Miss O'Day."

I didn't have a lot of experience with women like Mrs. Hill, but I had a feeling it wasn't every day that she invited a poor tenement girl to take tea with her in her private room. The whole thing made me stiff and uncomfortable. Even if I was just here for a servant's job, wouldn't I meet with Mrs. Walker in her sitting room instead?

I lowered myself to the edge of the delicate chair, but I didn't rest or relax. How could I?

Mrs. Hill sat on the chair opposite me, studying me like she had last night. Now, in the light of day, she seemed to be getting a better look. And I had a better view of her, as well. She was a little older than I had thought last night, with deep wrinkles around her eyes and lining her mouth.

She suddenly frowned. "Are you married?"

I shook my head.

Relief lowered her shoulders. "I hadn't even wondered until now, but that would have ruined everything."

It was my turn to frown, but she continued.

"Where do you live?"

I wasn't sure why I felt so embarrassed to admit the truth. I hadn't chosen to live there. "Lower East Side, in Five Points."

Her eyebrows darted up. Everyone knew about Five Points.

"Mr. Charles Dickens visited there," she said. "He came to America in the '40s and wrote about the squalor. Is it as bad as he claimed?"

How could I tell her about Five Points? It was only four miles from her home, but it could have been a world away. There was nothing that would ever cause a woman like Mrs. Hill to wander into Five Points. And I wasn't sure who Mr. Charles Dickens was, so I didn't know what he'd said about it.

"'Tis all I've ever known, ma'am," I finally told her, wondering if I would get the job now that she knew the truth about me.

"You live there with your family?"

"Aye. My uncle and aunt and cousins."

"And your parents?"

My parents? How did I tell her about them when I didn't even know? Had my mother died in the gutter, like Aunt Orla claimed she would? Was my father a client of hers? Wealthy, poor, married, single? I had no idea.

"I'm not sure, ma'am," I said, not able to meet her gaze. "Me mum sent me to America with me uncle and aunt for a better life."

"And has it been a better life, Miss O'Day?" Mrs. Hill asked, her voice low, serious.

I looked up at her and saw curiosity in her gaze. Slowly, I shook my head. It hadn't been a good life—though I didn't have anything to compare it to.

"My father was a Scottish immigrant, and he lived a very difficult life as a fur trader," she said. "My mother and I didn't see him for months out of the year." She looked around the room at the splendor and said, "I can't imagine what he would think if he saw where I live now in a room first built in France and then reassembled here."

Why was she telling me this? I would never have guessed that she hadn't been born into this lifestyle. She looked like she fit in perfectly—whereas I had never felt more out of place.

I was trying to get up the courage to ask her why she'd invited me to come when there was a light knock on the door.

"Come in," Mrs. Hill said.

The door opened and I expected the maid with our tea—but my heart leapt into my throat when I saw Mr. Alexander Paxton-Hill standing there. My surprise brought me to my feet.

He was wearing a simple black suitcoat and white shirt with a green vest and black tie. He wore no hat today, and his dark, curly hair looked as if he'd run his hand through it a few times.

But it was his surprise—and maybe even his disappointment—that made my cheeks warm.

"Miss O'Day," he said formally, without the teasing from last night. "I didn't think you'd come." He moved into the room to stand in front of the fireplace and address me. "Has she told you her harebrained idea yet?"

Frowning, I looked to Mrs. Hill.

"Have a seat, Miss O'Day," Mr. Paxton-Hill said as he crossed his arms and looked at his aunt. "You'll want to be sitting when you hear this."

I slowly lowered myself to the chair and looked between them. Mr. Paxton-Hill did not look pleased, though Mrs. Hill appeared quite happy with herself.

"I want to adopt you, Miss O'Day," she said with a wide smile. "And marry you off to an English duke."

I stared at her, wondering if I had heard her incorrectly.

"What?" I managed to ask.

"My aunt is suffering from a malady that has attacked many of the *nouveaux riches* here in New York City," Mr. Paxton-Hill said as he addressed me. "The old set controls society, those who are in and those who are out. According to Mrs. Astor and Ward McCallister, if you have gained your wealth within the past two generations, then you are not fit for proper society. You are too new—too inexperienced and in poor taste. In short, you are out."

Mrs. Hill lifted her chin and pursed her lips, looking toward the window. I could see years of frustration and discontent in her gaze.

Mr. Paxton-Hill continued. "So, the newly rich are fighting back. They built the Metropolitan Opera House, because Mrs. Astor and the other nobs would not allow them to have a box at the Academy of Music. The old set did not allow them into the Patriarch Balls, or the Assembly Balls, either."

I listened quietly, having heard a little bit about how the Metropolitan Opera House had been built. But the lives of these people did not affect my day-to-day living, and though I had been taught how to read by mission workers in Five Points, I had no access to newspapers. Mrs. Hill's existence was as foreign to me as mine would be to her. I thought about all the people I knew, those who fought every day just to survive, and could not fathom what he was telling me.

"The only way to *become* someone," Mrs. Hill interrupted, fire in her eyes, "is to rise in the ranks among them."

I stared at her, wondering if she was teasing me. Did she really think this was a problem?

"Nine years ago," Mrs. Hill continued, "Miss Jennie Jerome went to England and married Lord Randolph Churchill, the third son of the Duke of Marlborough, and *became* someone. Then others followed, including Consuelo Yznaga, who married Viscount Mandeville. She'll be a duchess one day. And do you know what all of them have in common?"

I was still staring at her. I had no idea.

"They were welcomed into Mrs. Astor's society after their marriages. More importantly, their families were welcomed into society, as well."

Mr. Paxton-Hill watched me intently—yet I couldn't quite grasp how this had anything to do with me—or why he seemed so upset that I was here.

"My aunt has been fighting to gain entrance into society for the past decade," Mr. Paxton-Hill said to me. "But she does not want to go to England and remarry herself."

"Heavens no," Mrs. Hill said. "I was married once and once is enough for me. Besides, I have no wish to live in Europe."

"And," Mr. Paxton-Hill continued, "because she has no daughter to sell for a title—"

"Sell?" Mrs. Hill gave him a look. "Really, Alec."

"What?" he asked her. "That's what these families are doing. Giving their daughters away in marriage, with large dowries, to gain a titled son-in-law, so they can come home and be the parents of the next duchess of something or other."

"It's much more civilized than all that. People have been marrying for wealth and position for centuries." She wrinkled her nose and turned back to me. "But Alec is right. I have no children and no wish to remarry or start a family. Even if I did, I'm much too old for all that. And I'm not just doing this for my own social gain—I'm also doing it for the business that pays for this home and our very existence." She looked at her nephew. "Alec inherited the hotel business from my husband when he passed away last year and he's struggling to keep up with all the other rival hotels and resorts going up in Newport and Coney Island. He needs this as much as I do—everyone who works for us needs this."

Mr. Paxton-Hill looked down at the crackling fire. There was a look in his blue eyes that I knew—a look that transcended status or wealth.

He was unhappy.

I still hadn't wrapped my mind around Mrs. Hill's first statement, about what she wanted to do with me—and I was almost too afraid to ask—but I had learned that if I didn't speak up for myself, no one else would.

"What exactly would you like from me, ma'am?" I asked her.

Mrs. Hill glanced at Mr. Paxton-Hill for a moment—as if making a final decision—and then said to me, "I want to make you my daughter, Miss O'Day—legally. I want to adopt you, train you, and take you to Europe, where I hope you will make a fine match. In exchange for your agreement, you will have all the finest things money can buy. A home, good food, a whole new wardrobe of clothing, and security. You will never want for anything a day in your life."

My lips parted—this time I had heard and understood her completely—yet I was still confused. "Why me?"

"You're stunning, Miss O'Day," she said, almost in disbelief. "Has no one ever told you how beautiful you are?"

I put my hand to my cheek. Aunt Orla said I looked just like my mother, but she had made my mother sound cheap and ugly. Men often propositioned me, and one had offered me a spot in his Mulberry Street brothel, saying my looks would draw in the men. But I hadn't felt uncommonly beautiful. Instead, I felt dirty and without any real value.

"You haven't been told," Mr. Paxton-Hill said, quietly, almost surprised.

"Your beauty is rare," Mrs. Hill said to me. "And, beyond that, you have a kind soul, Miss O'Day, I can see it in your eyes and your behavior. When I first started to think of this plan, I told Alec I needed to adopt a young lady from a good background. But I soon realized that no one with a pedigree would be amenable to that plan. I needed to find someone who could be completely pliable. Someone fresh, with no prior history in society. I decided to start looking high and low for just the right person—and the moment I saw you last night, I knew you were the one."

I wrapped my shawl closer to my body, trying to comprehend everything she was saying. "You don't need a chamber maid?"

Mrs. Hill's laughter echoed through her sitting room. "Heavens, no. Those are easy enough to come by. What I need, Miss O'Day, is something much more difficult to find. I need someone I can turn into a lady. I need a beautiful face, a kind heart, and a willing spirit."

My tattered gown hadn't been washed in months. I ran my callused fingers over the rough material, wondering what it would feel like to wear a fine gown, take a hot bath, and eat more than cabbage, potatoes, and ham. But even as I wondered, I knew it was a foolish dream. How could I ever pass for high society? How would *I* attract the attention of a duke?

"I'd only let you down," I said quietly to Mrs. Hill. "I don't know how to dance or speak or sit at a fancy dinner table."

"All of that can be learned," Mrs. Hill assured me.

"Even if I learn it," I said, unable to look her or Mr. Paxton-Hill in the eyes, "I'll still be me."

There was a pause, and I glanced up in time to see Mr. Paxton-Hill and his aunt share a look—one I couldn't read. But when she rested her gaze on me, she said, "That's precisely why I've asked you, Miss O'Day. You're humble and unassuming. If I asked a young lady who thought too highly of herself, I would have nothing but trouble. If you are willing, I can turn you into exactly what I need you to be."

That same look of concern and disapproval flitted across Mr. Paxton-Hill's face, but he didn't speak.

"What must I do—" I was almost too afraid to ask—"if I attract a duke?"

"Why, marry him, of course, and become his duchess." Mrs. Hill smiled as she stood and walked across the room to offer me her hand.

"Just say yes. You don't need to worry about a thing. I'll take care of all the details. You just do as I say and we'll both get what we want."

"What do *you* want, Miss O'Day?" Mr. Paxton-Hill asked me.

I slowly wet my lips. No one had ever asked me what I wanted. When I was small, my aunt had belittled me when I whispered my heart's desires, so I had learned to keep them close. They were safer that way.

"Do you want to get out of Five Points?" Mrs. Hill asked me.

"Aye."

"Do you want to wear fine clothes, ride around in a fancy carriage, attend operas and balls and dinner parties?"

I found myself nodding. I had never even dreamed of those things, but they sounded grand.

"Then you will get what you want, if you listen to me and do as I say."

Could it be that simple?

"Will you agree to become my daughter?" Mrs. Hill asked, not giving me much time to contemplate her offer.

Mr. Paxton-Hill looked as if he was holding his breath.

I would be a fool to say no—and, if I agreed to go to England, it would give me the opportunity to look for my mother. Surely, if she was still alive, I could find her.

That thought alone gave me the courage to nod.

"Aye," I said, my cheeks burning with excitement and nerves. Emotions I rarely felt flooded through me, like an elixir I wanted to drink over and over. Anticipation, expectancy . . . hope.

Mrs. Hill took my hand and squeezed it as she pulled me to my feet. Her grin stretched across her face, and she looked a decade younger. "How wonderful! How marvelous! Alec, did you hear that? I'm to be a mother." She laughed and it was the sound of pure joy.

For a moment, I felt the same thrill. I was going to have a mother—and not just any mother—but Mrs. Maude Hamilton Hill, one of the wealthiest widows in New York City.

But then my gaze collided with Mr. Paxton-Hill—Alec—and the elation was replaced by uncertainty and fear.

He did not look as pleased as his aunt.

But was he upset with her—or with me?

3

The tea tray was forgotten as Mrs. Walker was called into the room and told about the arrangement.

Alec quietly slipped away.

Mrs. Hill wanted complete secrecy. No one must know my identity. The staff would be told I was Mrs. Hill's long-lost niece, come to stay with her in New York City. The maid I spoke to when I first arrived would be offered a promotion in the house for her silence. And when the time was right, Mrs. Hill would announce my adoption, and we would proceed from there.

Until then, Mrs. Walker was to appoint a lady's maid for me, one who could be trusted with the secret, and if there was any gossip among the staff, it was to be shut down immediately.

"Do you have someone in mind for Miss O'Day's lady's maid?" Mrs. Hill asked Mrs. Walker.

"I think Deidre would be a good choice," Mrs. Walker said. "She's smart and hardworking. She keeps to herself."

"Excellent. Please have her draw a bath for Miss O'Day and send Brown in to me. I'll need to find a gown for Miss O'Day to use until we can get a suitable wardrobe made for her."

"Yes, ma'am." Mrs. Walker left the room as Mrs. Hill walked to a door on the side and motioned for me to follow her.

"You'll use Mr. Hill's old bedchamber," she said to me. "I'd prefer if you didn't traipse through the house to get to my room for your daily lessons. The less the staff sees you, the better."

I followed her into a room that held no bed—only dresses, shoes, hats, and other ladies' accessories.

I'd never seen anything like it—not even in a store.

We moved through the dressing room and into another cavernous bedchamber, this one with dark cream wallpaper and thick, dark woodwork. The ceiling was so high, the room echoed, and a large canopied bed sat in the middle. Red damask drapes fell from a dark wooden frame to the floor.

"I purchased the bed from Versailles," Mrs. Hill said. "It belonged to King Louis XIV."

"A king slept in this bed?" I asked in disbelief.

She lifted a shoulder and then went to the window to open the shutters. "This entire room was purchased in France, from the Château de Chantilly, and brought here. The trim, the flooring, even the finials around the lights." She turned and looked around the room. "It should do for now. After your bath, we'll discuss our plans. We have so much to accomplish and so little time to do it. I intend to take you to Europe in April or May."

April was five short months away. Could I be ready to attract a duke by then?

Mrs. Hill left me without another word. I stood in the middle of that large, French room and tried to catch my breath as nerves filled my stomach and made me feel ill.

What had I just agreed to? And how would I tell Uncle Charlie and Aunt Orla what I had done? They'd think I was overreaching my station again—which I was. But how could I say no to this offer? Even now, I wanted to pinch myself. This couldn't possibly be me. This couldn't be my life.

I closed my eyes tight and then slowly reopened them—but I was still standing in Mr. Hill's bedroom, near King Louis XIV's bed.

A slight knock was followed by the entrance of Mrs. Walker and another maid. This one was a bit older than the one I'd met at the servants' entrance, perhaps in her early thirties.

"Miss O'Day," Mrs. Walker said, "this is Deidre Gallagher. She'll be your lady's maid."

Deidre offered a small curtsey at the same time I did—but Deidre paused as she looked at me with a funny stare.

Was I not supposed to curtsey to the staff?

Warmth filled my cheeks.

"I'll draw a bath for you, miss," Deidre said as she went through a doorway I had not even noticed yet.

"Brown is assisting Mrs. Hill," Mrs. Walker said. "She'll have a gown ready for you when you're done."

"Brown?"

"Mrs. Hill's lady's maid. They're referred to by their last name. You'll call Deidre Gallagher."

"Gallagher?"

"Yes. And I'm Mrs. Walker and the butler is Higgins. You'll be meeting the other staff eventually—there are thirty-five of us—but, for now, we're the only ones you'll associate with."

Gallagher, Brown, Higgins. My head spun.

Soon, Gallagher returned to fetch me for my bath.

She led me into a bathroom behind Mrs. Hill's dressing room, between the two bedchambers. The bathroom was twice as big as our apartment on Mulberry Street, and everything was pristine white.

Large windows let in natural light and a massive clawfoot tub sat against one wall.

Steam spiraled from the tub, fogging the mirror and windows.

I had never been in a real bathtub. All my baths had been in the summer months, in the river, where it was cool and refreshing. How hot was this water? Would it scald my skin?

"Let me help you, miss," Gallagher said as she began to unbutton my dress.

I pulled back, putting my hands up to stop her. "I can undress m'self."

"Very well," she said, her voice devoid of emotion.

I couldn't tell what she thought of me. She had to be surprised at my appearance. She had to have questions.

Slowly, I undressed myself but left my chemise on as I stood near the tub.

"Everything must come off, miss," she said.

"Everythin'?" I'd never bathed naked before. It would have been indecent in the public baths.

"Yes, miss."

I wanted her to stop calling me *miss*, but I was afraid to make the request. Surely she was more educated, more skilled and refined than I was. Why hadn't Mrs. Hill asked her to become her daughter. Why me?

Embarrassment warmed my cheeks as Gallagher just stood and stared at me. She wouldn't question me or challenge me—I could see it in her eyes—but she was judging me. She was probably laughing at my lack of knowledge about baths and wondering about her own misfortune in having to care for me.

With a deep breath, I decided that I would have to pretend I knew what I was doing. I couldn't question everything Gallagher told me. I would just have to do it, even if it felt strange or uncomfortable.

I stripped off the last of my undergarments and watched as Gallagher left the bathroom, holding my threadbare items between her pinched fingers.

With her gone, I wasn't sure how to proceed but decided the best course of action would be to get into the water. Slowly, I lifted one bare leg in.

The water was warm and pleasant as it pooled around my skin—not too hot and not too cold.

I pulled the other leg in and then lowered my body into the tub.

Warmth enveloped me from my neck to my toes. The smell of roses wafted up to my nose and I closed my eyes, feeling something like bliss for the first time in my life.

The bath was marvelous and every muscle in my body relaxed, easing into the weightlessness of the water.

Without even realizing it, I sighed.

What other wonders would I experience in Mrs. Hill's home? My mind began to race with the possibilities—but I suddenly saw Aunt Orla's sneering face in my mind, chastising me for indulging in fantasies.

But this wasn't a fantasy. This was real.

Soon Gallagher was back, and she told me she would help me wash my hair.

It was another glorious experience as she poured warm water onto my head, lathered soap through my hair several times, and then rinsed it clean.

Even the soap felt extravagant and luxurious. It was soft against my skin and smelled like flowers. Nothing like the harsh soap I used at home.

Before long, Gallagher had a plush robe ready for me, and I stepped out of the bath. After drying my hair with a towel, she led me into Mrs. Hill's large dressing room, where an outfit was waiting for me, including brand-new undergarments of the finest cotton I'd ever seen.

In quick succession, Gallagher helped me into drawers, stockings with garters, a chemise, and then a rigid corset.

"Such a small waist," she said, almost to herself, which was her only comment since we'd started the process. I couldn't tell if it was a compliment or just a passing remark.

After the corset came a padded bustle, which I'd never worn before, followed by a petticoat with stiff ruffles down the backside, a yellow skirt with flounces, tucks, and a small train, and then a long-sleeved matching bodice with a square neckline. Mrs. Hill was taller and plumper than me, so Gallagher had to make do, but it was easy enough to draw the skirt tighter around my waist and adjust the bodice to fit.

Gallagher turned me to face the full-length mirror, and though my hair was still damp around my shoulders, I hardly recognized the woman before me.

I had never looked in a full-length mirror. It felt like I was meeting a stranger.

I *was* beautiful, with a creamy complexion, dark brown eyes, thick brown hair, and delicate features. There was a natural rosiness to my cheeks, and my lips were a soft pink. The warmth of the bath had heightened my color, I was sure, but for the first time, I could see what Mrs. Hill saw in me. Though it was only external—she could never see the ugly truth on the inside. No matter how pretty my gown, or how nice I smelled, the truth would eventually seep out of me. Uncle

Charlie and Aunt Orla saw it, and Mrs. Hill would realize it one day, too.

I just hoped that when it happened, I could find a way to repay her—because now that I had tasted such delight—in little under an hour—I was convinced that I was spoiled for the life I had once led.

By evening, I was exhausted. I had not slept the night before and Mrs. Hill had kept me engaged in conversation all afternoon. One-sided conversation, but I wanted desperately to know everything I could.

Thankfully, she had a tray sent up to my room for supper, since she didn't want the staff to know of my existence yet. I gobbled up the chicken in mushroom sauce, boiled potatoes, carrots, and lettuce salad. There was so much of it, I could hardly believe it was all for me. But the caramel custard was the best part. I tried to savor it, feeling the first twinge of guilt that I couldn't share it with my younger cousin, Imogen. She loved sweets, though we rarely had them.

Mrs. Hill entered the room as I finished. She was wearing a shimmering gold and black gown with a large bustle and a sweeping train. She was going out for the evening to a card party hosted by one of her friends.

"You look exhausted, Miss O'Day," she said as she stood behind a sofa across from me.

I rose, still unused to her presence.

"I have decided to call you by your first name," she said as she pulled a long glove onto her hand. "If we're to convince the world we've known each other for years, we'll need to start acting the part." She settled the fingers of the glove into place. "However—I'm afraid Keira won't do. We'll need to Americanize you as much as possible and given the disdain between the English and the Irish, we'll need to distance you from that heritage."

I lowered my gaze, feeling shame for something I knew nothing about, nor could I control.

"When I adopt you," she continued, "we'll make the name change legal. Of course, you'll want it to be something similar to Keira—but with a little softness. What do you think about Clara?"

"Clara?" I repeated, trying to wrap my mind around this change.

"Clara Day Hill," she said with an indulgent smile. "So you can keep a bit of yourself in the process."

Keep a bit of myself? Did I want any of my former self to remain? I had always suspected that God made a mistake when I was born. I hadn't been wanted by anyone, so perhaps I hadn't been wanted by Him, either.

Mrs. Hill was the first person who had ever chosen me—and the truth of it sank down deep into my heart. What was in a name, anyway? If this would hinder Mrs. Hill from adopting me, then I would not make a fuss.

"Clara Day Hill sounds grand," I assured her.

"Good." She lowered her chin. "And, Clara, you'll need to speak up. You're so soft-spoken. That will never do. The English aristocracy loves American women because they are confident, bold, and intelligent. That is your first order of business. When you're addressing people, you must tell them who you are and what you want with your words and behavior. Be in command of every situation—do you understand?"

I looked down at my hands, my cheeks growing warm at her admonition, and nodded. "Aye."

"Clara?"

I forced myself to look up at her.

"Let's try again. This time, look at me and speak clearly and directly—and say *yes*, instead of *aye*."

It went against everything I'd ever been taught or experienced. I had never been in command a day in my life. But I would try, for Mrs. Hill.

"Yes, ma'am."

She smiled—and her smile warmed me from head to toe. I had pleased her.

"Very good. Now, I'm off. I'll see you in the morning. Get some sleep. We will be busy tomorrow with the dressmaker."

With a swish of her skirt, she turned and left the room.

I sat for a moment, Louis XIV's intimidating bed beckoning me, but I didn't think I could sleep, because I had realized something important earlier that day.

I didn't have my mother's locket.

It was the only thing I could call my own. The only thing that connected me to her and to my past. And I wanted it. Besides that, Uncle Charlie and Aunt Orla would wonder where I had gone. I owed them some kind of explanation.

But how would I leave Mrs. Hill's house, travel to Five Points, and get back inside without someone telling her?

It was still light out, but the longer I waited, the more dangerous it would become. It was one thing to go into Five Points dressed in my old clothing—another to go dressed in the gown Mrs. Hill had loaned me. I would attract a lot of unwanted attention. But I didn't know where my old gown had gone.

I could send a note to my family, asking them to bring my locket to me, but they would never do it. And I didn't want them to get ahold of my nine dollars and fifty cents. If things didn't work out with Mrs. Hill, I would need every penny I could get.

That left one option. I would have to go on my own and hope I could get out of Mrs. Hill's house—and back in—without being noticed.

But what if Mrs. Hill came home before I returned? Would she think I had changed my mind? Or, worse, that I had stolen the dress from her?

It was a risk I would need to take. I couldn't have Uncle Charlie and Aunt Orla wondering about me—and I couldn't leave the locket behind.

I opened the bedroom door and looked out at the gallery. There was no one in sight, so I quickly left the room and closed the door behind me. It would be chilly without a shawl, but I didn't want to risk taking anything else from Mrs. Hill.

The next decision I had to make was which door I would use to leave the house. There was a greater chance of being discovered if I went out the servants' entrance—and I had no idea how to find it. So, I decided to use the front door—though I had no idea where that might be, either.

I crossed the upper gallery on slippered feet, marveling at the plush carpet beneath me, and went to the grand staircase. Surely the front door had to be somewhere near the stairs.

As I rounded the corner and began to descend—I paused.

Mr. Paxton-Hill was on his way up.

He stopped and his gaze was filled with surprise—and perhaps a bit of wonder.

"Miss O'Day?" he asked, frowning.

Dread filled me at being caught. What would he think when he learned I was leaving?

Slowly, he started up the stairs again, and I couldn't help but back up. I clasped my hands together, uncertain what to say—afraid of what he might say.

He stopped at the top of the stairs, taking me in from the hem of my yellow gown to the top of my hair. Gallagher had brushed the curls until they shone and then styled them gracefully atop my head.

"You—" He paused, as if trying to find the right words.

"I'm sorry," I said, glancing toward my bedroom door.

He was still staring at me. "You look lovely, Miss O'Day."

I glanced down at the gown, my cheeks getting warm at his compliment. "Thank you."

"Are you in need of something?" he asked. "Can I be of service?"

I nervously played with a ribbon on my gown as I glanced toward the stairs. Did I tell him the truth? I had to say something.

He studied me and I realized that he, unlike Mrs. Hill, had given me several choices in the past twenty-four hours. Nothing he had said or done would indicate whether he would try to dictate my actions. Perhaps he would even help me.

"I left somethin' at home," I told him. "Somethin' important to me. And I should tell me aunt and uncle what has become o' me."

He blinked in surprise. "You haven't told them?"

"How could I?"

"I hadn't even realized. Yes. You should tell them—immediately. They'll be worried about you, I'm sure."

Maybe not worried—but curious, at least.

"I'll accompany you," he said.

I shook my head, imagining what might happen to Mr. Paxton-Hill if he walked down Mulberry Street in that expensive suitcoat as darkness fell.

"Please," he said, "allow me to do this. I'll have the carriage brought around."

"No." I continued to shake my head. "I've been goin' home me whole life—alone."

"But now you have a—" He paused, as if surprised at his own realization. "A cousin to see to your welfare."

I had a cousin—Sean—who would be better suited to my welfare in Five Points than this dandy.

"Allow me the honor, Miss O'Day."

"Honor? To go to Five Points?" I might have laughed if he wasn't so serious—and kind.

There was a hint of surprise in his eyes when I said Five Points, but he rallied and nodded. "Of course."

A carriage would get us in and out much faster—and we could be back before nighttime shrouded Five Points in darkness.

"Aye—but we must hurry. Five Points is no place for a nice carriage after dark."

Ten minutes later, after insisting I borrow a cloak from Mrs. Hill's dressing room, Mr. Paxton-Hill and I were in the family carriage on our way to my old neighborhood.

I sat across from him in the elegant vehicle, marveling at the details in the upholstery and the comfort of the conveyance.

"How has Aunt Maude treated you?" he asked me. "You look tired."

"I was up all night sewin' before I come."

His eyebrows jumped. "You haven't slept since I saw you last night outside the opera house?"

Shaking my head, I looked down at my rough hands. So much had happened since then.

"I'll see that she lets you sleep in tomorrow."

"Thank you for your kindness, Mr. Paxton-Hill."

"Please," he said, "call me Alec."

I nodded, though I couldn't imagine calling him by his given name.

"And may I call you Keira?"

I parted my lips to say yes—but then I remembered what Mrs. Hill had told me earlier. "Mrs. Hill has changed me name to Clara."

Alec stared at me, his frown deepening. "Clara?"

I sensed his disappointment again—but was he disappointed in me or in Mrs. Hill?

"You'll let her change your name?" he asked.

Something broke inside me—a dam I had not realized was being held back. Emotions surfaced that had been lying dormant my whole life, and somehow, I knew that this man would understand. That he was someone I could talk to—trust.

"I would let her change everythin' about me if it meant I could have freedom from Five Points. Where I come from, me name means nothin'. If I can have a name that means somethin'—to someone—then I'll gladly take whatever she offers me."

He nodded as if properly chastised, but then he said, "Do not let her change everything about you . . . Keira."

His gaze was so raw, so penetrating, I had to look away.

Soon, we were entering the Five Points neighborhood. People looked up at the carriage with surprise and suspicion.

My heart began to beat an erratic rhythm as we drew closer to Mulberry Street. I could smell it before I could see it.

And when Alec glanced out the window, I looked away from him, not wanting to see his reaction. Would he think less of me after seeing where I came from? Would he tell Mrs. Hill to cast me out? Surely he'd realize what a mistake she had made.

When the carriage finally came to a stop, I began to open the door, but Alec reached out and placed his hand on mine. There was undisguised shock in his face—but there was also empathy there, which was much different than pity, and it caught me unaware.

"Allow me," he said.

His touch was soft and reassuring. Everything about this man was refined.

I moved back and allowed him to exit the carriage, apprehensive at what he must be thinking.

For a moment, he looked at the neighborhood—and I could see it all from his perspective.

Rats feeding off a dead, rotting horse, sagging timbers, dirty children, and sewage running through the street.

But when he turned back and offered me his hand, there was nothing but respect in his eyes.

4

Alec helped me from the carriage as people stopped and stared, though I wouldn't let it bother me.

When he started to follow, I turned and said, "You can wait here."

"A gentleman never allows a lady to go unescorted." He smiled, somehow making me forget the filth all around us. "If your family has questions, I want to be there to answer them."

It wasn't a good idea—but I could see he wouldn't change his mind.

We entered the tenement and climbed up the rickety stairs. I was self-conscious of my dress, my shoes, even my hair. I didn't want to get any of it dirty, for fear of Mrs. Hill's displeasure.

But mostly, I was conscious of Alec.

Slowly, I opened the door and found Aunt Orla at the table, cutting fabric. Polly was at her station, sewing, and Imogen was sitting at my spot.

All three looked up—and I felt their shock all the way to my toes.

It was rare that Aunt Orla was speechless—but she slowly rose from the table, her mouth hanging open—and said nothing.

"Aunt Orla." I tried to swallow my nerves. "This is Mr. Alexander Paxton-Hill."

Alec took off his bowler hat and nodded at Aunt Orla, a lock of his dark hair falling down his forehead. "How do you do?"

She blinked several times but didn't respond.

"And these are me cousins," I said quickly, "Polly and Imogen."

The girls stared, much like Aunt Orla, taking in my gown, my hair, and the man beside me.

"Charlie!" Aunt Orla finally squeaked. "Charlie!" she said again, this time louder.

Uncle Charlie came out of the bedroom in his underclothes, clearly pulled from his sleep.

"What is it, wife?" he demanded.

"Look," Aunt Orla said, pointing at me. "Look at Keira."

Uncle Charlie glanced at me, and all traces of sleep disappeared from his face. "Keira," he said, "what happened?"

I looked at Alec and saw that he was trying to school his features. No doubt he was shocked at what he saw—but he didn't let it show.

"I met Mr. Paxton-Hill and his aunt, Mrs. Maude Hamilton Hill, last night outside the Metropolitan Opera House. Mrs. Hill offered me a . . ." I didn't know how to explain—and wasn't sure I wanted them to know all the details. "A position," I finally said. "I'm to move into her home and start immediately." I looked down at my gown and touched the fine satin fabric. "She'll take good care of me."

Uncle Charlie hadn't taken his eyes off Alec. He narrowed them now and said, "I think I know what's goin' on."

Alec lifted his chin—just a fraction.

Aunt Orla's gaze seemed to clear, too, and she looked at me with disdain. "So the duchess found herself a man to keep her in finery. How long has this been goin' on behind closed doors?"

My cheeks burned with shame. "'Tis not like that."

"On my honor," Alec said, taking a step forward, "Miss O'Day is my aunt's guest and has been treated with nothing but respect."

I could see that my uncle and aunt would not be persuaded to believe the truth, so I said, "I've come for me things."

"What things?" Aunt Orla asked.

"The locket."

She lifted an eyebrow, as if unimpressed.

Walking past her, I went into the bedroom, where Patrick was asleep on the pallet, and found the loose board in the floor.

"How do we know you'll take good care o' her?" Uncle Charlie said in the next room.

I held my breath and worked faster, embarrassed that Uncle Charlie and Aunt Orla would question Alec.

"Miss O'Day will want for nothing," Alec said.

"And what happens when you tire of her?" Aunt Orla asked. "She won't come crying back to us, I can tell you that much."

"She will never have reason to come back here," Alec said, his voice filled with conviction, "as long as I have breath in my lungs."

My heart skipped a beat at his declaration as I reached into the dusty floorboards and pulled out the small box I stored there. I opened it, just to make sure nothing was missing, and found my locket and my money. Just as quickly, I replaced the board and rejoined them.

Alec looked relieved at my arrival.

"I suppose Imogen will have to pick up your slack," Aunt Orla spat. "I always knew you was good for nothin'."

Alec stiffened beside me as shame warmed my cheeks. This was the only family I'd ever known. A strange part of me was afraid to leave them—to leave this—because it was all I knew. But the other part never wanted to look back.

"Goodbye," I said and met Uncle Charlie's gaze. "And thanks."

"Get out o' here," Aunt Orla said. "You've always been an ungrateful child."

Uncle Charlie's uncertainty toward Alec turned to sadness as he nodded at me. "Go on with you, Keira. Best that you leave."

Tears threatened to fall, but I held them in place as I looked from my uncle and aunt to my cousins and then to the piecework on the table.

Alec held the door open for me, but when I saw the tears in Imogen's eyes, I went to her and gave her a quick kiss, slipping a dollar into her hand. "For something pretty," I whispered, then I turned away from my family and left the apartment.

Neither one of us spoke as we walked down the steps and out to the carriage, guarded by the driver and footmen who looked relieved at our arrival.

Alec helped me inside and climbed in behind me.

We were silent as the carriage pulled away from 36 Mulberry Street.

I couldn't meet his gaze—afraid of what I might see there.

He was quiet for a long time.

When he finally spoke, his voice was low and gentle. "Did you get what you went for?"

I opened the small box, embarrassed by the paltry amount of money inside, and took out the locket. It was on a delicate gold chain—though I had never tried it on before. I'd only ever held it.

"This belonged to me mam," I told him.

"May I see it?"

I had never let anyone else hold it—but I found myself handing it over to Alec.

He took it and looked it over with care.

"It's very beautiful—and looks like solid gold."

My eyebrows lifted. "Do you think so?"

Nodding, he handed it back to me. "Whoever bought that spent a great deal of money on it."

I looked at the locket with new eyes. I wasn't sure what I thought of it before, but I hadn't considered that it was solid gold. Who had purchased a solid gold locket for my mother?

"What do the initials stand for?" he asked me.

Running my finger over the engraved initials, I said, "I'm not sure. I think N is for Nellie—'twas me mam's name."

"And the B?"

I shook my head and shrugged.

"Not your father's name?"

I finally looked up at Alec. The sun had started to set, and it cast a golden light into the carriage. He was wearing his hat again, causing the curls to peak out from underneath.

I was embarrassed to admit the truth—a truth I had no control over, though it stained me nonetheless. "I don't know me father's name."

He nodded as if he understood. But did he?

I slipped the locket back into the box and held it tight between my hands.

We traveled in silence for a few more minutes as we left the putrid smell of Five Points behind. The only noise was the *clip-clopping* of the horse's hooves and the sounds of the city around us.

"Sometimes," Alec finally said, "God gives us opportunities we don't see coming."

I looked up at him, surprised by his talk of God. Outside of church, I rarely heard people speak of Him.

"We might not think we're up to the task, but I think that's the point." He studied me in the dying light, and I could see that he was speaking from experience. "When I inherited my uncle's business a year ago, at the age of twenty-four, I was in over my head and had no idea what I was doing. My father is a minister—Reverend Jonathan

Paxton—I was not raised in a cutthroat, business-minded household. But I saw the opportunity for what it was—what it is—and I am trying my hardest to make the most of it." He leaned forward. "If you are anything like me, you're afraid you won't be up to the task, either. But I think you will be surprised, Keira."

I stared at him. "Do you think I have what it takes to attract a duke?"

His blue eyes filled with something I couldn't quite define. "You have more than enough of what it takes."

For some reason, my cheeks grew warm, and I had to look away.

If Alexander Paxton-Hill believed I could do this—then I would believe it, too.

The next morning, as I slowly woke up, I was first aware of the comfortable bed I slept in. Then I was aware of someone in the room with me.

Opening my eyes, I found Gallagher laying a fire in the fireplace.

What a strange thing to wake up to—a maid *and* a fire.

"Good morning, miss," she said when she noticed I was awake. "I've set out a dress for you, but if you don't like it, I can find another."

I glanced at the dressing table and saw a pink gown lying next to it on the chaise lounge.

"What about the dress I wore yesterday?"

"There's no need to wear the same gown two days in a row." She went to the windows and opened the shutters, allowing in daylight. "Mrs. Hill has ordered breakfast in her room, but first you must dress. I have a bath drawn for you."

"Another bath? Why?"

She frowned, as if she didn't understand my question, and my cheeks warmed, remembering that I couldn't let on that any of this was strange. I would take a bath whenever it was offered.

But first, I had to use steps to climb out of the king's bed.

Within half an hour, I was bathed and dressed, with my hair twisted into an updo that seemed much too fancy for the likes of me. Though I wouldn't question Gallagher.

When I was ready, I stepped into Mrs. Hill's dressing room and was about to knock on her bedroom door when I heard Alec's serious voice.

"There's only one reason I'm not putting an end to this," he said.

"Really, Alec," Mrs. Hill responded, "as if you could stop me."

"I could strongly discourage you."

"So why don't you?"

"Because of Garfield."

"That loathsome man," Mrs. Hill said as silverware clinked against china. "I would prefer you never speak his name in my company. He was the death of Edmund."

I had heard Mrs. Hill refer to her husband as Edmund. Until now, I hadn't wondered how he had died.

"If we do not secure the interest from the right people," Alec continued, "I fear Garfield's resort will put ours out of business within the next two seasons. When Uncle Edmund built the resort in Newport, there were none like it. But now that Garfield's is finished, we have serious competition."

"What about the renovations? Won't that make our resort more appealing to the right crowd?"

"I fear it will only cause our demise sooner. Even if we pour a million dollars into our resort, the newness and modern amenities of Garfield's resort will outshine ours."

"Rest assured, Mr. Garfield does not move in the right circles, either."

"No, but I have heard rumors at my club."

I couldn't help but lean closer to the door, knowing I should not eavesdrop, but unsure what else to do. I couldn't interrupt them—could I?

"What rumors?" Mrs. Hill asked.

"Mrs. Garfield has plans to take Louise to England during the London season—and if she succeeds, and marries Louise to the right man, the Garfields will gain the support they need from New York society."

"And that's why you've agreed to my plan? So we can compete with the Garfields?"

"Precisely," Alec said.

My heart pounded hard at the weight of the responsibility I had undertaken. What if I couldn't succeed? What if this Garfield girl won the hand of a duke and I came home with nothing? Would Mrs. Hill cast me out?

Mrs. Hill sighed. "I am not worried. Clara far outshines Louise Garfield in every way. She's thinner, her hair is thicker, her face is prettier, and she's sweeter."

My cheeks burned at her bold assessment of me, but I noticed that Alec was silent on the matter—was it because he disagreed with Mrs. Hill?

"I hope you'll be home more often in the evenings," Mrs. Hill said in a quieter voice.

"Please do not lecture me about my club again."

"I don't wish to lecture you, but Clara could benefit from your time and attention. She will need all the help she can get."

"I'm not certain I'm the one who should give it to her."

I could no longer eavesdrop—afraid I might hear something I shouldn't.

Knocking on the door, I waited until Mrs. Hill called for me to enter.

"Come in, Clara."

My hands were trembling as I entered her room.

Alec rose from where he was sitting near the fireplace—in the chair I had occupied yesterday—but I couldn't meet his gaze. I'd worried about what he thought of Five Points—and now me.

"Good morning," Mrs. Hill said.

"Good mornin'."

Mrs. Hill did not rise from her chair but offered me a smile. "Today, we will start to break you of that accent. We cannot introduce you at court sounding like an Irish immigrant."

My lips parted as Alec cast a disgruntled look at his aunt.

She didn't seem to notice.

But I wasn't thinking about my accent—all I could think about was the other thing she'd said. "I'll be goin' to court?"

"Of course. No one is anyone in England without being introduced to Queen Victoria. I've already sent letters to friends in London about where we'll live and who we'll associate with—but don't worry about any of that. As your mother—" she paused and smiled at me "—it is my job to take care of all the little details."

She motioned to a chair next to Alec. The breakfast tray was on the table between them. "Have a seat and get something to eat. The dressmaker will be here at eleven."

"That's my cue to leave," Alec said.

"Nonsense." Mrs. Hill motioned to his chair. "You should stay for a while. I want to discuss a few things with you and Clara."

Alec took his seat again, but he had finished his meal, so he simply waited for his aunt to continue.

"First," she said as she poured me a cup of black tea, "Clara, you must call me Aunt Maude."

I nodded. That would be easy enough.

"And, second, I've decided to change some plans. Instead of hiding you away in your room, I believe the fastest way for you to acclimate to this lifestyle is if you interact with the servants—throughout the house. We'll eat breakfast in the breakfast room starting tomorrow, and luncheon and supper in the dining room. We'll use the front parlor for our morning lessons and the music room for our afternoon lessons. I don't want you interacting with any of them alone right now, except Gallagher, so either myself or Alec will always be with you."

Apprehension wound around my heart, but I nodded anyway.

"I would like you to start reading extensively, as well. You'll want a wide range of books to draw upon for conversation and you'll need access to the library. You do read, don't you?"

I nodded, my cheeks growing warm. Did she intend for me to go to the free circulating library on Bond Street? I had been there once, though it wasn't easy to get to and I rarely had time enough to read. But it had been thrilling to visit.

Alec glanced at me, and I finally met his eyes. I saw no trace of disdain for me or for what he had learned about me yesterday. But his gaze did search mine, though I wasn't sure what he was looking for.

"During the day," Aunt Maude continued, "I will conduct lessons in deportment, meal etiquette, parlor conversations, and the like. In the evening"—she turned to Alec—"I do wish you would help teach

Clara lessons in dancing, dinner conversation, parlor games, and flirting."

"Flirting?" he asked as he frowned at Aunt Maude.

"Yes," she said as she lifted her teacup. "And you don't need to limit the lessons to a single time and place. Flirting should come naturally to Clara, in all settings, therefore, I would like you and Clara to practice it whenever possible." She took a sip of her tea. "And try different tactics, approaches, and the like. One never knows when one will be in a situation with a potential suitor. Clara must be prepared for everything."

My cheeks burned at the thought of flirting with potential suitors—but more so at the thought of flirting with Alec.

When I finally got the courage to look at him again, I found he was watching me—but I couldn't tell what he was thinking.

"Clara should tour the house," Aunt Maude continued. "If you have time this morning, before the dressmaker comes, would you see to it, Alec? I have letters to write, and you could begin your flirting lessons."

My heart galloped at the thought.

"I suppose the office can get along without me for an hour or so," he said.

"Wonderful." Aunt Maude motioned to the food in front of me. "Finish your breakfast so Alec can take you on a tour."

My nerves had intensified to the point I'd lost my appetite. "I'm not hungry."

"Very well—but you must put on a few pounds before we leave for Europe. Shouldn't she, Alec?"

He smiled at me. "I believe Miss Clara is perfect as she is."

Warmth gathered in my cheeks, and I lowered my gaze.

"And what should you say to that, Clara?" Aunt Maude asked with all seriousness.

I was speechless.

"He just flirted with you," she said, nodding for me to respond. "How do you flirt back?"

Of course. I felt foolish.

I forced my gaze to return to Alec's.

If I was going to succeed and help Aunt Maude and Alec, then I would have to play the game. I had watched my cousin Fiona flirt with her husband during their courtship and knew enough to get by—though, with the stakes so much higher, it would be a different level of flirting than Fiona's.

Especially when they were men so high above my station. Anxiety overwhelmed me—but all I had to do was think about returning to Mulberry Street and I found the courage I needed.

"You're too kind, Mr. Paxton-Hill."

"Well," Aunt Maude said, a little disappointed. "It's not impressive, but it's a start. And remember to curb your accent, Clara. Emulate the sound of our voices and practice every chance you get. Now, be off on your tour and if you run into any of the staff and are forced to interact, let Alec speak for you."

Alec stood and offered me his hand, a teasing gleam lighting his eyes. "Are you ready to be dazzled by my brilliant personality?"

Was he flirting again? I had no idea how to respond, so I simply smiled and allowed him to help me stand.

He took my hand and slipped it into the crook of his elbow as he led me out of Aunt Maude's room.

Flirting might be the hardest lesson of all.

5

"Where shall we begin?" Alec asked in a playfully serious voice. "Flirting should come easily, as Aunt Maude suggested. It should be the natural result of conversation between two people who find each other desirable. It's meant to attract—without becoming too intense."

My cheeks were so hot, I was afraid they would give away my embarrassment. I found him very attractive—but there was nothing natural about what I was doing right now.

"Are you uncomfortable on my arm, Keira?" he asked me, easing away.

I nodded—and then shook my head—and then nodded again.

Alec laughed, but his eyes were thoughtful. "You are quite charming with your bright pink cheeks."

Was he flirting again? Or was he being sincere?

"If I make you uncomfortable, please tell me." He grew serious. "I never want you to feel uncomfortable with me."

I kept my arm in his and he walked me around the gallery, past all the pictures that had stared down at me the day before.

"Flirting should be interspersed through general conversation," he said next. "So, what shall we talk about?"

"The house?" I asked.

"Yes, of course." He smiled. "I had almost forgotten we were taking a tour."

He didn't sound at all like he was unhappy giving me his time and attention. Was he just pretending, for my benefit?

"My aunt and uncle built this home three years ago," he said. "Before that, they lived on Madison Avenue, but Aunt Maude wanted a better position in society—as you've come to realize—and she had this home built. It is one of the most expensive houses in New York City. Most of the rooms were imported from Europe, as were most of the furnishings. From palaces, castles, and chateaus. There might be more royal furniture in this home than in Versailles."

He chuckled and I smiled, but I could not comprehend such wealth.

"Shall we go downstairs?" he asked as we came to the staircase.

I nodded and asked, "How long have you lived here?"

"Since I moved to New York two years ago."

"You're not from here?"

"I'm from Boston. Uncle Edmund was my mother's brother. They were both raised in a wealthy home in Boston—my grandfather was a merchant. Edmund took the family money and invested it in real estate and hotels. My mother married my father, a minister. It was a love match, but my grandfather was very upset, and he disowned her. I am their only child and because Edmund and Maude had no children, I became my uncle's heir. He sent me to Harvard and as soon as I graduated, I was called here to apprentice with Uncle Edmund. When he passed away last year of a heart attack, I stepped in and took over."

"I'm sorry."

"Not as sorry as I am." His light-hearted banter had ended, and I suspected he had forgotten we were supposed to be flirting.

"You're not happy with the business?" I asked.

He turned at the bottom of the steps toward the front of the house. The main entrance was just as large as the gallery above and if I tilted my head up, I could see all the way to the stained-glass ceiling.

"I would be ungrateful if I said I wasn't happy."

"No—you would be honest, and there's nothing wrong with honesty."

Alec looked down at me and I was at a loss for more words. His blue eyes were so intense and full of emotions I couldn't identify. I'd never met anyone like him. Kind, thoughtful, intelligent—yet mysterious and filled with depth.

"This is the front parlor," Alec said as we walked into another oversized room with delicate furniture and expensive-looking wall coverings. "It opens to the music room behind it and the back parlor beyond that. When all three rooms are open, they make a large ballroom."

"Does Aunt Maude host balls?"

"Every year at Christmas."

Christmas. Just two months away. Would she expect me to attend? My legs felt weak at the thought.

We walked from the front parlor through the music room and into the back parlor.

"What do you do with the business?" I asked, curious about the life he led beyond these walls.

"I am the president of the eight hotels we own. There are three here in the city, one in Newport, two on Coney Island, one in Philadelphia, and one in Boston. I oversee all the major decisions regarding them and supervise the renovations being done to the resort in Newport. It's the most luxurious of our properties and the one that provides our largest income."

Eight hotels? I couldn't fathom that kind of responsibility. "If you aren't happy with the business," I said, picking up our earlier conversation, "what would you rather do?"

"It doesn't matter what I'd rather do," he said, a little stiff, though not unkind. "My path was set for me when I was young, and I haven't had the luxury of dreaming."

Alec and I were more alike than I'd realized.

We turned left in the back parlor and walked into a massive dining room along the backside of the house. The table was so large, I couldn't count the number of chairs around it without stopping. Above our heads, a mural had been painted on the ceiling with cherubs, clouds, and something like a Greek god shooting lightning out of his finger.

Large windows lined this room from floor to ceiling.

We walked through it silently and then he opened the door, and we reentered the front hall again. "What shall we talk about next?" he asked. "I'm supposed to be teaching you how to flirt, remember?"

"Perhaps I already know how to flirt," I said with a little smile and a lifting of my eyelashes in his direction. I'd seen Fiona do it a dozen times and had tried to perfect it—though I felt foolish now.

He paused as his face grew serious again. "Perhaps you do, Miss O'Day."

We looked at each other for a heartbeat and then he motioned for me to enter a room on the right. "Shall we continue to practice in my favorite room of the house?"

It was a library.

I paused just inside the enormous room, trying to take in the sheer number of books before me. There were thousands of them, on floor-to-ceiling shelves, surrounding a huge fireplace that dominated the center of the outside wall. There were little nooks and crannies with window seats, comfortable chairs, tables, and potted plants. And ladders, on both sides of the room, to get to the books on the upper shelves.

A hush fell over me.

People had libraries in their homes?

"If I hadn't had a life laid out for me," Alec said quietly, "I would become a scholar and perhaps a professor and spend all my time in a library."

He had an intelligent light in his eyes—I had noticed it right away. He'd been to Harvard. His father was a minister. He ran a large company and wanted to be a professor. His apparent brilliance was yet another thing that intimidated me and enthralled me all at the same time.

I, on the other hand, had only been educated by mission workers who had come to Five Points to teach the children basic letters and numbers. I knew enough to get by—but had never read a whole book.

Alec walked a few feet, looking at the books, and then turned to me and said, "What about you? If you weren't going to be a duchess." He smiled—but it didn't quite reach his eyes. "What did you hope to be, Keira?"

I felt vulnerable under his blue-eyed gaze, in an unfamiliar gown, in a room I had not even realized some people owned. How could I explain to him that I had never had the luxury of hoping to be something I wasn't—yet dreams had beckoned me, nonetheless?

I'd never shared my dream with anyone, for fear they'd laugh at me and steal the only joy I possessed. Somehow, I sensed—hoped—Alec wouldn't laugh.

"I dream of going west," I said quietly.

"West?"

"Beyond the Mississippi." I wasn't sure what was beyond the Mississippi—only freedom. "All I want is a cabin somewhere, near a stream and far away from New York City. With one enormous chair, where I can sit and sew to get by. It would be lovely."

He studied me for a moment, in that quiet way of his, and my heart felt like it quit beating. Would he laugh at me?

"I could see you in a cabin, by a stream, sewing."

"Could you?" My heart fluttered to life again. He was the first person who had envisioned it with me—and somehow that made it feel more real—more attainable.

"Would there be a library in your cabin?" he asked.

I smiled. Before now, I had never dreamed of a library in my cabin—but I nodded. "Aye."

"I like your dream, Keira."

"And I like yours, Mr.—"

"Alec."

Both of us were silent and I felt shy again, so I turned to the books and ran my fingers along the spines.

For the first time in years, my nails were clean.

A clock chimed somewhere in the house and Alec looked toward the door. "I should get to the office. They'll wonder what's keeping me."

I hated that our time together was at an end.

He walked across the room and joined me.

"Well?" I asked, lifting my chin, acting bolder than I felt. "How did me first lesson in flirtin' go?"

He grinned. "I think you're a natural." He offered me his arm to leave the library. "You're one of the most charming young women I've ever met and if it was up to me, I wouldn't change a thing about you."

I looked up at him, to see if he was serious—but I saw the hint of teasing in his gaze and knew he was only practicing with me again.

But I had no idea what to say.

The dressmaker stayed for hours and brought with her dozens of readymade dresses that were fitted for me. I hardly said a word as Aunt Maude made several selections. I lost count of how many gowns were left and how many were being ordered. There would be custom-made undergarments, shawls, hats, and more. Aunt Maude said we would go shopping for reticules, shoes, umbrellas, and ribbons.

And all of it would be mine.

I wanted to protest the expense but knew it wasn't my place. If she wanted to spend the money, she would. And I was under the impression that money was no worry—unless Mrs. Garfield married her daughter to a duke and people started going to their resort instead.

I struggled to wrap my mind around the sheer waste of it when I knew that Imogen was sitting at my workstation for hours a day, earning pennies for each shirtwaist she sewed, and only owning one hand-me-down dress. I should have given her my entire nine dollars and fifty cents when I left the apartment yesterday. At least then she might have something to give her a bit of hope for the future.

The dressmaker stayed until suppertime. Before she left, she helped me into an evening gown of fine blue silk. It had a large bustle in the back, with layers of fabric, a tight-fitting bodice with gold silk thread, and golden embroidered leaves.

Gallagher styled my hair high atop my head and placed a blue clip in the shape of a butterfly just behind my ear, before handing me my long, black gloves.

As I looked into the mirror again, I was starting to believe that all of this could be real. It was both exciting and terrifying.

"You'll want to go to the back parlor," Gallagher said to me. "Mrs. Hill will be waiting there for supper to begin."

Aunt Maude had told me what to expect. She said that they dressed for supper each night and gathered in the parlor before the butler, Higgins, came in to announce dinner.

From Alec's tour earlier, I knew right where the back parlor was.

I left my bedroom and walked across the short distance in the gallery to the head of the main stairs.

The dress felt heavy and burdensome with the layers of fabric, the tight corset, and the bustle.

And I felt shaky.

What would I talk about at supper? Several times that day, Mrs. Hill had chastised me for not speaking clearly or loud enough. She criticized my accent and had me practice several words over and over again.

I was exhausted.

But I had agreed to this, and I told myself it had to get easier every day.

So I descended the stairs and walked across the front hall to the parlor.

When I entered, I found Maude sitting on the sofa, sipping from a small glass and staring into the fire.

But Alec wasn't there.

"Clara," she said as she pulled her gaze away from the flames. "How lovely you look tonight. Come join me."

I tried not to let my disappointment show. Where was Alec? Would he not join us? I recalled Aunt Maude's words to him earlier, asking him to be present. He had told her that he didn't want to be lectured about his club. Was he at his club now?

The dress felt awkward as I tried to take a seat. There was so much fabric to manage that I felt like I was sitting atop a small mound.

"Here," Aunt Maude said as she set aside her glass. "Let me show you."

She stood and demonstrated how to move aside the bustle with a quick flick of her hand before taking a seat.

"Now you try," she said.

I practiced several times and then finally was able to settle my dress properly.

"See," she said with an approving smile. "You're doing quite well."

"Will Alec be joinin' us?" I asked her.

"'Will Alec join us this evening?' is the proper way to speak and enunciate the words. You try."

I repeated the phrase, trying my hardest, but it didn't sound anything like hers.

"We'll have to hire an elocutionist," she said with a sigh. "And to answer your question, I don't believe Alec will join us. He often dines at his club and doesn't return until late in the evening."

My heart sank a little more.

"Now," she said, "I have some news. I was able to secure passage for us on the SS *Oregon*, leaving New York on March 26. We will arrive in France a week later and visit the House of Worth for your London season wardrobe."

"I'll have *another* wardrobe?"

"Of course. One doesn't go to London for the season without a Worth wardrobe." She waved aside my concerns and said, "Then we'll arrive in London right after Easter, when the season starts. I have secured help from the Viscountess, Lady Mandeville. She is arranging a home for us and will work on our introduction to court."

I nodded, though I felt sick to my stomach just thinking about it.

"Before that," she said, "we will work at home on your lessons and have you ready to debut at my Christmas ball. There, we'll announce that you've been adopted. I've already spoken to my lawyers, and everything is moving along nicely. They believe the adoption will be final before the end of December."

"Adults can be adopted?" I asked—though it was a question I should have asked before now.

"Anyone can be adopted. It's not unheard of for a widow to adopt an heir or heiress, to secure their fortune."

My head was spinning, but I was torn from my thoughts as the door opened and the butler, Higgins, stepped into the room. "Dinner is served, madam."

Before either of us could respond, Alec appeared behind Higgins, wearing a black evening coat and white vest.

Both Aunt Maude and I looked toward him with surprise.

"I'm sorry to be—" He paused as I rose to greet him. He looked me over in the blue gown and his admiration shone from his gaze. "You look lovely tonight, Ke—Clara."

I had been practicing how I would respond to him. I bent my head in acknowledgment and said, in an accent as similar to Aunt Maude's as I could manage, "Thank you."

Aunt Maude rose, pleasure on her face. "You didn't stay at the club tonight."

"And miss a pleasant evening in the company of New York's finest ladies?"

She smiled. "Alec, take Clara's arm and show her how she'll be escorted into dinner at the parties we attend."

He gave me a short bow and then offered me his arm. "May I escort you into dinner, Miss Hill?"

I nodded, still uncomfortable with the new name, and took his arm. I felt just a little less awkward than I had earlier that day.

Aunt Maude led the way out of the parlor and down the hall to the dining room.

We followed behind her at a slower pace.

"Every time I see you," Alec said to me, "you look lovelier and lovelier. How is that possible?"

Was he flirting again? I needed to learn how to respond without embarrassment.

"'Tis the gowns," I said. "There are so many o' them—*of* them—and they're so expensive. If I didn't look lovely, Aunt Maude should ask for her money back."

He laughed and then shook his head. "I don't think it's just the gowns, Keira." He said my name quietly, so Aunt Maude wouldn't hear. "You're glowing."

"I'm happy."

He grew serious. "Then I'm happy."

We entered the dining room. Aunt Maude sat at the head of the table, while I sat at her right and Alec took a seat at her left, across from me.

"The man of the house usually sits at the head," Aunt Maude said to me as a footman stepped forward and laid her napkin on her lap. "But this is my home, so I sit here."

"This isn't Alec's home?" I asked.

"I'm only a guest," Alec corrected.

"But I thought you inherited the business. I assumed the house came with it."

Something uncomfortable passed between Maude and Alec.

"Yes," Alec said. "I inherited the business, but Uncle Edmund left the house and a generous allowance to Aunt Maude."

"It isn't proper to speak about such things at supper," Aunt Maude said as she nodded at Higgins to begin the meal and then glanced at one of the footmen, as if gauging how much they were listening to our conversation.

The staff still didn't know my identity—and no doubt she didn't want them gossiping about me after the meal.

I had never sat at such a grand table or been served by footmen. If I thought the meal last night was lavish—this one was extravagant. Soup, fish, salad greens, vegetables, meat, bread, and more were served in various courses. Aunt Maude showed me which silverware to use, while Alec watched with a secretive smile—that teasing gleam always present.

The meal felt like it lasted a lifetime—but when it was finally over, Aunt Maude said it was time to move to the back parlor for evening entertainment.

"Alec?" she asked, frowning as she touched her temple. "Will you see to Clara?"

He nodded as he extended his elbow to me once again.

"After dinner," he said, "the men usually recline with brandy and cigars in the billiards room or at the table and the women retire to the parlor for gossip as they wait for us. But with just the three of us, I'll join you in the evenings after supper."

"You'll come again?" I asked.

His smile was so warm—so sincere—my heart fluttered. "I would not miss an evening of your company, Miss O'Day."

"Does that mean you'll be staying away from that club of yours?" Aunt Maude asked.

Again, something passed between them, but Alec only smiled. "I'll be home as often as possible."

Before we entered the parlor, Aunt Maude stopped in the hall and let out a sigh as she touched her temple again. "My head is aching tonight. I hope you won't mind if I retire early."

"Of course not," Alec said.

"Please see to the evening activities without me." She laid her hand on my arm. "Clara has much to learn, so I trust you'll do your part to see that she's instructed in parlor etiquette."

He nodded.

"And," she said as she started to walk away, "don't forget to flirt."

We stood still—neither of us responding to her. What did I say to such a comment?

As she walked up the stairs, Alec turned me toward the back parlor. "It's not usually proper for an unmarried man and a woman to be alone together."

My pulse ticked up a notch at his words. "Then why is Aunt Maude going to bed?"

He glanced toward the stairs, his gaze inscrutable. "I imagine she thinks of us as cousins—though I'm struggling to see it that way."

I wasn't sure what he meant.

We moved into the parlor, and it felt large and imposing with just the two of us.

"Do you play an instrument?" he asked me.

I shook my head.

"Do you sing?"

I opened my mouth to say no—but that wasn't true. "Sometimes, for meself."

"Wonderful. It's desirable for a young lady to perform during evening entertainments."

"I will need to perform? In front of a duke?"

He laughed. "Even dukes are just men."

There was so much to learn.

Alec took a seat at the piano and ran his fingers along the keys. The sound filled the room with a melody I'd never heard before.

He played piano, too?

"Do you know 'I'll Take You Home Again, Kathleen'?" He began to play the familiar song, its gentle, haunting beauty coming alive beneath his fingers. Then he joined the piano with his voice, and it was mesmerizing.

"I'll take you home again, Kathleen
Across the ocean wild and wide
To where your heart has ever been
Since first you were my bonny bride."

He smiled at me, and a wave of affection overwhelmed me. I hardly knew what to do with myself, so I began to sing.

"The roses all have left your cheek
I've watched them fade away and die
Your voice is sad whenever you speak
And tears bedim your loving eyes."

He stopped singing as he listened to me, a tender look on his handsome face.

When I hesitated before the last verse, he nodded with encouragement for me to continue.

"Oh, I will take you back, Kathleen
To where your heart will feel no pain
And when the fields are fresh and green
I'll take you to your home again."

He played the final notes and his hands rested on the piano, the sound slowly dying.

"That was beautiful, Keira." He shook his head, almost in disbelief. "I've never heard such a sweet and pure voice."

"Thank you." I looked down at the piano, not used to hearing so many compliments.

"If your blushing cheeks or sweet disposition don't win over a duke, surely your singing will."

I caught the teasing gleam in his eyes and decided I would give him back a little of his own medicine.

"And what about you?" I asked him, leaning against the piano. "You must have a line o' young ladies waiting for you to turn their way." It hadn't occurred to me that he might already be courting or engaged.

The realization stung more than it should after such a short amount of time.

Alec looked down at his hands and played a simple tune as he shook his head.

"You aren't interested in gettin' married?" I asked him.

"One day," he said, finishing the tune. "I'd very much like to be married."

"You haven't met anyone?"

"I've met many young ladies."

"And?" I watched him, surprised he wasn't forthcoming when he was usually so eager to tease and flirt.

Alec finally looked up at me, his blue eyes shining in the light of the piano lamp. "Most have only one thing in mind and that's to marry well. They don't usually care who the gentleman is, but what he has to offer. I'm not interested in being loved for my money or position."

I lowered my gaze, my cheeks warming with embarrassment. I was guilty of that exact thing, wasn't I? Marrying a duke for his title.

Alec laid his hand over mine and I lifted my eyes again.

"I didn't mean to imply that you're like the others, Keira." He slowly pulled his hand away and set it on the keys again. "You're nothing like them. I would hate to see you become a copy of all the rest."

"You hardly know me," I said, thinking of all the reasons I shouldn't stay as I was—yet realizing he knew more about me than most.

His smile was sad as he ran his fingers over the keys again, playing another tune.

"It's been a long day," he finally said as he lifted his hands from the piano. "I'm sure you're tired and Aunt Maude will expect you to be up early tomorrow for more lessons."

He stood and offered me his elbow.

I took it and he walked me out of the parlor, up the stairs, and to my bedroom door.

When we arrived, he let go of my arm and faced me.

"For what it's worth," he said, "we haven't known each other long, but the little I've learned about you has told me everything I need to know."

And, with that, he walked away.

6

"Clara! Wake up! What has gotten into? You must *never* fall asleep while socializing with others."

I opened my eyes with a jerk and sat up straight. "Pardon me."

Aunt Maude clicked her tongue with disappointment as she shook her head and glanced at the two ladies sitting with us in the parlor.

My cheeks warmed under her displeasure as I lifted my cards for the game of whist we were playing with Mrs. Walker and Gallagher.

For two and a half weeks, I had been working day and night on my lessons. On evenings like this one, when Aunt Maude needed extra people, she called Mrs. Walker and Gallagher to join us. They had come into the parlor after Aunt Maude and I had finished supper and looked almost as uncomfortable as I felt.

"It's your turn," Aunt Maude said to me. She was sitting across the table, holding her cards. Candlelight flickered from the holders on the corners of the table, sparkling off her jewelry.

I tried to focus on my cards, but my eyes were so bleary, I could hardly tell the spades from the clubs—and I didn't care. All I wanted was my bed.

Knowing Aunt Maude, she still had hours of work ahead of me.

I laid a high diamond, and she lowered her cards, more disappointment in her gaze. "You've just lost the trick for us," she said.

Mrs. Walker picked up the four cards and laid them on her ever-growing pile of tricks.

"I'm sorry." I tried hard to speak as she'd instructed me. "I'm so tired."

Aunt Maude set the rest of her cards on the table and nodded. "Perhaps we should be done for tonight."

My shoulders sagged in relief, and I wanted to cry with happiness. I had not gone to bed before midnight since arriving at the mansion and was expected to rise each morning at six.

"Mrs. Walker and Gallagher, you may go." Aunt Maude rose from the table as the ladies stood and bobbed a curtsey before leaving the room.

I also stood, but as I moved toward the door, Aunt Maude stopped me.

"We're not finished, Clara," she said. "Come join me on the sofa."

My feet ached from standing in uncomfortable shoes, my back was sore from wearing such tight corsets, and my head throbbed from the incessant lessons. Night and day, Aunt Maude had pushed me beyond comprehension.

I pulled myself over to her and lowered onto the sofa as she'd instructed—perched on the edge, my back straight, my chin up, and my hands folded in my lap—trying not to let my misery show.

"Have you finished *The Scarlet Letter*?" she asked me. "I thought we could practice your diction through discussing the book tonight."

In my spare time, when she was attending social events and wasn't offering lessons in dancing, walking, eating, singing, embroidering, history, social etiquette, or diction, she required that I read. I had finished *The Scarlet Letter*, but at the moment, I couldn't remember a single word I had read.

I stared at her as she looked at me.

"You haven't finished it?"

"I have." I finally crumpled as I bent forward and placed my face in my hands, letting the tears fall. "I'm just so tired."

She didn't speak for a moment, but then she finally said. "Pull yourself together, Clara. The life of a duchess will be far more grueling than this. One must never yield to the weight of her difficulties."

The clock struck ten and I forced myself to sit up straight. I should be used to hard work, after all. I used to sit with a needle and thread in hand for twelve hours a day most of my life. But this was different. It required mental and emotional energy, as well.

"You remind me of Alec," she said.

At the sound of his name, I rallied. Alec had been gone for almost two weeks, on business in Newport, I'd been told. I wasn't sure when he'd return, but the house was not the same without him. We'd only had a few days together before he'd left suddenly, without saying goodbye. One morning he was there, showing me the gardens—and that evening, Aunt Maude told me he had left the city.

"How do I remind you of him?" I asked, speaking carefully—slowly.

"He was just as overwhelmed as you at the beginning. Just as exhausted as he learned what was expected of him. But he adapted, and you will, too." She touched the pearl-drop earrings at my ears, and a smile tilted her lips. "I know I am asking a lot of you, but it's because I want this endeavor to succeed—for you, just as much as for Alec and me. You have a lifetime of education to learn in just seven months, and I cannot ease up, even just a little."

I wanted to hear more about Alec, but I didn't dare ask. Surely being raised by a minister and the daughter of a wealthy merchant, he should have already possessed the necessary skills to function in society.

The parlor door creaked open, and we both looked up.

As if being summoned by our conversation, Alec appeared.

My heart sped at the sight of him. The waves of his curly brown hair, the sparkle in his bright blue eyes, the way he carried himself with both ease and confidence.

I stood with Aunt Maude, conscious of my gown, my hair, my earrings—and the tremble in my hands.

"Alec," Aunt Maude said. "I wasn't expecting you back so soon."

Two weeks was soon? I had waited, every day, wondering if this was the day he'd return.

"I was called back to the city," he said to Aunt Maude as he crossed the room and took her hand before placing a kiss on her cheek. "I hope I'm not interrupting."

"Of course not," she said.

He pulled away from Aunt Maude and turned to me. Had he been my real cousin, perhaps he would have taken my hand and given me a kiss without hesitation.

The very thought made my cheeks burn.

"Hello, Clara," he said and extended his hand.

I rested my hand in his. *Would* he kiss me as he'd kissed Aunt Maude?

He lifted my hand to his lips and placed a kiss there. "You look lovely this evening."

I was speechless as I took my hand back and laid my other one over the spot he had kissed.

"Clara?" Aunt Maude lifted her eyebrows. "We've practiced this."

I blinked a couple of times and swallowed the nerves. Of course. This was part of my education. His compliments were part of the curriculum. "Aye—yes. Thank you, Alec." I blundered through my words, trying not to blush even more.

"I see you haven't been practicing the art of flirting while I've been away," he said, a twinkle in his eyes.

Something inside me responded to that twinkle and I returned his smile. "And who would I flirt with? Higgins?"

"That I would like to see." He laughed at the thought of the stodgy, serious butler engaged in a flirtatious conversation and I joined him. Poor Higgins.

Aunt Maude let out a sigh, and I knew she didn't approve of our teasing.

Alec sobered and said, "Your accent is changing." There was something wistful in his voice.

"I should say it is." Aunt Maude returned to the sofa. "We've been working around the clock to fix her elocution. It's probably the hardest thing I've done while you've been away."

I remained near Alec and tried to smile, though it was hard, thinking about the long hours of work we had done. The countless times I'd been corrected, feeling ashamed, embarrassed, and uneducated.

"You're tired," he said, concern softening his eyes. "Are you getting any sleep?"

He was the first person who had inquired after my wellbeing since he'd left.

I opened my mouth to respond, but Aunt Maude interrupted.

"Now that you're here," she addressed Alec, "I could use a break this evening. I was going to converse with Clara about Nathaniel Hawthorne's novel, but she's in desperate need of dancing practice. An instructor has been here every day this week, but she must put the lessons to use. I would like for you to practice in the front parlor. Peter is an excellent pianist. I'll have him summoned to play for you."

Dance? My feet and back ached at the thought of dancing. And with Alec? I would stumble through each step, I was certain. Embarrassment warmed my cheeks just thinking about it. I wanted to protest, but that had earned me nothing but a stern lecture in the past.

"What Clara needs is rest," Alec said to his aunt. "It's past ten o'clock. She should be in bed."

"Nonsense. The night is still young. When she's attending balls, she'll be up until two or three in the morning. She must get used to long evenings once we introduce her to society."

"Most debutantes sleep until noon so they can stay up that late. I doubt you've allowed her to sleep past six." There was an edge to his voice.

"Do not question my methods, Alec." Her edge matched his. "Clara is my daughter and my responsibility. Her success or failure is at stake, and I will do whatever is necessary to ensure she succeeds. You, of all people, should understand."

I looked between them as they stared at one another.

"Clara," Maude said, "please give Alec and me a moment alone."

Nodding, I left the parlor and closed the door behind me, relieved to step away from the tension that had coiled around the three of us. Were the two of them always at odds with one another? Why didn't Alec leave the mansion and strike out on his own?

I stood in the massive hallway, unsure if I should go up to my room or wait there for Aunt Maude to summon me.

"I cannot help you," I heard Alec say, his voice muffled, but still easy to hear.

My breath caught. I didn't want to eavesdrop, but I wasn't sure where to go.

"You cannot—or you do not want to?"

There was a moment of silence before Alec said, "I do not want to help."

"Is that why you ran away to Newport?"

Again. Silence.

"I do not understand your aversion to Clara," Aunt Maude continued. "But you must put it behind you. We cannot fail. I know it and you know it."

Alec had an aversion to me? He'd run away to Newport to avoid me. The truth stung and I took a step away from the door.

"My plan with Clara is just as important as your plan for the new hotel on Coney Island," Aunt Maude continued. "I need all the help I can get, and I'll expect you to put a smile on your face and spend time in Clara's company whenever possible—whether you want to or not. No more running away."

"She is in over her head," he said. "She wasn't made for this life."

Was I that repulsive to him? I caught my reflection in a tall mirror. Though I wore a lavish silk gown and was adorned with diamonds and pearls, I saw what Alec saw. I heard what he heard. The poor Irish girl from Five Points with the course accent and ill-mannered relatives.

How was I supposed to convince a duke I was any different if I couldn't even convince Alec?

I stepped farther away, not wanting to hear more. Their muffled voices rose with passion.

When things finally quieted, the door opened, and Alec appeared. He stepped out of the parlor and looked around the hallway until he found me.

His shoulders were stiff, and his head was held high—but when his gaze met mine, it lowered a notch, and he smiled at me.

It took all my strength to return the smile because I knew it wasn't real.

None of this was real.

Though he was very good at pretending.

He walked toward me, and I could see he was uncomfortable—possibly embarrassed. A grown man didn't like to be told what to do, even if Aunt Maude was like a mother to him.

The last thing I wanted was to be the object of their disagreement—or the person Alec was forced to be around when he wanted to be anywhere else but here.

I swallowed the uneasiness that crept up my throat and fought the urge to run. Where would I go? I had agreed to this charade, and I needed to stick to the plan. If I couldn't face Alec, how could I be presented to the Queen of England?

What was my alternative? Return to Five Points?

I shuddered just thinking about it.

Alec stopped in front of me, his blue eyes searching my face.

Was he wondering what I'd heard?

"I'm sorry," he said. "She is one of the most stubborn, single-minded women I've ever known."

"She wants what's best for you."

He made a sound and shook his head. "She wants what's best for the Hill name."

"Which includes you."

"I suppose." He ran his hand through his hair, causing it to turn into a riot of curls. "She expects us to dance, so she's sending for Peter, who is probably asleep in his bed. The poor man."

It was my turn to apologize. "I'm sorry."

He frowned. "Why are you sorry? You're the one who's exhausted."

"I know you'd rather not dance with me."

His lips parted and he looked confused for a heartbeat. "That's not—" He paused and then started over. "I hate seeing you exhausted and in pain."

"I'll be fine."

"One dance," he said. "And no more."

Was that all he could stand? I tried not to let my disappointment show, but it was impossible. I had to look down at my hands, so he wouldn't see the hurt in my eyes.

"Hey," he said as he set his fingers under my chin and gently lifted my face to look at him. There was a strange expression in his gaze. "Were you hoping to dance more than that?"

I swallowed and forced a smile. "I'll dance as many as you desire."

He stared at me for a moment and then shook his head. "What I desire is rarely what matters."

His response was strange, but I hardly had time to discern his meaning when he grinned and offered me his arm.

"Besides, you know what they say when an unmarried couple dances more than two times together."

I frowned and shook my head. "What do they say?"

He leaned closer, as if he was taking me into his confidence. "That they must be madly in love and an engagement is soon to follow. Unless you want the gossips to talk, you must never allow a gentleman such liberties."

I slipped my hand through his arm and allowed him to escort me to the front parlor, where the grand piano sat. "And what if the gossips talk?"

"Then your reputation could be ruined and your chances of marrying a duke will be reduced."

"For dancing with a gentleman more than two times?"

"That is only the beginning," he said. "Has Aunt Maude taught you ballroom etiquette yet?"

"She told me that a woman must never move about a ballroom unescorted and that a gentleman must take her onto the dance floor and off again." I spoke slowly, trying to ensure my words sounded proper. "A woman must never go anywhere without an escort. To be seen walking alone is frowned upon."

Peter, the footman, entered, smoothing back his hair. His eyes were sleepy as he offered a quick bow and then moved to the piano.

I wanted to apologize to him, but Aunt Maude had told me that I should never apologize or thank the staff for doing their job.

"What would you like, sir?" Peter asked Alec.

Alec looked to me. "What would *you* like?"

No one had asked my opinion in weeks.

"A waltz?" I said, uncertain.

"Is that what you want?"

It had been the easiest dance for me to learn, so I nodded.

"A waltz, Peter," Alec said.

Peter began playing a song I had heard earlier in the week. It was a hauntingly beautiful tune that had swept me away. I didn't know the words—or if there even were lyrics to the song—but I loved it. There hadn't been a lot of music in my life in Five Points, and if there was, it was Irish folk songs.

Alec bowed to me, and I curtsied, as I'd been taught by Aunt Maude. I lifted the train of my evening gown into my right hand and took a step toward Alec.

He paused for a moment, and I wondered if he was having second thoughts about dancing.

I stood, waiting for him, my heart thumping hard against my breastbone. What if he walked away? Decided he didn't want to honor Aunt Maude's request?

Finally, he took a step toward me, his face very serious, as he slipped his left hand around my waist.

I caught my breath. The dancing instructor had been close, but I had felt nothing.

This was much different.

Alec took my left hand into his and we looked at each other for a heartbeat before he began to lead me around the floor.

Just as I feared, I felt clumsy and awkward in his arms. My feet didn't want to move properly, and I couldn't seem to remember anything I'd been taught.

I stared down at my feet, trying to keep time.

"Keira." Alec whispered my real name.

I hadn't heard it since he'd left.

"Look at me," he said.

I did as he instructed.

His blue eyes were filled with compassion—and that twinkle I had come to recognize.

"Don't focus on your feet or what you've been taught. Listen to the music, feel your partner's movements, and, above all else, enjoy the journey."

"Journey?"

"A dance is like a journey," he said. "There is a beginning, a middle, and an end—and so much to discover along the way about the person standing opposite from you."

"And what are you discoverin' 'bout me?" My words lilted with an Irish brogue. I didn't know why I asked that question, slipping back into the cadence of speech I'd used since childhood. Would he think me too forward? Or would he think I was trying to flirt? After all, we were supposed to be doing that, too.

"You are inexperienced."

Embarrassment warmed my neck and cheeks and I had to look away.

But he wasn't finished. "You're a breath of fresh air, Keira O'Day. Sweet, gentle, and innocent. Unsullied by this world you've entered."

I looked back at him and saw the honesty in his gaze.

"It is my prayer that it will not ruin your tenderness," he said.

"Sure now, and you've forgotten where I grew up. There's nothing pure or tender about that."

"I could never forget where you grew up."

Of course he couldn't. He knew the worst part of me and would always know.

We finished the waltz and then Peter played a polka—but I was so exhausted, I almost collapsed. When Peter asked if we wanted a third dance, Alec shook his head.

"I believe we're done," he said to the footman. "You may retire."

"Very good, sir." Peter bowed and left the room, looking as relieved as I felt.

"You should go to bed," Alec said to me. "May I escort you to your room?"

I nodded and placed my arm through his.

We left the front parlor and entered the main hall. The wall sconces had been dimmed, and the house was quiet.

The stairway looked daunting as we came to the base of it.

But I drew up my strength with the hem of my gown, and we began to ascend.

Alec didn't rush me, for which I was grateful.

The silence stretched between us, so I said, "Did you have a successful business trip to Newport?"

He didn't need to answer for me to know it was disappointing. I could tell by the slope of his shoulders, the heaviness in his footsteps, and the way he let out a weighty breath.

"We have a business rival who is opening a hotel next to ours this summer and we're already seeing our reservations dwindle. We cater to a wealthy clientele, and they have expensive tastes. Garfield's hotel will be electrified. It would cost a fortune to electrify ours—and we couldn't have it done by the summer, even if we tried. We're also building a third hotel on Coney Island and that has cost more than we budgeted—much more."

Did I admit I had overheard him discussing this issue with Aunt Maude? What would it hurt?

"Mr. Garfield's daughter will be goin' to England, too?"

He looked at me, surprised. "You've heard about Louise?"

"Aye."

"Yes, she will be searching for her own duke." His words sounded strangely bitter. Was he in love with Louise?

"And if I find one first? Will that help your hotel?"

He was silent for a moment and then said, "That's what Aunt Maude believes."

I lifted my shoulders with renewed energy. "Then I will do my best to win the heart of a duke before Louise Garfield."

We came to the top of the stairs and Alec led me across the gallery to my room.

When we arrived, he turned to me.

"What do you want, Keira?" His gaze was intense as he studied me.

It was the second time he'd asked me that question, but this time, it felt different. Not simply what I wanted to do with my life—but what my heart longed for.

What *did* I want? Beyond freedom from Five Points, a little cabin next to a stream, and being able to live comfortably?

"I want to know where I came from."

"Aren't you from England?"

I shook my head. "I was born in England and raised by my Irish relatives. I want to know me parents. At least, me mother, if she's still alive. I want to know who I am."

The upper gallery was dim, but I could see Alec clearly. His handsome face was gentle as he smiled.

"I understand," he said. "But please, don't lose who you are in the process of trying to answer that question."

He lifted my hand and placed another kiss on top. Then, with a gallant and exaggerated bow, he said, "I have escorted you safely back to your room. My task is complete."

With a grin, he winked at me and then turned and walked across the gallery to his room on the other side.

His words had been meant to tease—or flirt—but they hurt more than I wanted to admit.

7

The sound of church bells woke me up on Christmas morning. Frost hugged the edges of the windows in my bedroom, but the air was warm. No draft or hint of winter inside the palace-like room on Fifth Avenue.

Aunt Maude wouldn't stand for it.

"Good morning, miss," Gallagher said as she opened the shutters a little wider to let in the brilliant sunshine. A fire crackled in the hearth behind her. "And Merry Christmas."

"Merry Christmas," I said as I sat up in bed and stretched.

Slowly, I lowered my arms as realization dawned.

As of yesterday afternoon, the adoption had been finalized. I was now legally Clara Day Hill.

But that was hardly the most exciting—or terrifying—thing about today.

For the first time since Alec and I had returned from Five Points, I would leave the house again. And I would interact with other people—society people—who must never know the truth about my identity.

"Mrs. Hill has decided you shall wear the burgundy cut-velvet silk with chenille fringe to church," Gallagher said in her brisk manner. We'd spent two months together, but I knew very little about her and she about me. Aunt Maude had cautioned me not to get close or personal with the staff and Gallagher made it easy. I wasn't even sure if she liked me.

"Is that her final decision?" I asked. "She's changed her mind half a dozen times since yesterday."

"I believe so, miss."

It didn't matter to me. I had dozens of gowns, and though I liked some more than others, I had tried to keep my own preferences to myself. There was little point in stating my opinions since Aunt Maude made almost every decision for me.

As I bathed and allowed Gallagher to help me with my church toilette, my excitement and trepidation mounted.

I had been living on Fifth Avenue for two months—two of the most grueling and tiring months of my life. And today the entire experiment would be put to the test. Not only would I be required to attend Aunt Maude's church, but this evening, she was hosting a dinner party. If all went well, we would start to pay calls on New Year's Day and hopefully, I would receive invitations to society functions.

The grandest coup of them all would be an invitation to Mrs. Vanderbilt's costume ball, to be held at the end of March. Three months away and it was already being hailed as the most remarkable and extravagant party the city had ever seen. Over a thousand guests would be invited. My performance over the next couple of months would determine if I was to be one of them.

And then, England.

But none of that was as important as what would happen as soon as Gallagher finished my toilette.

I would have breakfast, alone, with Alec.

As soon as I was dressed, I left my room and made my way downstairs toward the breakfast room. Aunt Maude would have her breakfast in bed, as was the custom for most married ladies. Since my arrival, she'd been eating breakfast with Alec and me, but now that I was officially adopted, she felt it important that we create a standard routine.

I tried not to look too eager as I crossed the front hall, slowing my step. I wasn't even sure if I could stomach breakfast with the butterflies wreaking havoc inside me. The last thing I wanted was to embarrass Aunt Maude or, worse, disappoint Alec—and it was making me feel ill.

Alec was sitting at the head of the table, leaning forward, his hands clasped, his elbows on the table. He stared out the window at the frozen world beyond, deep in thought.

The aroma of sausages, cinnamon, and fresh-baked pastries filled the small, intimate room, tucked into the corner of the house. Breakfast had been set on the sideboard, meant to be dished up as each family member arrived, but the lids were still in place. Higgins and the first footman stood silently by the door to the butler's pantry, waiting.

"Merry Christmas," I said as I stepped into the room.

Alec tore his gaze from the window and rose at my entrance. His hair was still damp, and his face freshly shaved. He was dressed in a fine, black suit, ready for church.

He took in my appearance, an approving smile lighting his face. "Merry Christmas, Clara. You look lovely this morning."

I'd had months of practice and now smiled easily at his compliment. "Thank you."

The footman lifted the lids off the silver chafing dishes and stepped back so we could fill our plates.

There were cheese turnovers and egg fritters, alongside sausages, cinnamon pear butter, crumpets, and stewed apples. I wasn't sure if I could eat a bite, but I filled my plate, conscious of Aunt Maude's reprimands to put on a little more weight before we traveled to France for my Worth wardrobe.

I also thought of my family in Five Points and the meager breakfast they would be eating. I had used my remaining money and sent Gallagher off to purchase gifts for Imogen, Polly and Patrick. They should have been delivered by now, and though I hadn't included a card, I suspected they knew where the gifts had come from. It was the least I could do as I enjoyed all this splendor. I only hoped I could do more one day.

The footman held my chair for me as I took a seat and then Higgins filled my glass with orange juice and Alec's with coffee.

"Thank—" Alec paused and then nodded at Higgins. "That will be all. You may join the others for your own Christmas breakfast."

"Sir?" Higgins asked with a frown.

"Miss Hill and I can serve ourselves."

Higgins continued to frown, but he bowed at the waist and then shooed the footman from the room, disappearing behind the butler's pantry door.

"I hope you don't mind," Alec said to me. "I can't abide having someone looking over my shoulder as I eat."

I grinned. "I don't mind in the least. I haven't eaten a single thing without an audience in two months."

"Aunt Maude will have my head when she hears." His eyes crinkled at the corners. "But it shall be worth it."

I reached for my fork, but Alec stopped me.

"May I say grace?" he asked.

I paused, a little surprised. I had been raised in a Catholic church and attended each week, but it had been out of obligation and tradition. Uncle Charlie and Aunt Orla never spoke of God or worried overmuch about what He thought of them outside Mass. Aunt Maude attended her church every week, as well, but it had been much the same.

"Grace?" I asked.

"I say grace silently before each meal, but I miss sharing it with my family, especially on Christmas morning. Would you mind?"

"Of course not," I said quickly, though I did feel a bit awkward. Was I expected to know how to say grace? Did he have a memorized prayer in mind? I worried my bottom lip, afraid I would start this day with a mistake even before I left the house.

Alec surprised me, again, by offering me his hand. "May I?"

With a frown, I took his hand and watched as he closed his eyes.

The pressure of his fingers against mine was all I could think about as I, too, closed my eyes.

His prayer was brief—yet heartfelt. It wasn't a memorized litany of words, but a prayer of thanksgiving and gratitude for our many blessings.

After he said amen, I slowly opened my eyes and found him smiling at me.

"Thank you," he said as he let my hand go.

I was speechless. I'd never heard anyone pray as he had just done. Could one talk to God as if they were speaking to a friend?

"You look surprised," he said, a smile in his voice and eyes.

Was this yet another thing I had not been taught? Warmth filled my cheeks, and I tried not to look as ignorant as I felt.

"Do you not speak to God, Keira?"

He only called me Keira when we were alone, which wasn't as often as it had been at the beginning. Every time he said my name, I felt a strange pang. It was a bittersweet feeling, since it was the name my mother had given me—yet it was connected to a past I wanted to forget.

"I speak to Him in church," I said, hoping that would appease him. "When I recite the Lord's Prayer."

"You believe He exists?"

"Yes." I knew God was there—I just wasn't sure if He was aware of me.

"You can speak to Him anywhere you like," Alec assured me, probably seeing the skepticism on my face. "He is not confined to a church building or to the clergy. He is present, everywhere, and He loves talking to His children. You can share your hopes and dreams, and your fears and frustrations. You can speak to Him as I'm speaking to you."

I tried not to frown, but I couldn't help it. His words were astonishing to me.

"Try it," he said with a chuckle. "I promise it's true. You can also read the Bible and see for yourself that it's full of people talking to God."

The thought of speaking to God or reading the Holy Bible was both exciting and terrifying. For as long as I could remember, I'd been taught that it was the priest's job to read and interpret the Bible for me. And that he would petition God on my behalf. Was it blasphemy to approach God on my own?

We began to eat our breakfast, but Alec stopped me once again.

"I almost forgot." He reached into his pocket and withdrew a small box wrapped in brown paper packaging. He set the box on the table and slid it toward me. "Merry Christmas, Keira."

I blinked in surprise. The only Christmas gifts I had ever received were second-hand gifts such as dresses, shoes, or books through the mission workers in Five Points.

No one had ever purchased a gift with me in mind.

"I didn't get you anything," I said.

"I didn't expect you to." He nudged the box a little closer to me. "There will be more gifts later, after church, but I wanted to give this to you now."

It took me a moment, but I finally reached for the box and untied the string. The paper fell away, and I lifted the lid.

Nestled on a bed of silk was a broach in the shape of a flower, with at least a hundred tiny pink diamonds glittering in the morning sunshine. When I looked up at Alec, he had a grin on his face, and he reached into his pocket and pulled out the silk flower he had purchased from me outside the Metropolitan Opera House the night we had met.

"I had it made to match the flower that introduced us," he said.

It was an identical representation, though one was made of silk and thread and the other of gold and diamonds.

"A fair trade, I think," he said as he pinned my silk flower to the lapel of his suit.

I was speechless. The flower I made had cost me pennies. The broach—I couldn't even put a price on it. But I was certain it could get my aunt and uncle out of Five Points for life. "I can't—"

"Don't make me beg you to accept my gift." He reached into the box and lifted the broach out. He placed it in my palm and closed my fingers around it, keeping his hand over mine. There was sadness in his expressive eyes. "I want you to have it, if for no other reason than to remember me when you're a duchess."

I slowly nodded and forced myself not to cry.

I wouldn't need a diamond broach to remember Alexander Paxton-Hill.

The tower of St. Thomas Episcopal Church loomed before us as we stepped out of the carriage. Bells tolled from high above as some of the finest-dressed people I'd ever seen entered the building. Passersby gawked at their expensive finery, but the social elite didn't seem to notice the attention—at least, they pretended they didn't. I wasn't sure I would ever get used to strangers staring at me. I'd spent a lifetime trying to blend in. Now, as I stood before the church with the cold December wind slicing through me, I felt conspicuous. A fraud. And everyone would know it as soon as I opened my mouth.

Every bit of me trembled, and not from the cold. I had never been more terrified. Everything Aunt Maude and Alec had taught me fled from my mind. I was Keira O'Day, the poor tenement girl, dressed up in a costume, trying to pretend to be someone else.

Aunt Maude led the way with a regal countenance as Alec offered me his arm.

"Just remember to breathe," he said.

I took a breath, but it felt like I couldn't fill my lungs.

We walked into the church, and it was just as cool inside as out.

The cathedral was magnificent. My gaze traveled to the heights of the curved ceiling, and I tried not to let my amazement show. The grandeur put every other building I had ever seen to shame. Yet, if I was Maude's niece, educated and refined as we were to pretend, then this church would be like all the others I had seen.

People spoke quietly amongst themselves as they found their pews. I knew the exact moment they noticed me on Alec's arm. Curiosity shone in their faces and then the speculation began and the whispering intensified. It was like a wave as it followed us up the aisle.

Aunt Maude had told me that the wealthy set in New York encompassed only about a thousand people, so everyone knew everyone else—at least by sight, if not by association.

I was trembling so violently, Alec set his gloved hand over mine and gave it a gentle squeeze of reassurance. I could almost hear him tell me to breathe again. Using my free hand, I touched the diamond broach at my neck, finding strength in his gift.

As we took our seats near the front of the church, I was thankful for the solid pew beneath me. But it was only a matter of time before I would have to face those curious eyes and convince them that I was one of them.

The Episcopal service was similar to the Catholic ones I had known my whole life. It was the only familiarity I had felt in months, and it filled me with comfort. I thought of Alec's prayer over breakfast and wondered what it might feel like to speak my own words to God. Would He listen to me? Did He care what I was doing? Would He help me?

As the choir sang "Angels We Have Heard on High," I bowed my head and whispered a fervent and heartfelt prayer. The first of its kind. I had never thought I could speak to God, but here, on Christmas morning, with Alec on one side of me and Aunt Maude on the other, I was desperate. My heart fluttered to think He might listen. That He might care. That I might matter to Him. And not because I wore an expensive gown or sat in this magnificent church. But because I was His child, as Alec said.

When the minister, Mr. John Wesley Brown, gave the benediction, I tried to listen to each word. To understand my place in God's creation. Could I know? Did He reveal that sort of thing to a person? I had so many questions for Alec, but I didn't want him to see my ignorance. He saw enough of that already.

Soon, the Christmas service was over, and everyone began to leave their pews.

"This is the moment we've been waiting for," Aunt Maude said to me. "Do not speak unless spoken to, and keep your answers brief. The less you say, the better. Stand up straight, keep your chin level, and do not look as if you are going to be sick."

Alec offered me an encouraging smile. "You're perfect."

I followed Aunt Maude down the aisle as the congregants visited, wishing each other a Merry Christmas. People glanced her way, but she seemed intent upon three women in the middle of the throng. Two of the women had a stately bearing and were in their mid-thirties or forties. The third was a younger woman, perhaps the daughter of one of them.

As soon as they noticed the three of us, they turned to greet Aunt Maude and then rested their gazes on me.

"Who is this divine creature?" one of the older women asked Aunt Maude. "I do believe all the eligible bachelors in the church are already wondering when they might call, and all the mamas of single young ladies are drawing up their battle plans."

That seemed to please Aunt Maude as she smiled. "Mrs. Vanderbilt, Mrs. Whitney, and Miss Whitney, this is my niece, Miss Clara Day Hill. She's recently come to live with me. Clara," she continued, "this is Mrs. William Kissam Vanderbilt, Mrs. William Whitney, and her daughter, Miss Evelyn Whitney."

On shaky legs, I offered them a curtsey, my stomach turning so violently I thought I might lose my breakfast. Could Aunt Maude tell?

"How do you do?" I managed slowly and as calmly as I could in the accent I had tried to perfect.

"How do you do?" all three of them responded.

"Your niece?" Mrs. Vanderbilt asked Aunt Maude. "I wasn't aware that you had a niece."

"Oh?" Aunt Maude said absently. "I'm sure I've mentioned her before."

"Hill?" Mrs. Whitney asked. "Then she's your husband's niece? I thought Mr. Paxton-Hill was your only nephew from your husband's side of the family."

"He is," she said without hesitation. "Clara is from my side of the family. I've adopted her, so she's taken on my last name."

"Adopted?" Mrs. Vanderbilt's eyebrows rose. "When did this happen?"

"It was just finalized yesterday, as a matter of fact. I've always wanted a daughter and Clara was orphaned, so I decided to make her my heiress."

Mrs. Vanderbilt and Mrs. Whitney studied me as Aunt Maude spoke, their calculating gazes taking in every detail. Miss Evelyn Whitney seemed a bit distracted and did not seem as concerned with my recent arrival. Did the older women believe I was Maude's niece? I didn't look anything like her, but that wasn't necessary.

"And where do you come from, Miss Hill?" Mrs. Vanderbilt asked.

We had prepared for this question, so I was ready with an answer. We'd chosen somewhere far away that hinted at a lack of refinement to cover my faux pas—yet familiar enough that it wouldn't seem far-fetched.

"St. Paul," I said.

"St. Paul?" Mrs. Whitney asked. "How primitive."

"Her father was a lumber baron," Aunt Maude explained. "St. Paul is a growing city, but it lacks the sophistication of New York. I'm eager to introduce her to society as soon as the holidays are through, and of course, she has much to learn."

"I'll be sure to send around an invitation," Mrs. Whitney said, "but we must be going. I see my husband and son waiting for us. It was a pleasure to meet you, Miss Hill."

"And you," I said with a nod, trying to hide the fact that I felt ill as I clung to Alec's arm.

The ladies moved past, and Aunt Maude turned her pleased face to me. "Very good, Clara. Those are two of the wealthiest and most influential ladies in New York—at least, among those outside Mrs. Astor's circle. An invitation to Mrs. Whitney's home is a major step in the right direction."

She paused, her back stiffening, as a family approached.

"Garfield," Alec said under his breath. "What does he want?"

The Garfield family consisted of Mr. and Mrs. Garfield and a young lady, who I presumed to be Louise Garfield. She was very pretty, with dark hair and blue, calculating eyes.

"Mrs. Hill," Mr. Garfield said as he nodded at Aunt Maude. "Mr. Paxton-Hill," he said as he acknowledged Alec. When his gaze landed on me, he paused.

"Mr. Garfield," Aunt Maude said with pride in her voice. "May I present my niece, Miss Clara Day Hill?"

"Daughter," Alec corrected her quietly.

"Oh yes," Aunt Maude said. "I've adopted Clara and made her my heiress."

Introductions were made and Louise and I curtseyed properly, though I felt her eyeing me like the competition I was.

"We're thinking about making a trip to Europe this coming spring," Aunt Maude said, as if it was a passing thought and not something we spoke about dozens of times a day.

"Oh?" Mrs. Garfield asked, pursing her lips.

"I've heard you're planning a trip, as well," Aunt Maude continued.

"Why, yes. We are."

"Perhaps we'll run into one another while we're there." Aunt Maude's voice was cool.

"Perhaps we will." Mrs. Garfield gave her husband a look. He blundered on about needing to get home to his Christmas luncheon and the family moved on.

"There is your greatest competition," Aunt Maude said to me under her breath once they were gone. "Louise Garfield was the talk of society last year when she debuted in New York, but her mother is shrewd and would not allow her to choose an American husband. She's saving her for something much bigger, I'm sure of it. And with the Garfield money, they will be able to pay top dollar to an English aristocrat when the time comes."

I watched Louise walk just behind her parents, every movement precise and elegant.

Was Louise eager to visit England and attract the attention of English nobility—or was she simply a pawn in this high-stakes games, like me?

8

Aunt Maude's simple dinner party was anything but simple. The staff had spent days transforming the mansion into a Christmas wonderland, until it looked and smelled like something out of a fairytale. Pine garland, red velvet ribbons, and silver bells adorned the stairs, the railings around the gallery above the foyer, and on every available surface. Dozens of Christmas trees, each bedecked with silver and gold ornaments, filled each room on the main floor, with the largest standing in the foyer at twenty feet tall. But the most impressive was the candlelight. Hundreds of candles twinkled from the trees, offering a soft light as I stood in the receiving line next to Aunt Maude and Alec. Footmen and maids stood at the ready with water buckets and mops, should the candles catch something on fire.

At least two dozen guests had arrived. The women were festooned in breathtaking gowns and lavish jewelry. One woman had a long golden chain, which she wore around her waist like a belt, with another chain dangling down the front of her skirt. At the bottom was an emerald the size of an egg. It looked heavy and uncomfortable, but it was meant to attract attention and it did.

"Why am I here?" I asked Alec, quietly, after Aunt Maude had turned to a guest.

He frowned at me, puzzled. "What do you mean? You're Maude's daughter now. She'll expect you at all sorts of social events."

"I thought I was needed to find a husband so Aunt Maude could enter polite society. It looks as if she's already there."

What more could she want?

Alec turned his back to the room, offering us a little more privacy. "These are the swells," he explained. "They're all new money. Some in banking, some in railroads, shipping, or real estate. None of them have ascended to Mrs. Astor's rank among the nobs."

"How do you know if you've arrived?" And why did it matter? They were all so wealthy, I couldn't begin to comprehend why it wasn't enough.

"A list was printed last year by Mrs. Astor's cohort, Ward McCallister," Alec explained. "He claims there are only four hundred people in all of New York City who are proper enough to be in fashionable society—and most of them are old money. The swells don't mean anything to Aunt Maude. She will not rest until she's on Mrs. Astor's list—and then she'll spend the rest of her life trying to stay on it."

"Do all of them want to be on the list?" I asked as I indicated the group.

Alec looked over the room and nodded. "Every last one of them. The men work hard to make the money, and the women work harder trying to show it off. Every woman in this room is trying to elevate her family's social status to support her husband's efforts."

Was that the kind of life I would lead once I married? Was it different in England?

Not for the first time, I wondered what I had agreed to. I didn't even know how to show off wealth. But it was the least of my worries about marrying a duke. There were so many other duties that would be required of me—I didn't even know how to ask about those. All Aunt Maude was concerned about was preparing me to capture a duke—she didn't seem to care what I would do once I had him.

A gentleman started to walk toward me from across the room, his gaze intent upon mine, and I stiffened. What if I said or did something to give up the ruse?

Alec also stiffened, but said quietly, "That's George Vanderbilt, the youngest of the Vanderbilt family. One of the most eligible bachelors in the city. You met his sister-in-law, Mrs. William Kissam Vanderbilt, earlier today at church."

Even before I had moved into Aunt Maude's home, I knew the Vanderbilt name. Everyone did. They were one of the wealthiest families in America.

I fidgeted, feeling the weight of my heavy gown and the lies I was wearing.

"Don't worry," Alec said softly, "I'm here if you need me."

"You mustn't feel obligated to take care of me."

"I don't."

After proper introductions were made, Mr. Vanderbilt gave me a small bow. "I hope you'll allow me to escort you into supper—unless Alec has claimed the honor."

I swallowed my butterflies and looked at Alec. Aunt Maude had made it clear I must not fall in love with an American, but she wanted me to flirt and become confident with men. Yet—the only man I wanted to sit with at supper was Alec. I had grown comfortable with him, even if he teased me and made my cheeks blush.

"I have no such honor," Alec said, his voice serious.

"Then may I have the honor?" Mr. Vanderbilt asked me. "I wanted to be the first to ask, since I'm certain I won't be the last."

I glanced around the room, filled with both married and single men. Some were looking in my direction and Mrs. Vanderbilt's words returned to me. *"I do believe all the eligible bachelors in the church are already wondering when they might call, and all the mamas of single young ladies are drawing up their battle plans."*

Mr. Vanderbilt stared at me, waiting for an answer.

"Thank you," I finally managed to say. "I would like that."

Alec helped me navigate a stilted conversation with Mr. Vanderbilt, making me wonder how I would endure an entire meal at his side.

When it was proper to move away from him, Alec took me to a small group of matronly ladies and reintroduced me, so I could remember their names. Thankfully, they seemed intent upon hearing their own voices, so I wasn't required to say much. And when I was, Alec ensured that I only needed to talk about things I was comfortable discussing.

Higgins announced supper was ready, so Mr. Vanderbilt found me once again and offered me his arm. As he led me away, I had a moment of panic as I realized we were leaving Alec.

But as I looked back, he was offering his arm to one of the matrons and stayed right behind Mr. Vanderbilt and me—and when we got to the long dining room table, he took the seat beside mine, so I was nestled between him and Mr. Vanderbilt.

"In case you need help flirting," he said, for my ears alone, as he leaned close for just a moment. "I will be right here."

My heart fluttered at his comment, but it gave me a boost of confidence to address Mr. Vanderbilt. Two months ago, when I'd first come to the mansion, I had no experience with this sort of thing. But Alec had taught me a lot, and if I could flirt with him, surely I could flirt with Mr. Vanderbilt.

I had practiced this moment for weeks. I knew exactly which silverware to use, which conversation to laugh at, and which topics to ignore.

And when I didn't, Alec swooped in to rescue me.

After the meal, the men stayed in the dining room for cigars and brandy while the women moved into the parlor.

Which meant I was alone without Alec's help.

As we left the dining room, I sent a lingering look to Alec, and he gave me the slightest wink of encouragement.

A young woman walked up beside me, a gentle smile upon her face. We'd been introduced when she had arrived with her parents, but she'd been sitting on the opposite side of the table, and we hadn't spoken.

Her pretty green eyes crinkled at the corners as she said, "I'm sure you don't remember my name. I'm Miss Annabelle Wellington."

"I'm Clara," I said, relieved that she'd reminded me of her name.

"It can be overwhelming meeting so many new people," she said with empathy. "We moved to New York three years ago and I still don't know everyone Mama thinks I should know."

We followed the other ladies into the hall.

"I don't know about you," Annabelle continued, "but I think making new friends is hard. I hope you'll allow me to be your friend, Miss Hill."

I finally gave her my full attention. Her offer seemed genuine as she studied me.

"I would like that," I said with a smile.

"I heard your aunt is planning to take you to England this spring," she continued. "We are also planning to go. It will be nice to have a friend there."

My heart warmed with relief. "I'm terrified," I confided in her.

"As am I. Mama insists we go, but I would rather not." She glanced back toward the dining room, where the doors were still open, and Alec was standing near Annabelle's father. "I already know what I want, and it doesn't include marrying a bankrupt nobleman."

Was she referring to Alec?

Before I could form a response to her statement, she said, "You and Alec appear to get along well. Did you know him before you moved in with your aunt? He never mentioned you before."

This I could answer honestly. "No. I met him in October, when I first arrived."

"October?" she frowned. "And we haven't been introduced yet?"

I didn't know what to say, so I glanced back at the dining room and found Alec watching us—but was he looking at me or Annabelle? Was he interested in Annabelle? I hadn't noticed him paying attention to her since her arrival—though perhaps I had been too preoccupied with myself.

The ladies settled into the parlor in small groups. As I listened to their incessant gossip, I counted down the minutes until the men would join us. I wasn't sure if I would get a chance to ask Alec about Annabelle, but I would try.

Aunt Maude sat with me while I worked hard to answer questions carefully. She would either stiffen beside me, or nod gently, depending on my performance. When the gentlemen finally arrived, I was exhausted and relieved to have Alec in the room again.

Annabelle was still at my side when Alec and Mr. Vanderbilt approached.

"Hello, Alec," Annabelle said.

He offered her a tight smile and replied, "It's good to see you again."

"Mother and I were surprised we were invited tonight," she said. "But we were thankful to be included."

"Your father and my uncle were good friends." His voice was a bit stiff. "Almost like family. Aunt Maude will never forget."

"That's what I'm afraid of." Annabelle's voice trailed away as Mr. Vanderbilt shuffled his feet uncomfortably and Alec lifted his chin.

The four of us stood awkwardly as I tried, in vain, to think of something to say. Alec had come to my rescue several times—couldn't I rescue him, too?

"Miss Wellington tells me she's going to Europe, as well," I said to Alec and Mr. Vanderbilt. "It will be nice to have a familiar friend there."

Mr. Vanderbilt smiled—but Alec's face remained a mask of indifference.

"Have you been before?" Mr. Vanderbilt asked me.

I shook my head, so he proceeded to tell me all about the pleasures of France and England.

The moment had been rescued, but Alec didn't relax as I had hoped he would.

Aunt Maude rose to announce it was time for the evening's entertainment, and I sighed in relief.

"Annabelle?" Aunt Maude asked, her voice level and even. "Would you sing for us?"

Everyone nodded their agreement and Annabelle's cheeks blushed prettily.

"Only if Mr. Paxton-Hill will accompany me," she said.

"Oh, do, Alec," one of the matrons said. "You and Annabelle make such beautiful music together. I remember when you sang in Newport last summer."

Alec did not look eager to play for Annabelle, but he was a gentleman and agreed. While he played the piano, Annabelle sang "Silent Night" and then "It Came Upon the Midnight Clear." Her voice was melodic and mesmerizing, and she sang with such purity, it was hard to take my eyes off her beautiful face. When everyone begged her for a third, she shook her head in humility and then turned to me.

"Let's have Miss Hill take a turn. I don't want to monopolize the entire evening. She's so lovely, I'm sure her voice will match."

I shook my head emphatically as panic engulfed me. Aunt Maude had said she would not ask me to sing tonight. It was too soon.

"Come, Miss Hill," said a lady with a commanding voice. "We'd all love to hear you."

"I couldn't," I said, looking to Aunt Maude for help.

She looked stern and nodded once, as if I *should* sing. It was the proper thing to do when several people had asked me.

I swallowed hard and then stood on shaking legs as everyone turned their gazes to me.

Terror filled my heart. I had never sung for a crowd before and the last thing I wanted was to be the center of attention.

"Would you like me to accompany you?" Alec asked, empathy in his gaze.

I shook my head. I couldn't ask him to ruin himself along with me.

"Are you certain?"

"Yes." I nodded, my voice quavering with nerves.

He nodded back and then took a seat on a sofa near Annabelle.

They were a splendid couple, both exceptionally good-looking and born into this lifestyle. It made me feel even more out of place.

I couldn't think of a single song I knew by heart, though I was certain I had known plenty before this moment. There had to be at least one Christmas carol I could recall. Perhaps "O Little Town of Bethlehem" would please the room?

I opened my mouth to begin singing, but the words stuck. Sweat gathered along my back and across my forehead.

I met Alec's steady gaze, and he nodded with encouragement.

Taking a deep breath, I started to sing, but it wasn't "O Little Town of Bethlehem." Instead, an old Irish ballad Uncle Charlie had sung slipped out of my mouth. I was so nervous, I hadn't realized it. I just wanted to be done, to get it over with, so I could sit down and let someone else stand in this terrifying place.

"O father dear, I oft-times hear you talk of Erin's Isle,
Her lofty scenes and valleys green, her mountains rude and wild.
They say it is a pretty place wherein a prince might dwell.
And why did you abandon it, the reason to me tell."

There were curious glances all around, but no one seemed alarmed that I had chosen an Irish ballad. Maybe they were happy it wasn't another Christmas carol, which they'd been listening to all day.

I couldn't remember the lyrics until they were coming out of my mouth, but I let my memory work for me as I continued.

"My son, I loved our native land with energy and pride,
Until a blight came on my land, my sheep and cattle died.
The rent and taxes were to pay, I could not them redeem,
And that's the cruel reason why I left old Skibbereen."

A few of the matrons frowned, but I lifted my gaze so I wouldn't have to look at them and pressed on to complete my task.

"Oh, it's well I do remember that bleak December day,
The landlord and the sheriff came to drive us all away.
They set my roof on fire with their demon yellow spleen,
And that's another reason why I left old Skibbereen."

As the words came out of my mouth, I slowly began to realize that perhaps they weren't appropriate for this parlor—or these people—and the more nervous I became, the more pronounced my accent became, too. But it was too late to stop now, so I started the next verse.

"Your mother, too, (God rest her soul) lay on the snowy ground.
She fainted o'er in anguish with the desolation round.
She never rose, but passed away from life to immortal dream,
And found a quiet grave, my boy, in dear old Skibbereen."

Aunt Maude's mouth fell open—terror on her face now, too.

There were several more verses, but they didn't get much better, so I simply let my voice trail away.

Silence filled the room as everyone stared at me. The heat from the candles made the sweat drip down my corseted back and the cloying scent of pine made my stomach turn. All I could think about was racing out of that room and running back to Five Points, where I knew my place—even if it wasn't a pleasant one.

But then Alec began to laugh—a hearty sound that filled the space with so much mirth, others began to chuckle.

"How clever, Clara," Alec said. "What a unique and entertaining song. Sometimes I feel as if I've heard them all—but this was a new one for me. Well done."

There were several heads nodding in agreement, and I knew I had a choice to make. I could either run from the room weeping, as I wanted—or I could pretend it had all been a gag. Something to make people laugh.

I had no choice but to do the latter—so I started to laugh with them, though I knew Aunt Maude would not be laughing with us.

The house was quiet as I stood in the front parlor hours later, watching the snow falling on the side lawn. Behind me, the wall sconces were dim, and the candles were still burning on the tree. Aunt Maude had excused the footman after all the guests had departed, though I knew he was only a bell pull away. No one was ever truly out of Aunt Maude's beck and call.

"I'm sorry," I said, unable to turn around and look at Aunt Maude or Alec, knowing I had disappointed them. "I don't know what came over me. I panicked."

"I detest excuses," Aunt Maude said, her voice cool. "If Alec had not lightened the mood, everyone would be talking about it tomorrow. Rumors would swirl about your origins and people would begin looking deeper. Your enemies would have ammunition, and your reputation would be ruined."

I had enemies?

"It was a simple mistake," Alec said. "She was nervous. She should not have been asked to sing tonight."

"I did not ask Miss Wellington to call on Clara. If I could have stopped it, I would."

"You could have stopped it," he said.

"Perhaps you should speak to Miss Wellington about improper behavior. She and you seem to be experts on the issue."

Silence followed her words, and I peeked over my shoulder to see Alec's response.

He was standing next to the hearth, his arm on the mantel, as he stared down into the flames.

What had Aunt Maude meant? Had Alec and Annabelle been part of a scandal? Together?

"As for you," Aunt Maude said as she stood and addressed me, "you came dangerously close to ruining everything tonight. I expect better from you. We'll resume lessons in the morning and will work night and day until you are ready."

I nodded, dreading the work, but unable to deny her demands.

"I'm exhausted," she said as she walked toward the door. "Good night."

"Good night," I said quietly.

After she left, neither Alec nor I spoke for several moments, but there was a question that had been burning inside me all evening.

"Who is Annabelle?"

He continued to stare into the flames and was quiet for so long, I was afraid he wouldn't answer.

Finally, he said, "She is—was—" He paused. "I was in love with her once upon a time."

Was he still in love with her?

"What happened?"

He turned to me, and I saw the pain in his gaze. "I wasn't good enough for her."

"How could that possibly be true?"

The look he gave me was a cross between tenderness and frustration at my naiveté.

"Annabelle's mother, just like Aunt Maude, has her sights set higher. She will take Annabelle to Europe in the spring to look for their entrance into the English aristocracy, just like so many others. Despite my uncle's close relationship with Annabelle's father, and their years of devoted friendship, I do not have a title, so I was turned away when I asked for Annabelle's hand in marriage."

A strange stab of jealousy tore at my heart. He had loved Annabelle enough to marry her?

I walked over to the hearth to face him, the train of my gown brushing against the thick carpet. "I'm sorry, Alec."

The depth of his sadness sliced through me as the firelight flickered over the planes of his handsome face. As his gaze caressed mine, he said, "It seems my lot in life is to fall in love with women who are out of my reach."

My pulse thudded as my heart begged to believe he meant me. Yet—I knew better than to hold on to false hope.

I couldn't look into his eyes, realizing I was ignorant and naïve about this, too.

"Do you still love Annabelle?" I asked, needing to shift the conversation back to solid ground.

"No." He was quiet for a moment before he whispered, "Someone else has captured my heart."

I could hardly breathe as I looked down at my hands, forcing myself to accept that he meant someone else. "She is a lucky young lady."

I felt his gaze upon me. "I hope she would think so, though I'm not certain she's aware of my feelings."

Swallowing, I asked, "Have you not told her?"

He didn't respond immediately, so I finally looked up. His expression was so intense, so full of longing and heartbreak, it was hard to hold his gaze—but I did.

"I am not at liberty to tell her how I feel—and I'm afraid she's not at liberty to return my affections."

I swallowed the nerves racing up my throat. The look in his eyes told me it *was* me that he spoke of, yet nothing in my experience had taught me that such a thing could be true. Even still, I whispered, "We are never without hope, Alec."

He studied me, as if trying to answer a question. "I fear she will never know the depths of my love for her, because even if I told her, she would not have the freedom to accept it." He let out a breath. "It would be torture for both of us."

I couldn't stand under the weight of his heartache—a heartache that matched my own. I had to get away, to be alone and grapple with the emotions that tossed me about.

"Good night, Alec." I left the hearth and started to walk toward the door.

"Keira."

I stopped in the doorway and took my time turning toward him.

He approached me, his eyes filled with so many emotions, I couldn't identify any of them.

When he stopped, he, too, was in the doorway. He looked up and my gaze followed his.

A bouquet of mistletoe hung from the trim and was tied with a red ribbon.

My heart beat hard as I realized why he had stopped me.

I lowered my gaze as he lowered his, and we were staring at each other.

He gave me time to walk away—but I didn't. I couldn't.

His gaze fell on my lips and made them tingle with anticipation. An internal struggle waged behind his eyes and when he finally lifted them again, I held my breath.

Slowly, tenderly, he placed a gentle kiss on my lips.

My pulse beat with affection as a tendril of pleasure slid through my chest and tightened into a coil of longing in my stomach. I wanted to wrap my arms around him and hold him close, but I couldn't.

Because I was planning to marry a duke.

I wanted to cry.

After a moment, he pulled back. Something sweet filled his face—and just for a moment, he seemed to forget.

But then his shoulders dropped and he took a step away, lowering his gaze from mine. "Merry Christmas."

Then he was gone.

I stood in the doorway as I watched him take the stairs two at a time and disappear.

9

"There's a gentleman caller to see you, miss," Gallagher said the next morning as I sat in my room reading Shakespeare's *Romeo and Juliet* before the warmth of my fireplace. Aunt Maude had woken with a terrible megrim and was in her room with the shades pulled. It afforded me a respite from our lessons, but I was still required to read. Shakespeare's story gave me a headache of my own, especially since I couldn't concentrate on the difficult words and phrases.

All I could think about—all I had thought about since last night—was my encounter with Alec. I'd never been kissed, and though it had been quick, it had still left me spinning for hours—even in my dreams.

But I had also thought about what he'd said concerning Annabelle. So much heartache, and for what? Money? Power? Position? It was a tangled web of greed, and I didn't want to be part of it, though I had agreed to be here. Would my heart be protected?

Above all else, I thought about what he *hadn't* said, or, rather, what he'd hinted at. My heart kept hoping...but my mind told me it was foolishness to even consider.

I eagerly put aside the book, hoping to put aside my thoughts, too.

"A gentleman caller?" I asked.

She handed me a calling card. "Higgins brought it up for you."

Mr. Geo. Vanderbilt.

My heart galloped at the simple name embossed in gold ink on a crisp white card.

"What does he want?" I asked Gallagher.

She rarely cracked a smile, but one tilted her lips at my question. "What does any young man want from a pretty young woman?"

I frowned.

"He's come calling, miss, the morning after he met you," she said. "So he must have romantic inclinations and wants to be the first to stake his claim."

Of course. Why was I so naïve?

"What should I do?" I asked her.

"You can meet with him, or I can send him away and tell him you're not receiving callers."

I worried my bottom lip. I couldn't accept Mr. Vanderbilt's pursuit, because I was destined for Europe. The only reason to meet with him was to practice my flirting, but that might lead to other problems and the last thing I wanted was to break his heart as Annabelle had done to Alec. Yet he had come all this way—and he *was* a Vanderbilt. I didn't want him rebuffed by one of the servants.

What would Aunt Maude want me to do? Should I disturb her? I hadn't made an important decision alone since I'd entered her house. Surely she would want me to accept his call, if for no other reason than his sister-in-law, Mrs. William Kissam Vanderbilt, was hosting a party she wanted me invited to.

"I'll receive him," I said as I rose from the chair and smoothed my morning gown. It was a lovely dress made of mauve cotton with layers of material drawn up and bustled at the back.

"You'll need a chaperone," Gallagher said. "It should be your aunt."

"I don't want to disturb her. Can you do it?"

She nodded, though it wasn't generally the job of a servant. The task often fell to a family member.

We left my room, and I tried not to look for Alec, but I found my eyes wandering through the gallery and down the stairs. Was he home?

The front parlor door was open, so I took a deep breath and was about to enter, when I heard Alec's voice.

I paused, causing Gallagher to pause, as well. If Alec was in the room, then I wouldn't need her, so I motioned for her to leave.

She nodded without hesitation and left.

"I've been busier than usual," I heard Alec say.

"Is that why you haven't been at the club?" Mr. Vanderbilt asked. "Rumor is that you've been preoccupied with a young woman."

Was the rumor true? Had Alec been talking about another woman last night, and not me? Pain sliced through my chest as the possibility took shape into a dozen different thoughts.

Alec was quiet for a moment and then said, unconvincingly, "You shouldn't believe everything you hear."

I didn't want to hear another word on the subject. Lifting my chin, I entered the room as if I had been walking steadily toward the parlor without stopping to eavesdrop.

"Mr. Vanderbilt," I said, pretending to be surprised.

Mr. Vanderbilt was sitting on the edge of a chair and Alec was standing near the hearth, almost exactly as he'd been standing last night.

They both turned at my entrance, looking concerned that I had heard them, but I would set their minds at ease and give them no foothold to feel uncomfortable because of me.

"Good morning, Miss Hill," Mr. Vanderbilt said as he rose from his chair, a bright smile on his handsome face. "You look lovely."

His compliment didn't warm my cheeks as Alec's would, but it pleased me and was an honor. Two months ago, if he'd passed me on the street, he wouldn't have looked twice.

Today, he'd come to call.

"Thank you." I didn't acknowledge Alec—I couldn't. But I wasn't sure if it was because of the kiss he'd given me last night or the rumor Mr. Vanderbilt had heard concerning him. "To what do I owe this visit?"

Alec remained standing near the hearth, waiting for Mr. Vanderbilt's response.

Mr. Vanderbilt looked uncertain as he glanced from Alec to me. He should have expected a family member to chaperone us, but perhaps he had been anticipating Aunt Maude. It was a little easier courting a woman without another gentleman present.

"I enjoyed myself immensely last evening," Mr. Vanderbilt said, "and was hoping to continue our acquaintance today."

I smiled, as I knew I should, and nodded. "Won't you have a seat?" I had planned to thank him for coming and then tell him I had no intention of accepting gentlemen callers—but with Alec watching, I didn't want Mr. Vanderbilt to leave too soon. Perhaps I could practice my flirting with him, after all, and show Alec that I wasn't as naïve as I used to be.

I took the seat opposite Mr. Vanderbilt and offered him one of my biggest smiles. "I had hoped to see you again."

It was the right thing to say. His face lit up with a grin and his cheeks turned a ruddy color. He was an attractive young man, in his early twenties, with gentle, dark eyes and a charming mustache. When he smiled, it lit up his entire face. "I hope you don't mind that I've come so soon."

"Of course not." I had practiced the art of using my eyes to flirt, since Aunt Maude told me it was imperative that I could communicate my pleasure or displeasure without uttering a single word. I did so now, letting him know I was pleased he was here. "I wasn't certain you would want to come after my song last night."

Mr. Vanderbilt's laughter was as charming as his smile. "On the contrary, Miss Hill, it was the song that made me sit up and take notice. Anyone can sing timeless Christmas carols—it takes a spirited young woman to choose an Irish folk song. I get so bored with evening entertainments—but not last night. I have a feeling I would never get bored with you."

He had found me to be spirited? The song choice had been made from frightened desperation—and nothing more. But I smiled nonetheless.

There was an awkward pause, so I said, "You mentioned last night that you've been to Europe. Do you enjoy traveling?"

"I travel extensively. I've been across the ocean a dozen times already."

I lifted my eyebrows, unable to imagine such a life.

"And you?" he asked. "Do you like to travel?"

"I was born in England," I said—but then realized it didn't match the narrative that Aunt Maude was telling, so I quickly said, "I came to America when I was just a baby, so I have no memories of it. I have not left New York since then, but I believe I will love traveling."

Mr. Vanderbilt spent the better part of twenty minutes regaling me with stories from his travels, telling me that I would enjoy this place or that. Several times, he even told me he would love to show me it himself.

Alec remained near the fireplace, not moving, nor giving any indication that he wanted to be part of the conversation.

I forced myself not to look at him—to pretend he wasn't even there.

"It sounds delightful," I said to my caller. "I would love to see some of the places you've mentioned."

"Perhaps you'll allow me to call on you in England—though—" He briefly glanced at Alec before continuing. "I hope you'll allow me to call on you before then."

I again refrained from looking at Alec. It would be foolish to encourage Mr. Vanderbilt, though it also seemed foolish not to. For a girl from Five Points, his attention was like a daydream—an impossibility. A Vanderbilt was interested in calling on me?

But I was no longer a girl from Five Points—at least, legally. I was a well-bred heiress to Mrs. Edmund Hill—and as her heiress, Mr. Vanderbilt was not an option. So I blithely evaded the question.

"Does everyone travel to Europe in the spring?"

He smiled, though I could see the disappointment in his eyes. He had wanted an answer from me, and I had not given it.

"Europe or Newport," he said. "There is very little socializing in New York City in the spring and summer. It's much too wretched a place to endure during that time. No one stays here."

No one? There were over a million people in the city. If he only knew what we endured during the hot months of July and August in Five Points. Living in a mansion like this one during the summer would be a delight.

I smiled and then rose, indicating that our meeting was over, and said, "It was so nice of you to come, Mr. Vanderbilt."

He also rose and nodded. "Thank you for receiving me. I do hope I may call again."

I had hoped he would take the hint from before, but clearly, he had not. I couldn't alienate him, for fear of being left out of his sister-in-law's party, but neither could I encourage him.

Alec watched me closely, his expression stormy.

For reasons I couldn't identify, I wanted to make him upset.

"I would like that," I found myself saying to Mr. Vanderbilt.

"Excellent." He grinned at me and then he turned to Alec and nodded his farewell before leaving the parlor.

I slowly sank onto the chair I'd been occupying and let the nerves have their way. I hadn't realized how tense I'd been until now.

"Don't be foolish, Keira," Alec said, not leaving his spot near the hearth. "Why would you encourage him when you know you cannot marry him?"

I clasped my hands on my lap and studied them as I tried to gather my wits about me. "He's a very charming young man. It will be nice to have his friendship."

Alec snorted—which caused me to finally look at him.

"He's too young," Alec said, "and besides, he gets bored easily and moves from one thing to the next. He hasn't taken anything serious in his life and won't start now. He'll toss you aside at the least provocation."

My anger at Alec was intensifying, and I wasn't sure why. I stood, my chest rising and falling quickly. "If I cannot keep the attention of Mr. Vanderbilt, how will I keep the attention of a duke?"

"A duke will be desperate—Vanderbilt is not."

My mouth slipped open at his harsh comment, and I took a step back.

"Keira, that's not what I meant." Alec moved away from the hearth, remorse in his face. "I'm sorry."

"I know what you meant," I said just above a whisper, my anger turning to pain. "Only a desperate man in need of money would take me seriously."

"That's not—no." He shook his head and swallowed. "I only meant that Vanderbilt has the luxury of choosing—" He paused again, clearly digging himself deeper.

"Please don't," I told him, holding up my hand, my accent deepening with my emotions. "I'm very aware of who I am and why someone like George Vanderbilt wouldn't be interested in me if he knew the truth."

"Keira—"

"I should not have encouraged him," I continued, "but I'm not as heartless as the rest of your kind." I turned away to leave, but he reached out and grabbed my hand.

"Please, Keira." He gently slipped his fingers through mine. "I didn't mean what I said. I don't like George Vanderbilt, and I allowed my dislike of him to influence my words. Trust me when I say I didn't mean them."

My hand tingled from the pressure of his, but I refused to look at him. I had never felt the emotions that were stirring in my heart, and I wasn't sure which way to turn. Alec was my only friend in this house, and he had been kind to me. I owed it to him to listen.

"Why don't you like Mr. Vanderbilt?" I asked.

He softly tugged my hand until I turned to face him. "My dislike for him is a recent development," he said quietly.

I needed to change the subject as I disentangled our hands. "Aunt Maude is planning a debutante ball for me, before we leave for France."

"I know. She told me." He did not sound pleased.

"Don't you think I should have a ball?"

"It doesn't matter what I think."

"What does that mean?"

"It means that it's all—" He shook his head in frustration. This was a side of Alec I'd never seen before. He was usually affable and teasing, but something had changed recently. "If you want a ball, you should have a ball. If you want Vanderbilt—or your cabin by the stream—or a duke, then you should have it, Keira. It doesn't matter what I think." He moved toward the door and stopped. "I am going away again. I don't know when I'll return, but I'll be back in time for your ball."

"You're going away?" My pulse sped up. My ball wasn't until the end of February. Two whole months to navigate society without him? To endure Aunt Maude's endless lessons? To miss him? "Where are you going?"

"I'm going to Newport—" He paused, as if he wanted to say more, but then he shook his head.

"When are you going?"

"Now. This morning. I should be on my way already."

I walked across the room, trying to think of a way I might convince him to stay.

We stood facing one another as we had the night before.

The only difference was, last night had been bathed in candlelight, with falling snow brushing the windows. Now, the harsh morning light glared off the piles of snow—and the mistletoe was gone.

"Must you go, Alec?"

"I can't stay."

It wasn't an answer—not really.

But it was the only one he gave as he left me standing in the same spot he had left me the night before.

10

I stared at my reflection for a long time that late-February evening as I stood in front of the mirror in my dressing room. Aunt Maude had ordered a dress shipped to us from the House of Worth. It was a beguiling gown of silk, tulle, satin, and brocade in shades of cream and gold. Of all the gowns I'd worn since coming to Aunt Maude's four months ago, this was the most extravagant and expensive.

It was also the gown I would wear to my debutante ball, which was starting soon.

"Do you like it?" Gallagher asked as she stepped back and let me have a full look at myself. "Do you want anything changed? More tendrils around your face?"

My dark brown hair was styled high with a diamond tiara encircling it. As I moved my head from side to side, it twinkled in the lights.

"I don't require anything else." I had heard Aunt Maude say the same to Mrs. Walker many times—yet I couldn't leave it at that. I turned to my maid and offered her a smile. "Thank you, Gallagher. I don't know what I would do without you."

"You're welcome, miss," she said with a slight curtsey. She began to clean up the mess we had made with my toilette, but she paused and met my gaze in the mirror. For a moment, her guard came down, and she said, "You've come a long way, and you've made our kind proud."

Our kind.

I didn't know if I should thank her or ignore her, so I simply smiled.

I was no longer the woman who had walked out of Five Points and onto Fifth Avenue four months ago. I was no longer Keira O'Day—yet I didn't feel like Clara Day Hill, either. I didn't know who I was anymore.

Gallagher was about to leave the dressing room when I called out to her, "Has Mr. Paxton-Hill arrived?"

She shook her head. "I don't think so, miss."

I tried to smile and then nodded for her to leave.

Two months and not a word from Alec. Months of dancing, singing, speaking, reading, and deportment lessons had transformed me into a proper young lady. I had made calls with Aunt Maude to important homes, met dozens of people, danced at several balls, attended church, and visited the opera on three occasions. We had hosted two small dinner parties since Christmas, I had received gentleman callers, including George Vanderbilt, and Aunt Maude had taken me to Delmonico's Restaurant. We had gone shopping, drove in Central Park on fair days, and spent hours upon hours preparing for my debutante ball. And all that time, he had not written to me once. He sent letters to Aunt Maude, and she mentioned him in passing from time to time, but he hadn't sent me a card or a note. I wasn't even certain he would be at my ball tonight.

I lifted my chin, trying not to let my thoughts ruin the evening, and left the dressing room. There was something else I needed to complete my ensemble tonight—something I had stared at for hours but had never worn in my life.

Lifting the top of my jewelry box, I pulled out the gold locket from my mother. Among all the lovely and expensive jewelry I now owned, none compared to this in personal value—though the flower pin Alec had given me at Christmas was a close second.

I slipped the locket around my neck and looked at it for a moment, reminding myself that this was one of the most important reasons I had for following through on my promise to Aunt Maude. The closer we came to leaving for Europe, the more anxious I became to look for my mother. Would she want to meet me? And could she tell me who my father was?

The dressing room door opened, and Aunt Maude appeared in her own beautiful ball gown. It was a rich burgundy with a long train. A burgundy feather plumed from her updo, and her neck, wrists, ears, and fingers dripped with jewels.

She took me in from head to toe, nodding her approval, until her gaze landed on my locket. "What is that?"

"It belonged to my mother."

Stepping closer, she lifted it for a better look. "It's beautiful, but not appropriate for tonight. Where is the diamond choker I told you to wear?"

"Please," I said, never having asked for a favor from her before. "Could I wear the locket?"

Our relationship was not warm, but nor was it unpleasant. I knew my role and she knew hers. Rarely did we cross the lines. There was no affection between us, almost more like an employer and employee. I had been hired for a specific job, and I was fulfilling my duties. She was benevolent and kind, but also firm and demanding. She called me her daughter, but I knew better. I was her pawn in a strategic social game and nothing more.

"Not tonight," she said. "Perhaps at another ball. Tonight, I need everything to be perfect."

My chest rose and fell, with the weight of the locket reminding me of the past. It wouldn't pay to fight her, and I didn't want to make her angry. Not tonight when there were far too many other things to worry about.

I took off the locket and set it back in my jewelry box before retrieving the diamond choker and stepping in front of the mirror. As she helped me put it on, she said, "You've done a marvelous job under my tutelage, Clara. There isn't a trace of your former self present."

She was right. But there was one thing still out of our grasp. I had not received an invitation to Mrs. Vanderbilt's fancy dress party. If my debutante ball was a success, there was no reason I wouldn't have the invitation in hand by tomorrow morning.

"George Vanderbilt is getting serious," Aunt Maude said as she looked into the mirror with me.

I didn't respond, since there was no use denying it. George called regularly, and though I had told Alec I would turn him away, Aunt Maude felt it imprudent. George and his brother Cornelius II were among the only swells on Mrs. Astor's Four Hundred list. Somehow, they had earned a place amongst the fashionable elite. George didn't seem to care about the list, but it still mattered to Aunt Maude. Being associated with him was crucial.

"What if I married George?" I asked her. "He's on the list. Wouldn't that put me on the list and, by association, you?"

"Don't be naïve, Clara. You should know better by now." She adjusted the diamonds around my neck. "There are eight Vanderbilt children and only two of them are on the list. If one could earn a place by association, the rest would be there." She shook her head. "The only way to get on the list is to find a duke and become royalty. Mrs. Astor cannot turn a duchess's mother away."

George was so kind and good to me. He'd become a dear friend over the past two months, and though I hadn't encouraged him romantically, I knew he had it in mind. "I don't want to hurt George."

She waved aside my comment. "It's all part of the game. We know what we're getting into when we begin to play. George is no different. He's not guaranteed that you'll marry him. He knows he has competition. Let him fight for you—and, in so doing, it'll elevate your status. Then, when we're in England, you can marry a man of my choosing and George will have to accept that he has lost the game."

My conscience pricked and I looked down at my gloved hands, clasped in front of my waist. "I don't think I can knowingly break his heart."

Aunt Maude put her hands on my shoulders and turned me to look at her. "You've known your duties since you agreed to this job. It's not personal. Hearts should not get involved. It's all for the sake of financial security. Do not think of it as anything less."

I blinked several times and took a deep breath before I nodded my acknowledgment.

This wasn't personal. This was for security—both hers and mine.

And Alec's.

"Louise Garfield will be here tonight," Aunt Maude continued. "I don't believe I need to remind you that she is your biggest competition. Alec has been working day and night trying to update our hotel in Newport to keep our clientele happy. But it's not just the amenities of a hotel that attract customers. It's the perceived status of the hotel and its inhabitants. Especially if they think there's a chance a nobleman might be in attendance, they will flock to that establishment. Alec tells me there are people waiting to see what happens in Europe this spring, before determining which hotel to patronize."

I frowned. Surely that couldn't be the truth. "Why?"

"Because they are wealthy, but not wealthy enough to take their own daughters to Europe. The closest they can get is meeting a nobleman who visits America. If you attract one, and we invite him to our hotel, the patrons will come. If the Garfield girl attracts one of higher standing, and invites him to their hotel, the patrons will go there. We will not settle for anything less than a duke—though a prince would be best."

A prince? It was all so ridiculous. Even months into the process, I was still flabbergasted by the way wealthy people lived their lives and what they perceived to be important.

"And don't forget that Annabelle Wellington will be here," Aunt Maude continued as she lifted her chin. "Her mother also has plans to capture the most eligible bachelor in England or France. But I have a better plan in mind. Last summer, Alec proposed marriage to her, and both she and her father were eager to accept. It was her mother who refused the match."

I lowered my gaze, not wanting Aunt Maude to see how this story affected me. I had thought about Annabelle and Alec countless times since Christmas, and it still pained me to imagine them together.

"If possible, I want you to encourage both Annabelle and Alec to rekindle their romance," Aunt Maude instructed.

I quickly looked up at her, to see if she was teasing.

She was serious.

"If we can get them to elope, then her mother won't have any reason to travel to Europe and Annabelle will be one less person to compete with."

Encourage Annabelle and Alec to fall in love again? The thought made me ill. I chose not to comment, hoping she'd forget she had asked me. I couldn't play matchmaker between them.

"Keep all your competition close." She continued her last-minute instructions as she handed me my fan and dance card. "But not too close. Learn their strengths and weaknesses—but never reveal yours. Do you understand?"

I nodded. This wasn't just about winning the best husband, it was about thwarting the plans of my competitors, and keeping allies like George close—but not too close.

What I really wanted was a real friend.

"Good." She stood back and looked at me one more time. "I believe you're ready, Clara."

Despite the hours of socializing I'd already done, there was a heightened level of nerves that hummed inside me. Hundreds of people had accepted Aunt Maude's invitation to my debutante ball tonight, and all of them would be watching me. Almost no one questioned the story we'd told about my origins, but many were still skeptical. Any little misstep could mean disaster.

"I'll go down first," Aunt Maude said as she moved toward the door. "Our guests will start arriving any moment, but I want you to make a spectacular entrance on the stairs. Come down in thirty minutes."

I nodded, knowing every strategy, every detail, every nuance of this evening was part of a larger master plan.

A plan that felt more and more dishonest with each passing day.

Thirty minutes later, I left my bedroom and entered the upper gallery. It was half past ten and the wall sconces burned bright. Conversation mingled with laughter from below and the string quartet played a soft melody. The dance would begin at eleven, dinner would be served at one, followed by more dancing. It would prove to be a long and arduous night, but I'd attended enough balls to know what to expect.

I didn't hate them, but I would prefer a quiet parlor with a handful of guests.

My dress was heavy and difficult to move in, but it was sleeveless, which made it cooler for the warm ballroom.

I stood for a moment, taking a deep breath as my gaze slid across the gallery to Alec's bedroom door. Every time I walked out of my room, my eyes searched for him, though I knew he was in Newport.

Tonight, my heart galloped, wondering if this time I would see him emerge.

I waited—a minute. Two minutes. Five.

Perhaps he was already downstairs.

With a light step, I walked to the top of the stairs and saw all the guests assembled below in the large hall. I scanned each face, looking for Alec, but found unfamiliar gazes turning toward me.

Strangers intermingled with a few people I'd met or come to know the past two months.

George stood at the foot of the stairs and glanced up at me with a smile.

I forced myself to not feel disappointed and returned his smile.

Everyone turned to watch me walk down the stairs. The lights were bright, and the scent of fresh-cut flowers made me want to sneeze. Floral garland was attached to the railing, making it impossible to use as I tried to maneuver in the massive gown. My heeled shoes were a little taller than I was used to and while I should have been focusing on my steps, my gaze continued to scan the crowd.

It felt like it took an hour to descend those stairs, but I was eventually at the bottom, and I was joined by Aunt Maude and George.

"You look stunning tonight, Miss Hill," George said as he bowed over my hand. "A dream in gold."

"Thank you," I said as I allowed him to kiss my gloved hand.

"Will you allow me the honor of the first dance?" he asked. "I've been waiting here since I arrived, hoping to be the first to speak to you."

Where was Alec? Why wasn't he waiting at the bottom of the steps for me? I had wanted to save the first dance for him, but it would be rude to tell George to wait for my answer. Instead, I looked at Aunt Maude, who gave me a slight nod. George was a nob, and he would do quite nicely for her purposes.

"I would like that," I told him, though my heart longed for someone else to ask me.

He grinned and wrote his name at the top of my dance card.

Aunt Maude pulled me away from him to introduce me to the rest of my guests. My mind whirled with names and faces as I tried to focus.

My dance card filled quickly, and with each penciled name, my disappointment mounted. If Alec didn't appear soon, I would have no dances left for him.

"Where is Alec?" I finally asked Aunt Maude when I had a moment to breathe.

Aunt Maude's features hardened. "He was unable to make it tonight."

"Why?" I shook my head. "He must know how important this evening is to all of us."

"Put a smile on your face and pretend all is well, Clara. We will talk about it later."

More pretending. More secrets.

At exactly eleven, George appeared at my elbow and offered me his arm.

He escorted me onto the dance floor while the rest of the guests assembled along the edges of the ballroom. All the walls had been opened to allow the three rooms to become one. And though I was familiar with the house, it felt like I was in another world.

What would Aunt Orla and Uncle Charlie and my cousins think if they saw me now? What would Imogen say? I wished she could be with me, knowing how much she appreciated fine and beautiful things.

I wished my mother and father could see me now, too. I wanted them to know I was worth something—perhaps not to them, but to Aunt Maude and George Vanderbilt.

There was a time I had hoped I meant something to Alec, too, but his absence from my life hinted otherwise.

As the musicians began a waltz, I lifted the train of my gown and allowed George to spin me around the dance floor. He was a magnificent dancer, so confident and handsome, and he seemed to only have eyes for me. I smiled up at him, trying to remember that I was happy.

The evening progressed from one dance to the next, but they all started to blend. When we stopped for supper, George escorted me into the dining room. He sat to my right, a place of honor, and I knew that by morning the gossips would speculate that we were engaged.

Would he ask me to marry him? Now that I'd had a proper debutante ball, I was considered ready for the marriage mart. Surely George knew why Aunt Maude was taking me to Europe. He couldn't be completely naïve.

After the meal, there was more dancing. My feet and back ached, but I kept a smile on my face, knowing how much money and time Aunt Maude had given toward this ball. The flowers alone had cost her five thousand dollars, a sum of money that would take over a decade for Uncle Charlie and his family to make. To know that they would be cast into the garbage tomorrow felt like a sin. Newspaper reporters were writing scathing articles about the excess and waste of parties like this one when the average New York family was living off less than four hundred dollars a year. And they weren't wrong. For party favors, Aunt Maude has chosen gold cigarette cases for the men and diamond necklaces for the women. The food, the champagne, the party favors, flowers, invitations, musicians, and extra staff had cost over fifty thousand dollars.

And all for what? To impress each other? It was a foolish way to live and the more I experienced it, the more I disliked it.

But it wasn't my money, so I said nothing.

Just before five in the morning, the musicians announced the final dance of the ball. I wanted nothing more than to climb into my bed and sleep for days, but I soldiered on and saw that George had written his name for the last dance, as well as the first.

He found me near the punch table and offered his arm to me.

"I hope you don't mind that I took the last dance without asking," he said as we began to waltz.

"Of course not."

His smile was warm and affectionate. "I've loved getting to know you these past two months, Clara."

"And I you." I was so tired of talking, but it was almost over.

"I imagine you'll have several callers in the morning."

There had been many young men who had asked if they could call, and I had said yes to all of them. Aunt Maude wanted it to appear as if I was the belle of the season.

"I suppose I will," I said.

"I hope—" He paused.

I finally gave him my full attention. If things had been different, I could have fallen in love with George. He was kind and generous and would be easy to love.

"I hope," he continued, "that you'll not give any of them encouragement to pursue you."

I studied him, waiting.

"I had rather hoped you'd reserve that for me," he continued.

For weeks, I had practiced my response to him, but it seemed to stick in my throat.

"Don't speak now," he said. "I would rather wait and hear a yes, than get my answer now and hear a no."

I smiled at him, thankful he was preceptive enough to understand where I stood. "You are very dear to me."

Those appeared to be the right words because his hand pressed a little tighter to my back and his gaze filled with pleasure.

When the final dance concluded, the guests took their leave, and I was finally free.

Twenty minutes later, I stood with Aunt Maude in the ballroom for a moment, listening to the silence.

"The staff will come in soon and begin the cleanup," Aunt Maude said with a sigh. "You'll want to get a few hours of sleep before your callers arrive."

I groaned at the thought.

Aunt Maude looked at me out of the corner of her eye. "Remember you're respectable now, Clara, and respectable people don't moan."

Duly chastised, I smiled.

She left the parlor, and I stood for another moment taking in the empty ballroom, wondering how I had been so fortunate as to have this opportunity. Because no matter how difficult or unpleasant, it was a far better life than the one I'd been leading.

"I'm sorry, Keira."

I spun at the sound of the familiar voice and found Alec standing in the doorway, still wearing his outer coat and hat, a small traveling bag in hand. The early morning light was just starting to glow on the horizon outside the windows, but the wall sconces were still shining.

Alec stared at me for a moment, taking in the sight of me, and then slowly lowered his bag. He took off his coat and set it on the back of a chair, putting his hat on top.

"Why weren't you here?" I asked.

"I'm sorry," he said again. "If I could have been here, I would have."

I frowned. "I don't understand."

He stood in front of me, admiration shining in his eyes. "You look beautiful."

I'd been complimented all evening, but his was the only one that truly mattered.

"Thank you."

"I know I'm too late—but could I have the final dance?"

"There is no music."

"We don't need music."

I hadn't seen him in so long, there was an awkwardness between us, but I didn't want it to last, so I lifted the train of my gown and stepped closer to him.

He took me into his arms, pausing for just a moment as his gaze caressed my face, my hair, my gown, and then we slowly began to waltz around the empty room.

And he was right. We didn't need music.

11

I had fallen in love with Alexander Paxton-Hill.

Joy and elation should have filled my heart at the knowledge, but pain and disappointment overwhelmed me. I couldn't have Alec, even if he wanted me in return. I had made a promise to Aunt Maude, and I needed to see it through. She had even asked me to play matchmaker between Alec and Annabelle.

Yet how could I hide my feelings from him?

I caught a glimpse of a small army of maids and footmen who had gathered at the entrance to the ballroom with brooms, mops, buckets, and rags.

My cheeks grew warm at being caught dancing without music and I slowed my steps.

I could have danced with him all night.

Alec glanced at the doorway and gently brought our waltz to an end.

He smiled at the staff and then offered me his arm. "I'll escort you to your room."

We walked out of the ballroom and into the foyer as the staff entered to begin the arduous task of cleaning up after the party.

Neither one of us spoke as he led me toward the stairs.

"I don't want to go to sleep, yet," I said to him as we came to a stop.

"Aren't you tired?"

I had been tired—exhausted. But seeing him and dancing with him had given me a burst of energy I couldn't explain. I shook my head.

He smiled at me. "What would you like to do?"

I'd grown bold over the past two months as Aunt Maude had taught me the art of authority—within reason. "Why didn't you write to me?"

Alec let out a sigh and took a step back, causing me to loosen my hold on his arm.

I frowned, confused by his behavior now and over the past two months. "I thought we were friends, Alec."

"We are friends, Kiera."

It felt good to hear my name again.

"But, perhaps," he said, "the foyer isn't the place for this conversation."

"Then come with me to the library." I put my hand on his arm and tugged him gently.

We walked through the shadowed hall to the library, the train of my cream and gold skirt trailing behind me. When he opened the door, there was enough light outside to see that it was snowing. The coals from a fire in the hearth the night before were still warm, offering a soft glow in the room.

I entered and he followed. He paused a moment before shutting the door.

When he turned back to me, the tension that had coiled during our kiss under the mistletoe had returned and it tightened in my belly. I crossed my arms and rubbed my gloved hands over my bare skin, suddenly feeling cold.

He went to the fireplace and stirred the coals before adding a few more logs to the fire.

"Why didn't you write to me?" I asked, my voice lower.

Alec slowly rose from the hearth, but he did not turn around to look at me. "I think you know the answer, Keira."

Shaking my head, I took a step closer to him. "I don't."

He put his hand on the mantel, as if to steady himself.

"I missed you," I whispered, taking another step closer, wanting to be near him.

Finally, he turned, and his blue eyes were filled with longing. "How can you not know I'm in love with you?"

My lips parted as the truth settled into my aching heart. I swallowed as my chest rose and fell on short breaths. "Alec—"

The door to the library opened and a scullery maid appeared, an ash bucket in her hands. Her eyes grew wide. "Pardon me," she said as she took a step back and closed the door.

Alec went to the door and opened it again. "We're just leaving," he told the girl. "Come and do your task."

She looked as uncertain as I felt.

"We cannot have the staff gossiping," Alec said in a low tone as he rejoined me by the fireplace and offered me his arm.

We passed the maid as we left the room and walked slowly down the hallway.

"Alec," I said again, trying to wrap my mind around what he'd said. I had hoped—almost believed it to be true—but to hear it on his lips was overwhelming.

"Please don't," he told me, stopping near a darkened alcove. The months apart had been a strain on him, causing lines to crease around his eyes. "Nothing can come of my feelings. I should not have spoken."

My lips parted as a thousand wishes poured from my heart, begging to be spoken. I wanted to tell him I loved him, too, yet the words stuck in my throat.

"I have only returned for a short visit," he said, looking down at his hands. "I am needed back in Newport as soon as possible. I told Aunt Maude I wouldn't be here for your party—" He paused and finally lifted his gaze to my face. "But I have something very urgent I need to discuss with her and at the last minute, I tried to get here in time for your ball. But I was delayed." He let out a breath. "You should go to bed, Keira. I'm certain you'll have callers here in a few hours, perhaps even an invitation to Alva Vanderbilt's ball, and you need some sleep."

I swallowed and glanced toward the library. "But what about—"

"There is nothing else to talk about. I was a fool to say something." Sadness deepened the lines around his eyes as he offered me his arm again. "Come. I will take you to your room and then I will go freshen up to speak to Aunt Maude as soon as she's awake."

I wanted to beg him to speak to me of love, but he was right. He could not act upon his feelings and neither could I. It would be foolish for me to tell him I was in love with him, and the weight of that knowledge crushed me.

Taking his arm, I allowed him to walk me up the stairs and lead me to my room.

Before I opened the door, I turned to him again, my mouth open to speak, but he bowed and said, "Good night, Keira."

And then he walked away.

Gallagher arrived in my room at eleven that morning to wake me up and start my toilette. I had slept so little after returning to my room, I felt groggy and irritable as she opened the shutters and stoked the fire.

"Your aunt has told me to not let you sleep past eleven," she said. "She's expecting several gentlemen callers here after luncheon."

Despite their name, morning calls were not usually made until one or two in the afternoon. It was another thing that had baffled and confused me.

I wanted to groan and protest the social obligations, but that would only force Aunt Maude to come into my room and demand my compliance. I didn't want to upset her or give her reason to regret adopting me. The alternative to living here and obeying her wishes was a life I didn't want to think about. Sometimes, when I allowed myself to think about my life in Five Points, my back ached as it once had from stitching piecework all night, and I could almost feel the prick of the needle in my fingers.

"Is Mr. Paxton-Hill still at home?" I asked, sitting up, not sure whether I wanted her to say yes or no.

Seeing Alec after the ball and finally acknowledging to myself that I was in love with him, and hearing he loved me, had left me feeling unmoored.

"Aye," she said. "He's speaking to your aunt now."

"Will he join us for lunch?"

"I couldn't say, miss." She had brought one of the pink day dresses into the room with her. It was beautiful, with layers of delicate silk, ivory-colored lace, and pearl buttons.

Did I want to see Alec before he returned to Newport? In the four months I'd been in Aunt Maude's home, I'd only spent a few weeks in his company, but his impact on my life and my heart had been enormous. Perhaps it would be best if I didn't see him again. I'd known from the first day that my course was set for England and I couldn't let my heart get entangled with his.

Yet I wanted to weep at the thought of not being with him again.

With resolve, I decided the best thing to do was focus on getting to Europe, meeting a duke or prince, and finding my mother. Those were things I could control.

By noon, I was bedecked in the beautiful pink gown and Gallagher had styled my hair in an updo that was elegant, yet simple. I wore pearl earrings to match the buttons and, despite the pit in my stomach, my cheeks displayed a delicate pink shine.

As I stepped out of my room, I had decided I didn't want to see Alec again. It would be easier to push him out of my mind and heart if I wasn't forced to converse with him or have his handsome, blue-eyed gaze on my every move.

"Clara?" I turned toward Aunt Maude's room, where the door was open and Alec was standing. "Aunt Maude would like to see you."

My pulse picked up its rhythm and excitement filled my midsection at seeing him again, despite the resolution I'd just made. Frustration and anger at myself soon followed. I couldn't let Alec affect me this way.

His face was serious as he stepped aside to allow me to enter her sitting room.

I forced myself to walk past him without looking in his direction. Every time I thought about his declaration in the library, I wanted to either throw myself into his arms, or pretend I'd never met him.

Aunt Maude sat on one of the chairs by her fireplace, her elbow on the armrest as she stared into the fire.

"Good afternoon," I said to her. "I hope you slept well after last night's success."

She didn't greet me with her usual calm, and the lines of her face were hard and unreadable as she turned away from the fire.

I paused. "Is something wrong?"

"Sit down, Clara," Aunt Maude said. "We have something we need to discuss with you."

My legs began to shake at the severity of her voice.

I slowly lowered myself into the chair across from her as Alec joined us.

"Alec asked me not to discuss this with you," she said, "but as my legal daughter, I believe you should be privy to the same financial information that Alec and I know."

Frowning, I glanced at Alec and found him watching me.

"It seems we're in a very dire situation," Aunt Maude continued. "Alec has been in Newport overseeing the major renovations on the Ocean House, the most prestigious hotel we own."

She didn't know I had previously overheard her and Alec talking about the issues they were having with their hotel in Newport, so I let her explain the problem to me. When she was done, she said, "The costs have been greater than anticipated, and with the other hotel we're building on Coney Island, and our living expenses—"

"It is more than your living expenses," Alec interrupted her.

She gave him a look that suggested they'd been in disagreement about something.

"It's your extravagant spending on things that aren't necessary. Like gold cigarette cases and diamond necklaces for party favors at the ball."

"What do you expect of me?" she asked him. "I must keep up appearances, so no one notices our financial desperation."

"Spending fifty thousand dollars on one party, ten thousand dollars on a wardrobe for Clara, and untold other expenses on this upcoming trip to Europe is not 'keeping up appearances.' It's foolishness while we're trying to expand our business."

"You know why we're going to Europe, it's to secure—"

"I'm quite familiar with why you're going to Europe."

I had never seen Alec so severe with Aunt Maude, but it was clear he was desperate and worried.

Aunt Maude had taught me to sit with my back perfectly straight, but I started to slouch now, feeling that this was somehow my fault. The ball, the clothing, and the trip were all expenses incurred because of me.

"We need to secure the best match possible for Clara," Aunt Maude said, "and as soon as we're successful, we'll have all the clientele we need at our hotels. All of them. I promise it will work, Alec. I just need more time."

"And how will you cajole a duke or prince to marry Clara when you have nothing in the way of a suitable dowry for her? Most noblemen are making American matches because they need the money."

"There's the stock in our company."

"A company that sits on the brink of bankruptcy."

"They don't need to know that. And by the time it will matter, our company value will increase once again."

Alec pressed his lips together until the muscles in his jaw jumped. "I'm concerned that we won't have the time you need."

Neither spoke as they stared at one another. I wasn't sure why I needed to be here for this conversation. I couldn't tell them what to do, not only because I didn't know, but because it wasn't my place. Even if Aunt Maude had adopted me.

"So you see?" Aunt Maude said, turning to me. "Everything relies on the best possible match you can make in England."

My pulse pounded at the weight of her words.

"Don't put this on Clara," Alec said, taking a step forward. "She is not the one who has made poor financial decisions. This is not her burden to bear. The whole plan was preposterous to begin with."

"Are you suggesting I give up?" Aunt Maude asked.

My gaze met Alec's and the look of longing he'd had last night in the library returned. The knot in my stomach tightened as my own feelings stirred deep within my heart. I wanted nothing more than to tell him I loved him and that I didn't want to go to England and marry a duke. Was that what he was trying to get Aunt Maude to agree to?

Aunt Maude slowly rose from her chair, regaining the control she always demonstrated with Alec and me. "I see what this is about."

We both looked at her.

"Mrs. Walker told me that a scullery maid came upon the two of you in the library earlier this morning, but I didn't want to believe that you would go behind my back."

Alec's shoulders stiffened. "We've done no such thing."

I wanted to sink into the earth and not have to meet her angry and disappointed look. We hadn't done anything wrong, but I still felt guilty, because I had *wanted* to do something.

"I thought both of you understood the dire circumstances we're in and why it's necessary that my plan succeeds." She focused her gaze on me. "You, of all people, should understand this mission, Clara. I pulled you out of deplorable conditions and have given you everything your heart could desire."

My heart desired Alec.

"And you"—she said as she turned to Alec—"Edmund paid for your education at the best university in the country, and he left his entire life's work in your hands. And this is how you'll repay him? Having a clandestine meeting with Clara in the library?"

"It wasn't anything inappropriate or untoward. You asked me to teach her how to flirt."

Embarrassment warmed my cheeks. Was that all that had happened in the library this morning? Another lesson in flirtation?

The tension in Aunt Maude's face eased. "As long as that is all that happened."

"You have nothing to worry about where I'm concerned." He walked toward the door, which was behind me, and paused. "You are correct about one thing, Aunt Maude. Uncle Edmund entrusted his life's work to me. Stop spending so frivolously, or there will be nothing left of your husband's legacy to rub in my face."

With that final strike, Alec left the room.

I sat motionless in the chair, afraid to even blink for fear she would turn on me next.

Instead, she bit her bottom lip and looked to the side as she motioned for me to leave the room. "Get something to eat and then prepare for your morning callers."

Without waiting, I stood and was about to exit the room when Higgins appeared with a silver salver in hand.

"What is it, Higgins?" Aunt Maude asked.

He entered the room and presented the tray, which had a gold-embossed invitation on its surface. "This just arrived from Mrs. Vanderbilt's footman."

Aunt Maude's cares seemed to slip away as she took the invitation and opened it. Her eyes lit up. "It's an invitation for Alec, Clara, and I to attend Mrs. Vanderbilt's fancy dress ball in March." She rose from her chair as she read the invitation. When she lowered it, she said, "Clara, Mrs. Vanderbilt would like you to participate in one of the quadrilles. You'll begin to practice with the other young people at Mrs. Vanderbilt's home immediately."

Sweat started to gather on my brow. "What kind of quadrille?"

"I've heard there will be five themed and choreographed quadrilles to open the ball. Only four couples per quadrille, so that means there are only forty young people invited to participate—and you're one of them. It's a great honor!"

I was certain it *was* a great honor, but I had no experience with anything like it. What if I made a fool of myself with all of New York society watching?

"Higgins," Aunt Maude said. "Send for Madame Donovan immediately and tell her we've been invited to the most exclusive party in New York. I'm willing to pay whatever she asks to come here." After Higgins left, Aunt Maude turned to me. "There is no time to lose. We must have two fancy dress ball gowns designed for us. We won't know what theme you will dance in, so we'll have to wait until after your first practice this afternoon to find out." She tapped the invitation against her hand in thought. "Madam Donovan caters to Mrs. Astor's Four Hundred. She has never wanted to work with me before, but once she hears we've been invited to Mrs. Vanderbilt's costume party, and you'll be one of the quadrille dancers, she will be eager to accommodate us." She lifted her eyebrows. "Especially because I will pay her whatever she asks."

"But Alec said—"

"It is not your place to question how I spend my money." Aunt Maude's anger was swift, and she tightened her jaw. "It's *my* money. Alec is only being cautious. We will be fine." Her mood shifted drastically and she smiled. "My plan is working brilliantly. You'll make a splash here in New York and then we'll go to Europe, where you will be a sensation. We'll have every eligible aristocrat in England pounding down our door to propose to you."

The thought terrified me.

12

Mrs. Vanderbilt's French-chateau-inspired mansion was unlike anything I'd ever seen, even more impressive than Aunt Maude's home, if that was possible. I stood in a second-floor bedroom the night of the fancy dress ball with a dozen young ladies and their maids as we prepared for the quadrilles that would start thirty minutes before midnight.

Downstairs, the massive home was filled with over a thousand guests. I'd peeked out a window facing the street and saw hundreds of carriages blocking the road as their occupants waited to disembark in front of 660 Fifth Avenue.

The home was decorated with tens of thousands of flowers. Each room had a different color theme with flora draped over banisters, fireplace mantels, doorways, and tabletops. Gas lighting filled the rooms with a gentle glow and crystal sparkled from candelabras, vases, and statues. Mrs. Vanderbilt had allowed photographers to come in before the party to fill the newspapers with pictures of the opulence.

"There you are, Clara," Annabelle said as she appeared at my side. "I'm simply breathless! I just peered over the banister, and the foyer was crowded. There isn't an empty square inch to be had."

Annabelle and I had been put into the Louis XV–themed quadrille. We were both dressed in *robes à la Française*. My gown was a gorgeous pink silk with box pleats, which fell loose from my shoulders down to the floor behind me. The front of the gown was open, showing an intricately embroidered stomacher displaying little pink flowers and green vines, and a ruffled petticoat. Under the skirt I wore panniers over my hips and had pink slippers on my feet. My hair was styled high on my head with ringlets falling over my shoulders.

"I saw Alec," Annabelle said as I allowed Gallagher to assist me with long white gloves.

"Alec?" Despite my best efforts, I couldn't hide the pleasure from my voice.

I hadn't seen Alec since the morning we'd spoken about finances in Aunt Maude's sitting room, a month ago. He'd returned to Newport that afternoon and hadn't written.

"Are you surprised he's here?" Annabelle looked in the mirror nearby and pinched her cheeks to add color to them.

"Quite." I finished pulling on the gloves and adjusted them to fit better, trying not to look nervous about Alec. "I didn't know if he would return from Newport for the dance."

"He's traveling to Europe with you, is he not?" Annabelle's large blue eyes peered at me in the mirror. "And you're leaving in less than a week. Surely you expected him back soon."

I had put off thinking about Alec's return *and* the trip to Europe. After the last time I'd been with Alec, I tried not to think of him at all. Nothing good would come from our feelings for one another. The month he'd been gone had been good for me.

At least, that's what I tried to tell my heart.

"I've been too busy to consider Alec's plans." I lifted one of my shoulders, as if it didn't matter.

"Mama is spending all her time planning our trip to Europe to find a titled husband," Annabelle said with a sigh. "But the man I want to marry is right here in this house."

Aunt Maude's request that I try to persuade Alec and Annabelle to wed was unnecessary—at least where Annabelle was concerned. I was certain that if Alec proposed a second time, she would accept him immediately. *If* she could persuade her mama to allow the match.

"Five minutes," one of the maids said above the noise in the room. "You must start lining up now."

There was a moment of hectic movement as the young women gathered their last-minute accessories and checked their appearances in the mirrors one more time.

I'd spent the past four weeks coming to Mrs. Vanderbilt's mansion every day to practice the quadrille, and I had become acquainted with several young men and women in the process. Annabelle was my closest friend, though she was not a confidante. I could not take that chance.

"Find your partner," a dance instructor called to us as we assembled in the wide hallway. There had been three instructors hired to work with us, and they had drilled us incessantly. None of them wanted to displease Mrs. Vanderbilt, and neither did the rest of us.

A long red carpet ran down the length of the hallway, while gilded trim encircled the doors, the molding near the ceiling, and the frames around the massive paintings. Gaslights allowed me to search the room for George, who had volunteered to be my partner for his sister-in-law's party.

His brown-eyed gaze found mine in the crowd and he smiled.

"You look breathtaking, Clara," he said as he joined me and offered his arm. He was dressed as an eighteenth-century French courtier in royal purple silk, with a purple plume coming out of his hat.

"Thank you," I said. "You look quite handsome."

I'd discovered that George was much more shy than I'd realized. He didn't gravitate toward groups of people, or people he didn't know, but kept to himself or spoke to close friends. During our daily practices, he'd either spoken to me or gone off into a quiet corner to read. At twenty-one years old, he was a similar age to the others who danced with us, but he seemed older. Much older.

"Are you nervous?" he asked.

I had to lean in closer to hear him, since the noise in the hallway had grown louder as people's excitement grew.

"A little more than I'd like to admit," I said.

He also leaned close—so close, I could smell the scent of his cologne. His ear was next to my mouth. "What did you say?"

As I repeated myself, he turned, and our faces were only an inch apart.

His gaze focused on mine and warmth filled his eyes. "I don't know if you can hear me, Clara, but I'm in love with you, and I want to marry you."

I heard him clearly—and my heart hammered. Even if I had not heard him, the look on his besotted face would have told me everything. We'd spent hours together, both here and at Aunt Maude's where he continued to call on me. And when we weren't practicing the quadrille, we saw each other at social events. There was an easy camaraderie with George, and I'd known for the past couple of weeks that he was in love with me. But I pretended I hadn't heard him. Instead, I smiled and lifted my shoulders as if I didn't know what he'd said.

He looked like he was going to try again, but one of the instructors clapped his hands loudly. "Quiet! Please be quiet. We have some last-minute instructions for you."

The others stopped talking and George straightened next to me.

My pulse beat an erratic rhythm as I took the arm he offered and listened to the dance instructors tell us what they wanted us to do.

George Vanderbilt, a man from one of the wealthiest families in the world, had just proposed marriage. To me. Keira O'Day, a guttersnipe from Five Points. Would he still want me if he knew the truth? What about Mrs. Vanderbilt? Or Mrs. Astor? I'd heard that she would be present at tonight's event, a coup that would elevate Mrs. Vanderbilt's standing in polite society. What a scandal it would be if anyone learned the truth, that Mrs. Vanderbilt had invited a young woman from Five Points to dance at her ball.

Annabelle touched my shoulder from behind me and when I turned to look at her, she gave a pointed glance at George, her eyes wide and questioning. Had she overheard what had just happened? What about the others?

The hall clock struck once, indicating the half hour, and the instructors motioned for the members of the first quadrille to descend the steps. Our group would be the second, so we moved forward to take the place of the dancers who had just left.

My nerves thrummed as George and I stood at the front of the group. My gloved hand was wrapped around his elbow, and he pressed it close to his side. When I looked up at him, his gaze was filled with tenderness and longing. He smiled, and I knew that before the night was through, he would speak of marriage again. I would try to avoid the conversation, but it would be impossible to give him the cold shoulder. He was too dear to me for that.

Finally, it was our turn to descend the stairs. My legs were shaking so hard, I was afraid I would fall down the steps—but George was steady at my side. He grinned with pride as we entered the foyer, where the overflow from the ballroom watched.

I tried not to look for Alec, but I couldn't help it. There were so many people, it was almost impossible to discern one from the next.

George led me out of the foyer and into the center of the massive ballroom. The walls were covered in floor-to-ceiling mirrors and draped with yards and yards of floral garland. Where had they found so many flowers in March? It was inconceivable. The newspapers claimed that Mrs. Vanderbilt had spent over $250,000 on this one party.

There were three orchestras in the house, but the one in the ballroom would play the French minuet for us. We'd practiced for hours upon hours, until I dreamt about the dance in my sleep. Yet with all eyes upon me, I was suddenly drawing a blank and couldn't remember a single step.

George caught my eye as we took our place. He offered me an encouraging smile, with a slight nod.

I took a deep breath, feeling calmer in his presence.

We began to dance, and my body quickly took control. I held a fan in my hand and used it as part of the quadrille. We stepped, hopped, turned, and bowed in a beautifully choreographed pattern. George continued to smile as we met and then moved apart and then met again. He seemed completely unaware of all the people watching and only had eyes for me.

He was such a wonderful man. How could I turn down his proposal? It seemed ludicrous. He and I enjoyed discussing books while sitting quietly together in Aunt Maude's parlor. He was intelligent and passionate about science, art, forestry, and so many other topics. I never tired of talking to him. Unlike some of his other family members, he didn't see his wealth as something to be paraded about or exploited. He wanted to do good with the blessings he'd been given. Saying no to marrying him was just as preposterous as everything else I'd experienced since moving into Aunt Maude's house.

We danced for almost fifteen minutes, and when our quadrille came to an end, we bowed at each other and then at the audience as they clapped enthusiastically.

Mrs. Vanderbilt stood nearby with Mrs. Astor and both of their faces were very pleased.

George offered me his arm as we moved to the edges of the dance floor to watch the next group descend and enter the ballroom.

"You were magnificent," George said to me, leaning close, for my ears alone. "I almost feel sorry for all the other young women in our quadrille. No one noticed anyone else but you."

"George," I said, playfully chastising him.

"It's true. Look. They're still watching you."

I did as he suggested and glanced around the room. Dozens of men and women were still looking at me. But it was only one man who caught my eye and made me pause.

Alec.

It took another hour before the real dancing began. As soon as the Spanish-themed quadrille, the last one of the evening, came to an end, Mr. and Mrs. Vanderbilt walked to the center of the room and the orchestra began a waltz.

"May I have the first dance?" George asked me.

"Of course."

"And the last?"

I glanced toward the other side of the room where I had seen Alec, but everyone had moved and he had disappeared.

George waited, so I smiled and nodded. "I would be honored."

His grin was wide and infectious as he took my dance card and filled in his name, then whisked me onto the dance floor.

Here, we were surrounded by people, but no one could hear us as we moved over the parquet floor. I was not surprised when George spoke to me again.

"I'm in love with you," he said. It was obvious he was nervous, but he didn't let it stop him. "I've never met anyone like you, Clara. I love seeing the world through your eyes. You're intelligent, kind, and you make everything come alive in a way it never has before. I'm excited about the future and all the places we could see and experience together. I want to marry you, if you'll have me."

"Oh, George."

He shook his head, as if to stop me. "I know what you're going to say, Clara."

"Then why did you ask?"

"Because hope is a dangerous mistress. It makes us do and say things we know we'll regret, though we can't help ourselves."

My hand lay gently inside his and I squeezed it. "I care for you deeply."

"I know you do." He pulled me a little closer. "That's why this confounded hope inside me won't die."

"You know we're going to Europe."

"Of course I do."

"My aunt has her sights set on an aristocratic match."

"I would be blind and foolish not to know that."

"Then why do you ask me this question?"

He sighed, but there was a teasing gleam in his eyes. "Perhaps I had hoped you would be willing to elope."

I didn't even bother to respond to his statement. It was out of the question, for both of us. His family would disown him if he did something like that. And, despite my reservations, I'd made a promise to Aunt Maude. She'd spent so much money on me. I needed to marry a titled lord to help pay it back.

It was the reason I couldn't love Alec.

"Do you want to live in England and be married to a stodgy earl or duke?" he asked, his mood darkening.

It would be easy to pretend with George, like I did with all the others, but I didn't want to. "No."

"Then why are you agreeing to it?"

I gave him a look. "How many young women in this room have a choice?" For me, the alternative wasn't worth thinking about.

"I won't hide my affections, Clara," he said, pulling me even closer. "The whole world will know I'm in love with you. And no matter which earl or duke your aunt picks for you, he'll always know that you have my heart."

We were silent as we finished our waltz and when it was done, several men approached, asking to be placed on my dance card. I glanced around, looking for Alec, hoping he'd ask me for a dance.

He was standing near Annabelle, and they were laughing together as he wrote his name on her card.

Jealousy wrapped around my heart as men vied for my attention. I absently said yes to whomever asked but couldn't take my eyes off Alec and Annabelle. Her cheeks were glowing and her eyes shone as she smiled at him.

When Alec turned and caught my eye, he paused, but I couldn't read his expression.

Instead of approaching, smiling, or even acknowledging that he knew me, he turned and walked away.

Tears burned at the backs of my eyes, and I had to blink furiously to keep them at bay as the strains of the next dance began.

My partner found me and soon we were circling around the room.

I tried not to let Alec's rejection hurt. I'd never had his affection, so I shouldn't feel such pain at the loss of it.

Dance after dance, I faced a new, eager partner, all of them wealthy and among the social elite. Their compliments flowed like honey off their practiced tongues. It became sickeningly sweet and cloyed at my mood. If they knew me—the real me—they wouldn't be saying such things. How many of these men had noticed me on opening night at the Metropolitan Opera House when I had stood outside selling fabric flowers?

Only one. Alec.

My head began to hurt and I needed a break. I should have looked for Aunt Maude, my chaperone, to walk with me into Mrs. Vanderbilt's garden, but I didn't have enough time—nor did I have the patience to listen to her critiques.

I slipped through the crowd and moved toward the doors, stepping out into the cool evening.

There were torches around the beautiful garden, spilling light onto the hedge-lined paths. A large gazebo sat at the back of the property, along with benches throughout.

I moved away from the house, the cold March air making gooseflesh rise on my bare skin.

Several couples meandered through the parklike setting, though I couldn't make out their features. As I walked along the path, I noticed a man sitting on a bench under the branches of a weeping willow.

He stood, and though I couldn't see his face, I recognized the set of his shoulders and the way he held himself.

It was Alec.

I paused and a part of me wanted to turn and walk away. I wanted him to feel the rejection I'd just felt by him in the ballroom. And put my feelings for him behind me. Forever.

Yet—I could never do that to him.

"Keira." His voice was low, but it traveled toward me and caressed my heart. It was the way he said it—tender and gentle.

I moved aside the branches and slipped into the little shelter. The orchestra music filtered into the garden, and the torches danced in the breeze, but here, the light didn't reach us.

I stopped just inside the cover but didn't approach him.

"Hello, Keira."

"Hello, Alec."

"You stole the show tonight. You're a graceful dancer. All those hours of practice were worth the effort."

I didn't respond, my heart still sore from seeing him with Annabelle.

"I should get back." I turned to leave, but he moved forward and took hold of my hand.

Memories of when he'd stopped me on Christmas evening resurfaced and my heart pounded as I turned back to him.

"Don't go yet."

My breathing was shallow as he stood close to me, his hand still grasping mine.

"Why not?" I asked, my pain making me bold. "You had no interest in acknowledging me or dancing with me earlier. Why should I stay here now?"

"I'm sorry."

I waited for him to explain himself, but he didn't, so I started to leave again.

He held my hand, gently pulling me closer to him. "Please, Keira."

"I should return to George." I wanted to make Alec as jealous as I'd been when I saw him with Annabelle. "He proposed to me tonight."

Alec stiffened. "You cannot marry him."

"Why not?"

"You know why." His voice was hard. "Aunt Maude has different plans for you."

"Let me go, Alec." I tried pulling my hand away from him. "What do you want?"

His lips were pressed together, as if he was holding back, fighting an internal battle. Finally, he whispered, "You."

My breath caught as tears filled my eyes. "Is this another lesson? Will I admit that I'm in love with you and you'll laugh and tell me it was all a game of flirtation that I must learn before going to Europe?"

It was his turn to look surprised as he dropped my hand. "You're in love with me?"

Tears fell and I banished them with the back of my hand.

"Oh, Keira."

The way he said it was exactly how I'd said it to George, and it meant the exact same thing.

Disappointment overwhelmed me. "I should return to the ballroom." I took a step backward. "My dance card is full."

This time, Alec didn't stop me.

I wished I hadn't come into the garden. And I wished I hadn't agreed to Aunt Maude's plans.

It hurt too much.

13

The SS *Oregon* was said to be the fastest steamship on the high seas. As I stood on board the brand-new vessel, watching the endless Atlantic Ocean from the promenade deck, I didn't have a hard time believing it. Captain Perry was attempting to earn the coveted Blue Riband title for the fastest eastbound transatlantic crossing, from New York to Ireland, held by a previous ship for the past two years.

Wind tore at my gown and threatened to pull off my hat, which was held in place by two pearl-studded hat pins. I pressed my hand against it, marveling at the breadth of the Atlantic Ocean. It was a wonder that I had crossed this body of water one other time in my life, though I had no memory of it. All I knew was New York City. No doubt I'd been in third-class, with those below deck.

I was both thrilled and terrified to be on my way to Europe. All I could think about was my mother and whether I would find her. What if she was no longer living in England or, worse, had died? Thoughts of my mother soon turned to my family in Five Points. How were they faring? What would they think if they knew what I was doing with my life? I didn't have money of my own, but I was determined that as soon as I did, I would send some to my cousins. What good was wealth and status if I couldn't help Imogen out of poverty?

Gallagher stood behind me, near the outer wall of the ladies' drawing room. She did not like to get close to the railings, deathly afraid of falling overboard. She watched me with apprehension. I hadn't thought anything could frighten my intrepid lady's maid.

"Miss Hill." Mrs. Garfield approached, her daughter, Louise, at her side. "I thought I saw your name on the passenger list."

I gave a slight curtsey, as I'd been instructed, and nodded at Mrs. Garfield and Louise. I had seen them at several social events throughout the past few months, and most recently at Mrs. Vanderbilt's party. But we rarely spoke, especially when Aunt Maude wasn't with me.

"We heard George Vanderbilt tried to get passage on this vessel," Mrs. Garfield continued, a knowing smile on her face. "But every stateroom was full."

"I heard the same."

Mrs. Garfield shared a look with her daughter before turning back to me. "We were surprised an engagement wasn't announced before the ship left port."

"An engagement?" I frowned.

"Oh, don't be coy," Louise said. "Everyone knows George is in love with you. Surely he has proposed."

My cheeks warmed under their scrutiny, but I wouldn't give them the pleasure of knowing one way or the other. Instead, I simply smiled.

"No doubt he'll be on your heels as soon as we arrive in Europe," Mrs. Garfield purred.

"I don't know what Mr. Vanderbilt's plans are when he's in Europe," I told her honestly.

The two ladies shared another look before Mrs. Garfield asked, "Where is your dear Aunt Maude? I would expect her to be promenading with you this first day out to sea, so you could meet everyone on board."

"Unfortunately, Aunt Maude is not feeling well," I confessed. "Seasickness."

"That is unfortunate." Mrs. Garfield grabbed at her hat as a sudden gust of wind whipped at all of us. "I hope she'll be recovered enough to join us for supper."

"I do, too."

They continued past me, talking in low tones as they bent their heads together. Louise turned once to run her gaze up the length of my gown and lift an eyebrow before turning back to her mother.

With a sigh, I faced Gallagher. "I think I'll check on Aunt Maude."

She nodded with relief and then followed me as I entered the interior of the ship, thankful to be out of the wind.

The SS *Oregon* was only a few months old and boasted the most luxurious accommodations in the Guion Line. Beautiful woodwork adorned every room on the ship and plush carpet cushioned my feet as I made my way to one of the larger first-class cabins on the main deck. There were four rooms in our suite, one for Alec, one for Aunt Maude, and one for me. Gallagher and Brown, Aunt Maude's lady's maid, were sleeping in a separate cabin, as was Alec's valet, Mr. Timmons. In the center of the suite was a common sitting room with luxurious furniture, rich upholstery, and electric Edison lights. Everything was much larger than I had anticipated, with generous windows and comfortable beds. No expense had been spared.

I entered the sitting room, wondering if I would see Alec. We had spoken very little over the past week since Mrs. Vanderbilt's fancy dress ball. He'd spent every free moment at the office, preparing for his departure to Europe. Early that morning, as we'd left Aunt Maude's home on Fifth Avenue, he'd kept to himself as Aunt Maude had given me last-minute instructions about shipboard etiquette. Since our arrival onboard, he'd been scarce.

He wasn't in the sitting room and the door to his cabin was closed.

It was for the best. After both of us had confessed our feelings to one another, what more was there to say? Our circumstances would not change and it was torture to hope otherwise.

Gallagher entered the sitting room behind me as I walked across the space and knocked on Aunt Maude's door. It opened and Brown stood before me.

"How is she doing?" I asked.

"The same."

"Is that Clara?" Aunt Maude asked in a weak voice.

"Yes." I stepped into the room as Brown moved aside. "How are you feeling?"

Aunt Maude was lying on her bed, the covers drawn up to her chin. Her face was ashen, and her graying hair was in a single braid, worn over her shoulder. "Do not concern yourself with how I'm feeling," she said. "I want to know how you've spent your afternoon." She paused and closed her eyes as her face went pale.

Brown grabbed a bowl and raced to her side, pressing a wet cloth against her brow and waiting.

Whatever had come over Aunt Maude seemed to pass and she opened her eyes, taking a deep breath. "Well?"

I told her how I had toured the steamship with Gallagher as my companion, finding the grand saloon, the ladies' drawing room, several music rooms, and even the men's smoking room.

"And who did you see that we know?"

I recounted several passengers that I knew by name, including the Garfields, which made her wrinkle her nose in displeasure.

"The captain has invited us to dine at his table," Aunt Maude said when I was done. "I wouldn't be surprised if the Garfields are there, as well." She looked ill again at the talk of supper. "I probably won't be well enough to join tonight, since it takes me a few days to overcome seasickness. You and Alec will have to attend without me. Where is Alec?"

"He's in his cabin, ma'am," Brown said.

"Get him for me."

Brown left the room as Aunt Maude closed her eyes and seemed to fall asleep.

Gallagher had not followed me into the room, so I stood there in the silence. Waiting.

It wasn't long before Alec appeared at the open door.

Our gazes collided and he offered me a tentative smile. I had to glance away, afraid my heart couldn't handle the press of affection for him, or the embarrassment that warmed my cheeks at having told him I was in love with him.

"Aunt Maude?" Alec asked, moving closer to her bed.

Her eyes fluttered open and she moaned. "I hate sea travel."

"Brown said you needed to see me."

She took a deep breath and nodded. "The captain has asked us to dine with him, but I will not be able to join tonight. I want you to keep a close eye on Clara. Use the next few days to introduce her to other men on the ship and continue to coach her in flirtations."

"We've already been over this," he said. "Clara doesn't need more coach—"

"There is little I can do to further her studies while I'm lying in this bed. But if she is not moving forward, she is retreating. If there are any other issues you see arise while she is conversing or dancing with others, or yourself, correct it later in private." She looked between him and me. "Do I make myself clear?"

The last thing I wanted to do was spend time with Alec as he continued to teach me to flirt. It was too hard on my heart. But what could I say to Aunt Maude, especially in her current state of discomfort?

"Of course," I said to her.

Alec simply nodded.

"Go, please," Aunt Maude said. "I need to sleep."

Brown reentered the room as Alec and I exited. Gallagher must have gone to her room, because the sitting room was empty.

When Brown closed the door, it left Alec and I in the main room alone.

"You don't need to teach me anything," I told him as I went to a sofa and sat on the edge, my back straight as I lifted a copy of *Pride and Prejudice* off the tea table where I'd left it.

Alec stood for a moment and then sat on the sofa facing me. A beautiful arrangement of freshly cut flowers graced the table between us.

I looked down at the book.

"You can't avoid me for the whole voyage," he finally said.

"I would like to try."

He moved forward. "Please don't be angry at me, Keira. The last thing I want to do is hurt you."

I knew he was speaking the truth. The only reason I was feeling any kind of agony was because I had fallen in love with him—and couldn't have him. It wasn't his fault. He hadn't forced me to love him, and he hadn't forced me to agree to Aunt Maude's scheme.

I finally lifted my gaze, and I saw the pain in his. I would have to push aside my feelings and forget about them. We had a whole week ahead of us, and even longer in Europe. I couldn't shut him out of my life or ignore him, nor did I want to. Alec was good and kind. He didn't deserve my unfriendliness.

"I'm sorry," I said, softening my shoulders. "I'm not angry at you."

I was angry at myself.

"You have nothing to be sorry about." He was quiet for a moment and then said, "I've missed you, Keira."

"I've missed you, too." And that was part of the problem. I was already mourning the loss of Alexander Paxton-Hill from my life. Because if all went as planned, I might be married to someone else in just a few short months.

Something I didn't want to contemplate for many reasons.

The grand saloon was a glittering space, capable of seating all 340 first-class passengers for supper, though there were many empty seats, like Aunt Maude's. Alec and I sat at the captain's table, along with Mrs. Garfield and Louise and several other wealthy passengers. The room was on the main deck and had a tall cupola in the center of the ceiling, with massive windows to let in light and ventilation. Everything in the room was decorated in white and gold.

"Is this your first passage over?" Captain Perry asked me, since I was seated to his right.

"No, but the first of my memory. I was born in England and came to America as an infant."

"I've gone over half a dozen times," Louise said as she set her crystal goblet on the table, waving her hand as if my comment was absurd. "How odd that you've never returned to England before now."

I smiled at Louise, not elaborating. I hated to perpetuate the lie that I was a relative of Aunt Maude's from St. Paul, so I simply said nothing.

"You've chosen the best voyage," Captain Perry said to me, not shifting his attention to Louise as she had probably hoped he would.

"We're making great progress, and I have every confidence that we'll break the speed record."

I returned his smile. "What a wonderful accomplishment. You must be so proud."

"Where will your travels take you in Europe?" asked the gentleman on my left, Mr. Keeton. He was a wealthy, single financier from New York. He and Captain Perry had kept my attention all evening.

Alec sat across from me, next to Louise. There were a few couples, one other young woman, and Mr. Keeton. When Louise wasn't dominating the conversation, we'd enjoyed discussing literature, society, and history while dining on oysters, salmon with hollandaise sauce, lamb with mint sauce, cauliflower au gratin, and custard.

Through it all, Alec was quiet, his gaze often on me and the conversations I had with the captain and Mr. Keeton. Apparently, he was taking his orders from Aunt Maude seriously, though I doubted he would correct my blunders when we were in private. Alec never corrected me.

When supper finished, everyone rose from the table. The women would withdraw to the ladies' drawing room, while the men would go to the smoking room for cigars and brandy.

The last thing I wanted to do was spend the evening with the other women, gossiping and positioning myself for social dominance, but there were few other options, unless I wanted to go back to my room and be alone.

Alec caught my eye as he joined me and offered me his arm. Leaning close he said, "Would you like to walk along the promenade deck? I have no desire to join the men in the smoking room tonight."

"You read my mind," I said quietly, relieved to bypass the ladies' drawing room.

As the passengers exited the dining room, we walked up the grand staircase to the upper deck and then the promenade deck. It was quieter up there, with only a few couples strolling along, arm in arm.

The moon was full and brilliant as it reflected on the ocean, sending a trail of light in its wake. Thankfully, the wind had calmed, and the sea was peaceful. I continued to hold Alec's arm as he walked me along the length of the deck, farther away from the other couples.

Neither one of us spoke as we listened to the sound of the ship slicing through the water and crashing against the waves. The noise filled the night air as the ship lifted and lowered along its course.

"What do you think of ocean travel?" Alec asked.

"It's quite grand. I'm thankful I haven't gotten seasick."

"So am I. This is only my second time to Europe, and I've avoided being sick both times."

"Why did you come this time?" It was a question that had been on my mind for months, but I hadn't had a chance to ask him. "Don't you have work to do in Newport and New York?"

"I have contacts in Europe that I need to visit. We serve a British and French clientele as well as an American one. Besides, our general manager has been working for the company for decades. He and Uncle Edmund started the business together. He can manage alone for a while."

"I doubt that. Aunt Maude speaks very highly of the work you do."

He accepted my compliment without a word as we stopped near the front of the promenade deck and stepped over to the railing. I let go of Alec's arm and placed my hands on the rail. Taking a deep breath, I turned to him. "What is your assessment of my abilities tonight? Would you recommend any changes or adjustments?"

Alec studied me for a moment, the moonlight bathing his face in a blue glow. "You're perfect, just as you are." He smiled, though there was sadness in his eyes. "I thought you were perfect even before you started to change under Aunt Maude."

My cheeks grew warm, and I dipped my chin. "Alec—"

"I'm flirting with you, Keira, and when a man is flirting, your eyes will tell him everything he needs to know. Lower them, and it will indicate that you want him to stop. Meet his gaze, and it will embolden him to continue."

Slowly, I lifted my gaze to his, though this game we were playing was dangerous. We both knew it.

"Your eyes tell a thousand tales, and I want to hear them all."

"You are skilled at flirting."

He leaned on the rail, facing the ocean, and I knew he was struggling with his attraction to me as much as I was to him. "It's easy to do when I'm with you."

We were both quiet for a moment, lost in our thoughts. Whatever this was between us *was* easy.

"Do you feel ready for Europe?" he finally asked me, changing the subject.

"I think if I could pass muster at Mrs. Vanderbilt's ball, France and England will be simple. Queen Victoria isn't nearly as frightening as Mrs. Astor."

He laughed. "You might be right."

I smiled, though I knew I would be terrified to be presented to the Queen of England. "Sometimes I still pinch myself to believe this is all real. How did someone like me end up here, or in Mrs. Vanderbilt's ballroom, or in St. James's Palace?" I didn't mention George's proposal, but that still didn't seem real either.

"If ever there was a woman suited to the queen's drawing room, it's you, Keira O'Day. Even before you came to live with Aunt Maude, you held yourself with regal bearing."

"Are you pretending to flirt again?"

"I never pretend when I'm with you."

I clasped my hands on the railing, looking at the moonbeams sparkling on the water. We were playing with fire, but in this moment, I didn't care if I got burnt. "There is one thing I haven't learned yet."

He turned to me. "What is it?"

I wasn't sure what emboldened me. Perhaps it was the solitude, or the moonlight, or the fact that we were in the middle of the Atlantic Ocean, so far removed from everything I'd ever known. I turned to face him. "I don't know how to kiss."

He blinked, and for the first time since I'd met him, I think I truly surprised him.

"What if a suitor tries to take a kiss?" I asked.

"Has George tried to kiss you?" There was an edge to his voice.

"No." I met his gaze, thankful for the darkness in case there was color in my warm cheeks.

"No man should ever take such liberties with you." He took a deep breath. "Unless you're engaged."

"You did," I said in a low voice.

He opened his mouth and then closed it again. "That was different."

"Why?"

"It was a Christmas tradition."

"Was that all?" I whispered.

He stared at me for a moment and then he turned back to the railing, leaning his forearms on top.

"What about when I'm engaged?" I asked him.

"Your fiancé can teach you everything you need to know about things like that." His voice was dry. "By that point, you will have secured his promise, if not his heart, and the rest will come naturally."

"What if it doesn't?"

He straightened and ran his hand over the back of his neck. "Some things cannot be taught, Keira. They are an extension of the love and attraction two people share. You have nothing to worry about."

"What if my fiancé doesn't love me? What if he's not attracted to me?"

"That cannot be possible. Any man with eyes would find you attractive."

My cheeks grew warmer. "Then what of love?"

"It's a rare gift in our circles. If you find it, you are one of the fortunate few."

My heart pounded as I watched him, knowing he was right. I had found it, but it could never be acted upon.

"I spent the first part of my life unloved," I whispered, lowering my gaze to look at my hands. "I cannot imagine spending the rest of my life suffering the same fate."

"Keira." He gently reached for my hand. "It is my fervent prayer that you get everything your heart desires. You deserve it more than anyone else I know."

His touch was soft and tender. It sent a tingling sensation up my arm and into my chest.

I lifted my gaze to his and something powerful passed between us.

"Oh, I do apologize," an older woman said from behind Alec. "I didn't realize we were interrupting a moonlit rendezvous."

Alec pulled his hand away from mine and turned, revealing Mrs. Garfield and Louise.

"Well, well," Mrs. Garfield said. "Here I thought Mr. Vanderbilt's greatest competition was the aristocracy in Europe. I had no idea the real competition was much closer to home." She smiled. "Does dear old Maude realize what's happening right under her nose?"

"It goes without saying that nothing is happening between Clara and I," Alec said.

"You were holding her hand."

"I was comforting her."

Mrs. Garfield's sly smile made her look like a cat. "Is that what we're calling it now?" She lifted a shoulder. "I would hate for rumors to circle about Miss Clara before we get to Europe. You know, the British are even more concerned about reputations than us Americans."

I wasn't sure if it was true, but I didn't want to take any chances.

"Alec has always been a gentleman," I said.

"It doesn't matter to me. But I would be more careful the next time you have a *tête-à-tête*. Perhaps it would be best not to do it so publicly. Come, Louise, we should leave these two to return to their *comforting*."

As they walked away, Alec gave me an apologetic look. "I'm sorry."

I shook my head. "Perhaps it would be best to retire for the night."

He nodded and offered me his arm.

I needed to put space between myself and Alec—not only to preserve my reputation, but also my heart.

14

Victoria Station, in the heart of London, bustled with activity as I stepped off the train that had brought us from Dover that morning. A large glass and iron dome above revealed a cloudy sky and droplets of rain as people hurried about on the platform. Women in beautiful traveling gowns, men in top hats and watch chains, businessmen running to catch their evening train, hawkers selling their wares, and porters, all mingled together with customs agents.

"Be mindful not to soil your gown," Aunt Maude said as she came down the steps behind me, a porter assisting her. "London is nothing but soot and mud. Gallagher will spend most of her days keeping your wardrobe clean."

I nodded as I absently listened, my gaze connecting with every woman who passed by. Could my mother be among this very crowd? It wasn't likely, but my chances of passing her on the street were better here than anywhere else.

My gloved hand slipped up to the locket I wore around my neck. For the first time since the night of my debutante ball, I had put it on. Aunt Maude had protested that it didn't compliment my green traveling gown, but she didn't force me to put it away. Perhaps she saw how important it was to me. There was a part of me, perhaps naïve and overly optimistic, that believed if I *did* see my mother, and she recognized the locket, she might recognize me.

Alec exited the train last, holding Aunt Maude's traveling satchel.

After the SS *Oregon* had won the speed record, and safely delivered us to our destination, we'd spent a week in Paris, long enough for an extensive wardrobe to be acquired at the House of Worth. Aunt Maude had paid handsomely for the clothing to be rushed. We'd ordered twenty gowns, including the one I would wear to be presented to the queen. Those gowns, combined with the fifty I had brought from America, meant I had dozens and dozens of trunks.

I hadn't heard Alec or Aunt Maude discuss money again, but I imagined paying for so many new clothes was a strain on their financial situation. Guilt ate away at me, strengthening my resolve to find the best match possible in England. Everything depended on my success in the marriage mart. The last thing I wanted was for Alec and Aunt Maude to suffer.

Between dress fittings in Paris, we'd shopped along the Champs-Élysées near the Arc de Triomphe, attended a performance at the Opéra Garnier, visited the Louvre, promenaded through the Jardin des Tuileries, and toured the Notre-Dame Cathedral. There had been luncheons, a river cruise on the Seine, and a stroll through Montmartre to watch painters and view the construction of the basilica, Sacré-Cœur, which would preside over Paris from its place atop the highest point in the city.

It had just been the three of us, and the only words I knew to describe our magical time in Paris were that it was *like a dream*. But, like with all dreams, I had to wake up and face the reality set before me.

"Lady Mandeville is sending a carriage around for us," Aunt Maude said to Alec. "It should be waiting for us. The porters will see that our luggage is taken to 7 Buckingham Gate. Lady Mandeville has arranged for us to rent the house for our stay here."

"Buckingham Gate?" Alec asked as we moved away from the train toward the station exit. "That sounds expensive."

Aunt Maude stopped on the platform and turned to Alec. "I do not want you questioning anything I do here in London. Everything has been meticulously planned for months. Lady Mandeville knows what's she's doing and, if all goes as expected, every penny will be worth the investment."

Over the course of the past six months, I'd gone from feeling like a dirty street urchin, to feeling like a beautiful lady. Now, as the pivotal moment arrived, I felt dirty again. I was a human pawn in a dangerous, high-stakes game, and the more I understood it, the worse I felt. In essence, I was being sold for a title, which Aunt Maude would carry back to New York to lord over Mrs. Astor and Mrs. Garfield.

I held my locket, running my thumb over it as Alec caught my eye. The empathy in his gaze almost undid my resolve—but what choice did I have? I'd agreed to play this game, and now I was here, for better or worse.

After ensuring our trunks and luggage were accounted for, we left the station and found Lady Mandeville's carriage waiting for us as she'd promised. If I'd thought the station was busy, it was nothing compared to the street. Carriages, hansom cabs, carts, omnibuses, and more traveled over the wet cobblestone streets as pedestrians darted between the vehicles. A mist hung in the air as dark clouds blotted out what was left of the daylight. Everything looked drab and dreary as Alec helped Aunt Maude into the carriage. After assisting me, he stepped up, taking a seat on the opposite bench.

"I'll be anxious for my bed," Aunt Maude said with a sigh. "And eager to settle in for a few months before traveling again."

"When do you plan for us to return to New York?" I asked her.

"That all depends on your success. Perhaps you won't return to New York at all."

My breath caught at that thought as I looked out the window at the soot-covered buildings. Never return to New York? Of course I knew it was possible, but now it felt real.

"I will return before winter," she continued. "But let us not worry about that yet. We have much to accomplish."

I glanced at Alec, and he offered me a half smile, perhaps meant to encourage me, though it was also sad. He had never been agreeable to Aunt Maude's plans and seemed even less so now.

"I will only be here for a month," he said to me. "I must return home before the summer season in Newport."

"You'll be leaving so soon?" My voice betrayed my disappointment. Though we'd been together almost constantly since the night Mrs. Garfield and Louise had come upon us on the promenade deck, we'd managed to keep our emotional distance from one another. The thought of him leaving all together was too painful to contemplate.

"I'm afraid so."

"Alec will be here for the first round of social events," Aunt Maude said, "helping me chaperone you. But after that, hopefully he won't be needed."

Alec looked out the window, and I wondered if he felt like a pawn, as well.

As the carriage drove through the streets of London, I fixed my gaze outside, pushing away my trepidation and looking for my mother. I wasn't even sure what to look for, but I wanted to believe that if I saw the woman who gave me life, I would somehow recognize her. Afterall, Aunt Orla had said I looked like her. Fog had started to settle in, blanketing the streets, making it harder to inspect the passersby.

"You can see the spires of Westminster Abbey over there," Alec said to me as he pointed out the window.

I looked where he indicated and saw a faint outline of the gothic cathedral. Lamplighters were making their way down the street as we passed shops closing for the night.

It didn't take long before the carriage came to a stop in front of a massive townhouse with a white stucco façade and two columns holding up a canopy over the front entrance. Though it was growing dark outside, I could still see that the entire neighborhood was impressive and expensive.

"There is Buckingham Palace," Aunt Maude said as she pointed out the window on her side of the carriage, opposite the house where we had stopped. "It's the side of the palace, but we are still neighbors."

The footman jumped off the back of the carriage and came around to open the door. Alec stepped out first and then offered me his hand to help me alight from the vehicle. I stood on the sidewalk, looking up at the five-story townhouse in the thick fog.

When Aunt Maude stepped out of the carriage, she hardly inspected the residence as she lifted the hem of her gown and walked confidently toward the front door.

Alec offered me his arm and shook his head. I could only imagine he was calculating the cost in his mind.

The front door opened even before Aunt Maude stepped under the canopy and then an older man greeted her with a slight bow. "Good evening, Mrs. Hill. I'm Rodgers, your butler. I'm at your service, madam."

Aunt Maude didn't pause or hesitate but entered the house with full authority.

I took a deep breath, wishing I felt as confident as she did.

"One foot in front of the other," Alec said, gently squeezing my hand. "That's how we'll get through this."

His words were bittersweet, because he could only take me so far and then I would need to go on without him.

I woke up in a strange sort of daze the next morning, forgetting where I was for a moment. Sunshine poured through one massive window as Gallagher stood at the second one, opening the long, heavy drapes.

"Good morning," she said.

The bed I slept in was also enormous, with four posters and a canopy overhead. The room was large, with a fireplace, writing desk, and a sofa.

"Mrs. Hill sent me in to get you ready for your meeting with Lady Mandeville. She'll be here right after breakfast."

"Why so early?"

"Mrs. Hill says there's no time to lose."

Lady Consuelo Mandeville had been one of the first American heiresses to marry into the English nobility, bringing a substantial dowry with her. But Aunt Maude had told me that her husband, the Viscount Mandeville, the heir to the Duke of Manchester, had quickly squandered their fortune. Because of it, Lady Mandeville was willing to sponsor American heiresses to present to Queen Victoria and would introduce them to the most eligible aristocrats in England. For a handsome fee.

Aunt Maude and Lady Mandeville had been corresponding all winter.

There was little to be done, so I stepped out of the bed and tried to eat the breakfast Gallagher had brought in for me.

My thoughts returned to the night before, as Alec and I had toured the beautiful mansion. Despite being the heir to the Hill fortune and living in one of the most extravagant homes on Fifth Avenue, his eyes still lit with wonder as we explored 7 Buckingham Gate. There were dozens and dozens of rooms, with a library, conservatory, and several drawing rooms. Domed ceilings, rich walnut paneling, marble floors, and gold gilding made the home impressive. I had been tired but didn't want to go to sleep, knowing what I would face today.

After I was done eating breakfast, Gallagher helped me into a cream-colored morning dress. It had a bustle and a jacket, which fit snugly, but comfortably. Aunt Maude had allowed me to have a little more say in the clothing we had chosen in Paris, for which I'd been thankful. I loved to watch the process of creating such intricate designs, thinking of the piecework I'd done in our apartment on Mulberry Street. I didn't miss the work, but I did miss sewing. And every once in a while, my thoughts slipped back to that long-ago dream of living in a quiet house in the country as a seamstress.

How different my life had gone. Perhaps I would still get that quiet house in the country, if Aunt Maude's wishes came true, though I doubted it would be a small cottage by a stream. And it wouldn't be beyond the Mississippi. Had I known I could dream bigger, I might have thought about a place in the English countryside. Had God known my future? Was this an even bigger answer to my whispered prayers? I wasn't sure, but it was something to ponder.

"I'd like to wear the locket again today," I said to Gallagher as she finished my hair.

"Locket?"

"The one I was wearing yesterday." How could she forget when she was the one who had clasped it for me?

She stared at me through the mirror, her face a mask of confusion. "I forgot you were wearing it yesterday. I don't have it."

I turned, about to tell her that she had removed it from around my neck the night before, but I suddenly realized that she hadn't. I hadn't been wearing it last night when I undressed, and I was so unfamiliar with wearing it, I had forgotten.

My hand went up to my neck, as if I expected it to still be there. "What happened to it?"

"Did it fall off at some point yesterday? I don't recall you wearing it when you came in to prepare for bed."

Panic seized me as I stood and scanned the room. "The last time I recall touching it was at Victoria Station. Once we arrived here, I don't remember thinking about it again until now."

Had I lost it at the station?

"It was old," Gallagher said with a frown. "Perhaps the clasp broke and it slipped off."

"No." I shook my head and went to the bed, pulling back the covers.

"It wouldn't be there," Gallagher said. "I don't remember you wearing it when you came into the room last night."

"I need to find the locket. It's the only link—" I almost said it was the only link to my parents, but despite Gallagher probably knowing the truth about me, she and I had never talked about my origins.

A knock at the door summoned Gallagher and she spoke to a maid.

"Lady Mandeville is here," she said to me. "The maid will take you to the north parlor to meet with her."

"I cannot meet with her until I find my locket." I lifted the pillow off the bed to look beneath.

"I'll search for it," Gallagher said as she took the pillow from me. "If it's in this house, I will find it."

Fear nipped at my heart as I thought about the locket being lost at Victoria Station. If it had fallen off there, I would probably never see it again. "I pray it is here."

Gallagher nodded as I moved around her to follow the maid.

I scanned for the locket as we traversed through hallways, down two sets of stairs, and to the front of the house. Had Alec seen the locket? If he remembered seeing me wear it here in this house, last night, then my heart would at least be put to rest until we found it.

"Is Mr. Paxton-Hill at home?" I asked the maid right before she opened the drawing room door.

"I believe he's receiving Lady Mandeville, miss," the maid said with a nod.

Relief washed through me, though it was no guarantee. Alec might not have any recollection of seeing the locket.

I stepped into the room and found Aunt Maude and Alec speaking to a beautiful woman who looked to be in her early thirties. Her blond hair was twisted into an attractive updo, and her blue day gown was impeccable. If she was struggling financially, her appearance did not suggest it.

"There you are, Clara," Aunt Maude said with a pleasant smile as she lifted her hand to summon me over to the small group. "I'd like you to meet Lady Mandeville."

I stopped before Lady Mandeville and offered a practiced curtsey.

"Lady Mandeville, this is my niece, Miss Clara Day Hill. Clara, this is the Viscountess Mandeville."

"How do you do?" I asked her.

"How do you do?" Her voice had a cultured Southern drawl. "Your beauty precedes you, Miss Hill. Mrs. Alva Vanderbilt is a dear childhood friend, and she wrote to me about you. She said you are breathtaking, and I quite agree."

I wondered what else Mrs. Vanderbilt had told her old friend. Had she mentioned George? Did Mrs. Vanderbilt even know that George had been courting me? It would surprise me if she didn't.

"Thank you," I said to Lady Mandeville.

"Shall we have a seat?" Aunt Maude asked. "We have a lot to discuss."

I glanced at Alec as the ladies began to move to the sofas in front of the fireplace. "I'm missing my locket," I said to him quietly as I touched my chest where it had been lying yesterday. "Have you seen it?"

He frowned and shook his head.

"Do you remember—"

"Clara?" Aunt Maude interrupted me. "Please join us. Alec, this concerns you, as well."

Alec stiffened. "I had hoped to get some work done this morning."

"I'd like for you to hear our plans, so you know what to expect."

Lady Mandeville lowered her eyes, as if she was embarrassed that Aunt Maude was speaking so freely about what we were about to do.

"I hope you don't mind, Lady Mandeville," Aunt Maude said in her no-nonsense way. "We've corresponded for months and there is no use pretending that you've come for a social call. This is a business transaction, and I believe Alec should be present for the discussion."

Lady Mandeville cleared her throat. "People are usually more discreet about my services."

"We will be the height of discretion beyond this room," Aunt Maude said, lifting her chin just slightly. "But this is the command center, and I want all of us on the same page, so to speak."

"However you'd like to proceed, I am at your service, Mrs. Hill." Though Lady Mandeville spoke the words, I could tell it rankled her. She might be desperate for money, but she didn't want to admit it.

Alec slowly joined us, sitting on a chair near the sofas while I sat next to Aunt Maude. Everything about his mannerisms and countenance told me this was the last place he wanted to be, but Aunt Maude would demand that he stay if he tried to leave again, and we'd both learned it didn't pay to fight her.

"I've ordered tea," Aunt Maude said, "but I think we can do away with the small talk as we wait for it. Please let me know what you have planned for Clara."

Lady Mandeville glanced at each of us before she said, "Queen Victoria only hosts four drawing room presentations a year. Two before Easter and two after Easter. If anyone wants to enter high society in London, and a debutante wants invitations to aristocratic events, they must first be received by the queen. We've already missed the first two drawing room presentations, but the third one has been announced, and I secured a place for Miss Clara to be presented to Her Majesty."

Aunt Maude straightened her back and offered a pleased smile.

"The only problem is that the presentation will be in four short days."

My heartrate escalated. I'd thought I'd have more time to prepare.

"Do not fear," Lady Mandeville said. "From the moment you entered this room, I saw your natural elegance. I will spend the next few days instructing you on what to do during the presentation, but it won't be too difficult, and it will accelerate your entrance into society. Do you have a gown to wear?"

"Yes," Aunt Maude said, even though Lady Mandeville had addressed me. "We had it sewn for her in Paris."

"Wonderful. Now"—Lady Mandeville glanced at me again, clearly uncomfortable speaking so openly—"I have made a list of eligible bachelors who are in need of an heiress. But I just heard the most marvelous news yesterday."

Alec repositioned himself in his chair but did not speak.

I tried not to look at him, afraid I would give away my true feelings in front of Lady Mandeville.

"Ames Welby, the 7th Duke of Severton, has just arrived in London." Lady Mandeville's eyes widened with excitement. "He is a confirmed bachelor, or so we thought, and lives a very secluded life at Pickering Castle near Ravenscar on the coastal moors. I've heard rumors that he has finally decided to take a wife and he's in need of a wealthy one."

Ames Welby, the 7th Duke of Severton. As the name solidified in my mind, I had a strange, unsettling feeling come over me. This was the man. The one I would marry. I wasn't sure how I knew, but I just knew.

I glanced at Alec, but he stared down at his hands clasped on his lap.

"Not much is known about his family," Lady Mandeville warned, "but if it's a duchy you're after, then I believe we should move with all haste. I have heard that there are several other heiresses in town for the season and they'll all have their sights on the duke."

"Of course." Aunt Maude leaned forward with anticipation. "Whatever you think best."

No doubt she was thinking about Louise Garfield.

"I will secure an introduction to the Duke of Severton immediately," Lady Mandeville said, "and then I will make sure we are at all the right events where he will be invited, and I will introduce His Grace to Miss Hill as soon as possible." She paused and studied Aunt Maude.

"There is one way I can guarantee Miss Hill is welcomed into society here, and that she is placed in front of all the right people."

"Yes?" Aunt Maude lifted one brow.

"I can arrange a dinner party, here, with His Royal Highness the Prince of Wales."

Aunt Maude's eyebrows shot up.

"The prince is a good friend of mine," Lady Mandeville said as she examined her gloved hand. "And he is always eager to meet the newest and prettiest American heiresses." She glanced at me and then returned her gaze to Aunt Maude. "However, if we're being candid, I would require an additional . . . inducement to see that it is done."

Alec's head finally came up as he looked at Aunt Maude. This was already costing so much money. Could they afford even more?

"Whatever the cost," Aunt Maude said, her face a mask of indifference. "I believe we can come to a sensible agreement."

Alec's gaze slipped to mine, but he, like Aunt Maude, kept his emotions closely guarded.

15

All I wanted to do was look for my mother, but the first four days in London were a whirlwind of preparations, plans, and practices with Lady Mandeville. I'd performed the court curtsey, one deeper and lower than the others, so many times that the muscles in my thighs ached.

I stood in front of the mirror in my bedroom at 7 Buckingham Gate on Thursday afternoon, the day of the drawing room presentation, staring at my reflection. I was wearing a beautiful white gown with short sleeves and a ten-foot-long white train, with white gloves extended to my elbows. My hair had been meticulously arranged by a woman hired for that purpose, and three white ostrich feathers were placed on the left side of my coiffure, with a white veil covering the back of my head. I held a small bouquet of white roses, lily of the valley, and myrtle, with long white trailing ribbons.

I couldn't have been any farther from Mulberry Street. But as I stared at myself, feeling detached from Keira O'Day, I wasn't sure if I felt like Clara Day Hill, either. I wasn't quite sure who I was, or which version of myself I liked better. I felt more like a puppet or, better yet, an actress like my mother. I was wearing a costume and pretending to be someone I wasn't.

Was it wrong? Was it the plan God had in store for me all along?

My hand slipped up to my neck, where the locket had sat for just a few short hours. We hadn't had any luck finding it in the house or in Lady Mandeville's carriage, and my heart was broken. My only link to the past was gone. It might have some monetary value for someone else, but to me, it was priceless.

A light knock sounded at the door.

"Yes?"

"It's Alec," he said through the door. "May I come in?"

Gallagher had left me to find a sponge to remove a black mark on my white slippers, but we expected Lady Mandeville to arrive at any moment with her carriage. She would take us to St. James's Palace, where we would be received by the queen at four.

Butterflies filled my stomach at the sound of Alec's voice, and I quickly stepped over to open the door.

His face filled with awe when he caught sight of me.

My cheeks warmed, but I didn't shy away from his bold stare.

"Keira—" He paused and smiled when our gazes met. "You are stunning."

Love and affection filled my heart as I returned his smile, but the feelings were quickly replaced by a sense of sadness that had overwhelmed me since arriving in London. "Thank you."

He continued to look at me, but then he seemed to remember himself and said, "I brought you a gift."

For the first time, I noticed the small velvet box in his hand. He presented it to me, his smile turning into a look of anticipation and joy.

"Alec, you and Aunt Maude have already spent so much—"

"This hardly cost a thing." He moved it closer to me. "Please open it, Keira."

I took the box from him and slowly lifted the lid. Nestled inside, on black silk, was my locket. It had been polished and shined brilliantly.

"Alec!" I looked up at him. "Where did you find it?"

"I went to Victoria Station this morning. I apologize, but it was the first day I could get away. One of the porters had found it and turned it in to the stationmaster. They were so pleased when I arrived to claim it." He lifted it out of the box. "The clasp was broken, so I stopped at a jeweler and asked them to fix it. They also polished it and made sure the rest of the chain is solid, so it is as good as new, and you don't have to worry about losing it again."

With a soft cry, I threw myself into Alec's embrace, not caring if I crushed my feathers or wrinkled my gown.

He hesitated for a heartbeat and then wrapped his arms around me, holding me tight.

"Thank you," I whispered, tears falling down my cheeks. "This is the most precious gift anyone has ever given me."

"Your mother gave you the gift," he said. "I only ensured it was returned to you."

I didn't want to leave Alec's arms, but Gallagher or another maid might come upon us.

"Thank you," I said again, pulling away.

He handed me a clean handkerchief, which I accepted to wipe away my tears. Then he gently laid the locket in my hand, closing my gloved fingers around it. "I can't wait to see you presented to the queen." With another smile, he bowed and then walked away.

As I looked down at the locket, so many emotions swirled in my mind and heart. For all my life, the only memories surrounding this piece of jewelry had been linked to a faceless set of parents. Now, Alec's thoughtfulness and care would be linked to the keepsake, as well.

Two hours later, we sat in Lady Mandeville's carriage, waiting our turn to alight and enter St. James's Palace. My nerves were so frayed, I was afraid I might lose my lunch. The locket was securely stored in my room, and just knowing it was back, safe and sound, eased so many of the worries I had carried the past four days.

But it didn't make me less nervous.

"You're dreadfully pale, my dear," Lady Mandeville said as she touched my knee. "Are you quite all right?"

Across from us, Aunt Maude and Alec stared my way. Aunt Maude would also be presented to Queen Victoria today. She wore a white gown and two white feathers in her hair, to indicate that she had been married. Alec would escort us into the castle and then part ways with us to go into the queen's drawing room and wait with the other men before escorting us out.

"There's no reason to be nervous," he said to me. "You've faced Mrs. Astor, remember?"

My smile turned genuine as I thought of all the sincere compliments he'd paid me. Even if I failed today, at least Alec would still be proud of me.

When it was finally our turn to step out of the carriage at the North Gatehouse, I saw that twin octagonal turrets flanked the arched entrance like sentinels as a coat of arms stretched between them. The redbrick Tudor-style palace was weathered with time and had a fortress-like feel. I'd learned that after the death of Queen Victoria's dear husband, Prince Albert, she had all but abandoned Buckingham Palace and lived in mourning in the more formidable St. James's Palace while in London. Here, she held her drawing room presentations but withdrew from most other parts of society.

Lady Mandeville lifted the train of my gown and slipped it over my left arm so it would stay clean and fresh for the presentation. She handed one of two cards she carried to a guard, indicating who she was and the names of the women she would be presenting to the queen.

The guards let us pass and we walked through the entrance and into a courtyard before we were directed to step into the palace. Dozens of other women were making their way to the queen's drawing room, and we followed them, walking through several stately rooms.

My pulse beat fast, and sweat had begun to form little rivulets down my back.

Alec was instructed to part ways with us as we were shown to one of the antechambers to wait our turn. As I entered, the first person I saw was Louise Garfield with her mother and an older woman.

"Remember to take off your right glove," Lady Mandeville said as she adjusted the feathers in my hair and looked me over with a critical eye, probably unaware of who Louise Garfield was.

I slowly pulled off the glove, though it wasn't easy with the sweat gathering on my palms. Louise glanced my way but lifted her chin and turned back to her mother.

It didn't pay to mention her to Aunt Maude, because Aunt Maude had already seen her and set her lips into a scowl.

"Don't forget to bow to every member of the royal family who is standing with the queen," Lady Mandeville said.

"Who might be with her?" I asked.

"It is likely the Prince of Wales and his wife, Princess Alexandra. It will be obvious who is royalty. They'll stand alongside the queen."

The chatter inside the anteroom made it hard to think. I just wanted this to be over. Lady Mandeville had sent out invitations for a tea party in my honor at her house after the ceremony, and then we would attend a ball given by the Earl and Countess of Hawthorne later that evening, where Lady Mandeville hoped to introduce me to the Duke of Severton. It would be a long and arduous day, flanked on both ends by important, stressful meetings.

One after the other, the women waiting in the antechamber were escorted out by footmen. Louise left soon after we arrived.

The young woman in front of me looked especially nervous. She was beautiful, with blond hair and marble blue eyes. Her mother was also being presented, but she pinched and plucked and patted her daughter until the young woman pulled away in frustration, tears in her eyes.

How well I understood what she was feeling, and when she glanced at me, I offered her a sympathetic smile.

She returned the smile, blinking away the tears. "Are you an American, as well?"

"Yes. I'm Clara Day Hill." It was still hard to say my new name, but I extended my hand.

"It's nice to meet you," she said, taking my hand. "I'm Lily Parker."

"Are you just as nervous as me?" I whispered, leaning a little closer to her, relieved to find a fellow compatriot.

"Dreadfully."

"We'll get through this together."

Her grin was beautiful. "Let's."

The footman called her forward and she gave my hand a tight squeeze before she walked away.

"Good work, Clara," Lady Mandeville said as soon as Lily and her mother and sponsor left the room. "Keep your enemies close."

Lily Parker wasn't my enemy, but I didn't say so.

Finally, it was my turn.

"Lady Mandeville presenting Mrs. Edmund Hill and Miss Clara Day Hill," Lady Mandeville said as we stepped up to the footman and she showed him her second card.

"Come with me, please." He led us out of the room and down a long hallway to a set of double doors.

My heart was beating so hard, I thought I might faint.

Two pages came up behind me with long poles, so Lady Mandeville took my train from my arm and laid it on the ground. The pages slipped the poles beneath it and spread it out in a luxurious river of white silk.

When the doors opened, I had my first glimpse of the sumptuous drawing room with its red drapes and gilded furnishings. Lily was ahead of me with her mother and sponsor, curtseying in front of the queen. As she rose gracefully and moved aside, I wanted to cheer for her success.

Lady Mandeville handed the card to the Lord Chamberlain, and then we waited.

When Lily finished, the Lord Chamberlain said, "Lady Mandeville presenting Mrs. Edmund Hill and Miss Clara Day Hill."

This was the moment I'd been working toward since I met Aunt Maude outside the Metropolitan Opera House six months ago. If I messed up now, all our hard work would be for nothing. We would be shunned from the social season in London and forced back to New York in shame.

I wasn't ready—but Lady Mandeville and Aunt Maude were already walking forward, so I was forced to go with them.

The queen turned her attention to me as the other members on the dais shifted their gazes away from Lily. I glanced at the man next to Queen Victoria, who I presumed to be the Prince of Wales, and then to the woman beside him, who was probably Princess Alexandra. They were the only three on the dais up near the front. The others stood behind and were more than likely ladies in waiting.

There was some quiet chatter among the gentlemen flanking either side of the aisle we walked down. I wanted to look for Alec, but I didn't dare turn my head to the left or right, afraid I might trip if I took my gaze off the dais.

Thankfully we didn't have far to walk. Lady Mandeville curtseyed and then stepped back as Aunt Maude gave a low curtsey to the queen, placing her right hand beneath the queen's and kissing it on the top. As she rose and stepped aside to curtsey to the prince, it was my turn to step forward.

Lady Mandeville had said that I shouldn't say anything unless the queen addressed me first, but it was rare if she spoke, so I needn't worry about what to say.

The queen was so much smaller than I had imagined as she stood on the dais. I stepped forward, my body shaking, as she extended her hand toward me. Slipping my right hand beneath hers, I curtseyed low, my knee almost touching the floor, and placed a brief kiss on her hand.

My muscles were sore, and I was shaking as I stood straight.

"You are breathtaking, my dear," the queen said with the slightest smile softening her serious face.

Surprised, I didn't know what to say, so I simply nodded my head in deference to her and then took a sidestep to the right and curtseyed before the Prince of Wales. When I stood straight, I found him staring at me with his piercing blue eyes.

I took another sidestep and curtseyed before Princess Alexandra, whose gaze looked mildly interested. Soon, Lady Mandeville was at my side again, drawing my train up to slip it around my left arm, so I could walk backward toward the exit, because no one must turn their back to the queen. This would be the most difficult part of my task, and took the longest, but thankfully, the next debutante's name was called, and the royal family turned their attention to her.

All but the Prince of Wales, who continued to watch me as I backed out of the room.

When I finally reached the exit, Alec was there, and he guided us into the antechamber. A footman closed the door behind us, and I let out the breath I felt like I'd been holding the entire time.

"Well done, Miss Hill," Lady Mandeville said with glowing eyes. "A compliment from the queen and a keen interest from the prince! You are well on your way, my dear."

I was shaking so hard, Alec reached out and put his hand under my elbow to steady me. "Are you all right, Clara?" he asked quietly.

"I want to go home," I said to him, my voice weak.

He studied me for a moment, as if he knew I meant New York and not Buckingham Gate and gave me a sad smile.

"Now for the duke," Aunt Maude said.

Alec's hand tightened on my elbow, but was it from jealousy or the fear that I would pass out?

I had thought I knew what exhaustion felt like over the months I had trained under Aunt Maude. But the physical, mental, and emotional drain of being presented to the queen and then riding through Hyde Park in a sort of parade for others to gawk at us, followed by the tea party, and then the ball, did not compare.

I'd changed three times that day and was now wearing the most stunning Worth gown I'd ever seen. It was a red-wine-colored silk with gold roses embroidered into the fabric, and pulled back into an intricate bustle, with a gold-colored underskirt peeking from beneath. The decolletage was lower than I was used to, but still modest. I wore gold-colored gloves and slippers that matched the underskirt. Mr. Worth had said it complemented my brown eyes and hair, turning them to warm chocolate.

If the way Alec had been looking at me since we'd left 7 Buckingham Gate was any indication, I presented a beautiful picture.

After exiting the carriage, he offered me his arm as Aunt Maude and Lady Mandeville walked in front of us toward the large home of Lord and Lady Hawthorne, not far from Kensington Palace.

"I won't make the same mistake I made at Mrs. Vanderbilt's party," Alec said, for my ears alone. "May I have the first and last dances tonight, Miss Hill?"

"Certainly not," Lady Mandeville said as she turned to look at us, clearly overhearing Alec. "We must leave the first and the last dance for the Duke of Severton. I'm certain he will ask. Surely word of the queen's compliment has already begun to circulate, and everyone will be eager to know Miss Hill. You may take one of Clara's other dances."

I wanted to look at Alec to see if Lady Mandeville's words upset him, but I didn't dare. I needed to put him out of my mind—especially now that I was about to meet the duke.

Neither of us said a word as we walked up the steps and entered the mansion, where we were presented to Lord and Lady Hawthorne. After I was given my dance card, Alec took it from my hand and wrote his name on one of the lines before handing it back to me.

He'd taken the dance right before the midnight buffet.

I smiled at him, knowing this meant he wanted to escort me into the meal and spend that portion of the evening in my company. Next to the first and last dances, it was the most coveted of the ball.

Alec returned my smile. "We can still be friends, can't we?"

I nodded.

"There he is!" Lady Mandeville said quietly as we walked into the crowded ballroom. "The Duke of Severton. I was able to get an introduction two nights ago, so I can introduce him to Clara."

I wasn't sure which of the gentlemen she was referring to but my gaze scanned the room nonetheless. There were several handsome men, both young and old. For the first time, I wondered what he looked like. Was he one of the attractive men? His looks didn't matter all that much, but if I was going to marry him, I hoped he would be pleasant to look at.

Several people stared in our direction as they whispered, and I wondered if they knew who I was. Had the queen's comment circulated as Lady Mandeville claimed? Many guests at her tea party had asked me about it, but it was because Lady Mandeville had told everyone we spoke to.

"There's Miss Wellington, Alec," Aunt Maude said when she spotted Annabelle and her mother. "How fortuitous. You should go ask her for a dance or two."

Annabelle was here? I could use a good friend right about now.

"I'd like to meet the Duke of Severton," Alec said as he still held my hand secure in his elbow.

"There will be time enough for that later." Aunt Maude nodded toward the Wellingtons. "Perhaps it would be best if we met the duke without you."

"And there are the Garfields," I said to Aunt Maude. "Over by the window."

The other three looked in that direction and Lady Mandeville inhaled. "They're being introduced to the duke as we speak."

I shifted my gaze from Louise to the man she was speaking to, but before I got a good look, Aunt Maude grabbed my hand and began to tug me away from Alec.

"Alec, leave us," she said in an authoritative voice. "We have business to conduct."

I turned to him as she pulled me away, but he looked powerless to stop her.

"We must find a way to monopolize the duke's time," Lady Mandeville said in a low tone. "If it's about money, we need to let him know that you are willing to offer whatever dowry he asks for."

"That won't be a problem." Aunt Maude sounded earnest, but I knew better. How much money could she possibly offer when their financial situation was dire?

As we drew closer, and Lady Mandeville had a good look at Louise, she said, "So this is our competition? Clara is much prettier than Miss Garfield."

"She's smarter and more accomplished, as well," Aunt Maude assured her, though I wasn't so confident.

"There will be others seeking the duke's hand in marriage," Lady Mandeville continued. "We cannot let our guard down for a minute."

It felt like I was following two soldiers going to war, and perhaps I was.

The crowd split for a moment and I finally had the opportunity to see the man they had set their sights on.

And I was astonished.

He was handsome—breathtakingly attractive—with jet black hair and matching black eyes. And he was tall, towering over Louise and Mrs. Garfield, with a muscular frame and a commanding demeanor. But there was something dark and brooding about his countenance.

He didn't seem shy—but reserved or, better yet, aloof. As if he didn't want to be here but was forcing himself to be in attendance.

His hooded gaze met mine and I felt frozen to the floor, though it wasn't exactly fear that held me there. Curiosity made me want to know more about him, yet a sense of foreboding made me leery of what I might discover.

A scar sliced across his left cheekbone and disappeared into his hairline, but it did not diminish his good looks. On the contrary, it added to his allure and mystique.

He didn't look back at Louise or Mrs. Garfield as we approached, and they slowly faded into the crowd again, though I knew they wouldn't go far.

"Your Grace," Lady Mandeville said with a curtsey, "may I present to you Mrs. Edmund Hill and her niece, Miss Clara Day Hill?"

Aunt Maude and I curtseyed as the duke dipped his head in acknowledgment.

"How do you do?" I asked him.

"How do you do?" His voice was low and rich, with a bit of a gravelly sound to it.

"Mrs. Hill and Clara have just arrived from New York," Lady Mandeville continued. "And were presented to Her Majesty, the Queen today. Queen Victoria commented on Clara's beauty, though I am not surprised."

My cheeks grew warm as the duke studied me, saying nothing.

"We were so pleased to hear you had come to London for the season," Lady Mandeville continued. "It has been years since you've been here, has it not?"

"I have not been to London since I was a child," the duke said, finally pulling his gaze away from me.

"And your parents?" Lady Mandeville frowned. "I don't believe I ever had the pleasure of meeting them."

"They've both been dead for fifteen years."

Lady Mandeville lost her composure at his forthright words. "Well—I suppose I've only been in England for a decade, so I wouldn't have had that opportunity."

He didn't speak again, and we stood there awkwardly until Aunt Maude ventured to ask, "Have you been to New York, Your Grace?"

"No."

It was clear he didn't want to be here and was trying to use his bad mood to push us away, but I'd faced harsher people in Five Points, and I wasn't afraid of him.

"Would you like to visit New York someday?" I asked.

He looked at me and said, "No."

"Your home must be an extraordinary place if this is the first time you've been to London in years," I said, "and you have no wish to go abroad. You must tell me about it sometime."

"Do you dance, Your Grace?" Lady Mandeville tried again. "Clara has several dances available—"

"No, I do not dance."

"Well," I said, "what do you do?"

It felt impertinent, but if he was going to be rude, I could be rude.

Something flickered in his eyes—respect? Did no one ever challenge him?

"I like to study maps, Miss Hill."

"For all the places you never plan to travel?"

The corner of his lips came up in the faintest smile, but then it was gone again. "And what do you like to do with your time, besides badger unsuspecting gentlemen?"

It was my turn to smile, though I didn't try to hide it like him. "I like to read and sew and sing. I like a great many things, dancing among them. Do you not like to dance because you never learned?"

"I learned—I just don't like it."

"Perhaps you haven't had the right partner."

"Perhaps I haven't." I saw a challenge in his eyes. "Would you care to prove me wrong?"

I lifted my dance card and said, "Choose your dance, Your Grace, and I will be honored to prove you wrong."

He looked over the card and then wrote his name next to the first dance of the evening.

"Are you hoping to get over the unpleasantness as soon as possible?" I asked, looking at his bold signature. "Or make a lasting impression on me to carry throughout the night?"

This time, he actually smiled.

I curtseyed and he bowed, and then Lady Mandeville led us away.

"Well done," Aunt Maude whispered to me. "I can see that Alec has done a marvelous job teaching you the art of flirting."

As she said the words, I glanced up and found Alec watching us.

He simply looked away.

16

The sun had just crested the horizon as I quietly left 7 Buckingham Gate the next morning. We hadn't returned from the ball until after two, and Gallagher wouldn't come into my room to wake me up until eleven, when it was time to get ready for luncheon. I would be expected to receive callers after we ate lunch, but it was a quarter to six, which gave me a few hours to get away and look for my mother.

Crisp spring air greeted me as I walked along Buckingham Palace Road. I had asked a maid if she knew where the Adelphi Theatre was located and she'd given me directions. My aunt and uncle had said my mother used to work there, but even if she wasn't there any longer, perhaps someone had heard of her and could point me in the right direction.

Though it was early, the streets were already busy as I walked past Buckingham Palace and down The Mall toward the West End. I had also asked the maid if this was a safe area of London and her response had been, "The safest area you'll find, miss, though nowhere is completely safe for a lady in London."

I'd decided to take my chances without a chaperone. After all, I'd lived in Five Points and gone about my business on my own in one of the most dangerous neighborhoods in the world.

St. James Park was beautiful as the first rays of daylight splashed the landscape. Ornamental bridges, winding paths, and elegant swans graced the serene setting. To my left was the formidable St. James's Palace. I could still feel the Prince of Wales's eyes on me as I walked past it. Lady Mandeville had arranged for him to come to a dinner at our home in one week, and he had accepted. It was quite the coup for Aunt Maude, and she'd already started making plans. No expense would be spared for the prince.

It didn't take long to pass Trafalgar Square, where four large, bronze lions encircled a towering column. Behind it were two beautiful fountains and behind those was the National Gallery.

Just like in New York, the streets were full of people from every nationality and race. If the buildings didn't look so different, I would have felt right at home. The other difference was the amount of attention I was getting. It was much easier to move about New York in rags than it was in London in a fine walking gown. A beggar stopped me, asking for money, and when I said I didn't have any, he spit on the ground at my feet before moving away.

I continued down the Strand toward the Adelphi Theatre, my mind slipping to the Duke of Severton. The night before, he'd proven to be an adept dancer, and we had continued to spar as before, but he told me very little about himself. All I knew about him, I'd learned from Lady Mandeville, and she knew next to nothing. He had not danced with anyone else the whole evening and did not mingle with the others. Instead, he waited for them to come to him—and they had. Every eligible woman at the ball had been introduced to him, including Annabelle. Aunt Maude and Lady Mandeville considered it a triumph that I was his only dancing partner.

Before the midnight buffet, Alec and I danced together, and then he took me into supper. But Lady Mandeville had intercepted me before we could talk and brought me around the room, introducing me to other eligible aristocrats, mentioning the queen's comment about me to each of them. She said that we couldn't be content with only one proposal this season.

I hadn't spoken to Alec again until we were in the carriage on our way back to 7 Buckingham Gate. But even there, we had talked little, since Aunt Maude wanted to recount everything that had happened at the ball. She spoke of the duke ad nauseam, until I was so tired of his name, I wasn't sure I wanted to ever hear it again.

The duke had seemed so aloof and disinterested in the people at the ball. I was convinced that Lady Mandeville had misunderstood his reasons for coming to London. Was he truly looking for a bride? Or had he come to show his disdain for society?

It didn't really matter to me. I would let Aunt Maude and Lady Mandeville worry about capturing a coronet. Right now, all I cared about was finding my mother.

The theater wasn't far from Trafalgar Square. It was a simple brick building with several white columns holding up a canopy over the main entrance that read *Adelphi Theatre*.

The only door in front was locked. Disappointment tried to dissuade me, but I had known there might not be anyone at the theater this early in the morning. I walked to the side of the building where a narrow alley led to the back and decided I'd come this far, I wouldn't give up now.

It was darker the farther I walked down the alley. Garbage had been left where it fell and there was an odd stench. When I finally arrived at the back of the building, there was a door with a sign above that read *STAGE*.

With a trembling hand, I turned the doorknob and was surprised and delighted to find it was unlocked.

"Hello," I called as I opened the door and poked my head inside. It was even darker in the back of the stage. My eyes hadn't adjusted yet, and I couldn't make out any shape.

"Hello," called a man, though I couldn't see him. "What do you want? Looking for work?"

"No." I tried to steady my voice. "I'm looking for an actress who might have performed here a long time ago."

The man appeared from the shadows. He was an older gentleman with white hair and whiskers. His portly middle protruded over his waistband, and his trousers were held up by suspenders, but he wore no coat.

"An American, eh? You sure you're not looking for a job?" he asked me. "You've got a face for the stage."

"Thank you," I said, swallowing my nerves, taking a step back into the alley. "But I don't need a job."

He looked me up and down as he stepped over the threshold of the door and held it open. "You sure don't look like you need a job. That dress alone could pay for a month's worth of wages around these parts. I should know, I'm the costumier." He frowned. "Who did you say you were looking for?"

"I—I didn't. Not yet."

"Well, come out with it, then. I don't have all day."

"I'm looking for an actress by the name of Nellie O'Day. Have you heard of her?"

His face lit with something akin to adoration. "Sure, I have. She used to work right here at the Adelphi, oh, fifteen, twenty years ago now."

Relief overwhelmed me. I hadn't thought it would be this easy to find someone who knew her. "She doesn't work here anymore?"

"No. She gave all that up years ago." He scratched his head. "I haven't heard Nellie's name spoken in a long time. What did you say your business was with her?"

"I didn't."

He sized me up. "Say, you look like her. Any relation?"

"Perhaps a distant relationship," I said, wanting to be vague and feeling oddly relieved that I *did* look like her, after all. "Do you know where I might find her?"

"Well now, I don't think you'd want to go and look for her."

It was my turn to frown. "Why not?"

"I live and work around a pretty tough crowd, young lady, and I usually say what needs to be said. But if I had to guess, I'd say you are a well-bred gentlewoman, and I wouldn't want to embarrass you by telling you where Nellie is living."

If he only knew my origins and where I had grown up, he wouldn't be so hesitant.

"Please tell me," I said. "I need to find her. It's a very urgent matter."

He ran his hand over his whiskered cheek and then sighed. "Last I heard, Nellie left the theater and went into business as a brothel owner somewhere in Soho." He held up his hands. "That's all I know—and that's just hearsay, mind you." He glanced up and down the alley. "If I was you, I wouldn't linger 'round these parts too long. I have work to do. I hope you have some luck finding Nellie. If you do, tell her hello from Bernard."

Bernard? I looked at him closely, trying to see if there was any resemblance between him and me. Could he be the B from my locket?

Bernard closed the stage door, and I was alone in the alley. A chill ran up my back. Had my mother started a brothel? And, if so, how was I going to find her? I didn't know where Soho was, and I wasn't sure how I would get there.

But I hadn't come this far to stop looking for her now.

I retraced my steps toward the Strand and when I rejoined the street, a man caught my eye. "Alec?"

He was just walking past the Adelphi but stopped and turned at the sound of my voice. Fear blanketed his face, but it was soon replaced with relief and then anger. He jogged toward me, pulling me into his arms to embrace me.

"Keira," he said, breathing heavily.

My mouth slipped open in surprise as I let him hug me. "What's wrong?"

He pulled back, holding me at arm's length. "I saw you leaving the house this morning from my bedchamber window, but by the time I was dressed and running out the door, you had disappeared. I asked the first maid I found if she knew where you had gone, and thankfully she said you had asked her about the Adelphi Theatre and whether this was a safe neighborhood. She gave me directions, and I set out on foot as fast as I could."

"Did you run all the way here?" I was half teasing, but when I saw how serious he was, I sobered. "I'm sorry for scaring you, Alec."

"What in the world are you doing leaving the house by yourself?" He crossed his arms. "You should know how dangerous it is to walk around London alone."

"I lived in Five Points. I think I can manage a respectable part of London in the light of day."

"You never looked like that in Five Points." He indicated my ensemble. "You're almost inviting someone to attack you or pickpocket you at the least."

"You have no idea what I survived in Five Points." My voice choked as a memory flashed back of being cornered by a strange man in a dark alley. I'd fought and gotten away, but the thought of it had haunted me for years.

"You're right. I don't know what happened to you before I met you." He swallowed and shook his head. "I wish I had met you much sooner and helped you get out of there. But you're out now and it's my job to protect you until—" He paused.

"Until what?"

"Until it's another man's job."

We stared at one another for a moment and then he glanced at the theater. "Why did you come here?"

I licked my dry lips, not sure how much I wanted to tell him. He'd already seen the worst parts of me, why not tell him the rest? "My mother used to be an actress here."

He studied me, frowning. "Is she still here?"

"No." I played with the fingers of my glove. "The man at the stage door remembered her but said she hasn't been here for fifteen or twenty years. The last he heard, she—she started a brothel in Soho."

"Oh."

The look of surprise and shock on his face was too much. I turned away from him and started walking back toward Trafalgar Square, tears burning my eyes. I hated the reminder of who I really was, and seeing his response only made it worse.

Alec was suddenly at my side, slipping his fingers through mine as he held my hand. "I'm sorry, Keira."

I wiped my cheek with my free hand and couldn't look at him. "I know you think less of me—"

"I could never think less of you." He pulled me to a stop. "Don't you understand?" He gently turned me to face him. "There is no one I think more highly of than you. Nothing in your past could change how I feel about you, especially nothing that you had no control over." He lifted his hand and wiped a stray tear on my cheek with the back of his finger, swallowing his emotions. "I'm—I—" He paused and shook his head. "I only want the very best for you."

My skin tingled where his finger had trailed, and longing swept through me. That one kiss on Christmas had set a fire in my heart that could not be quenched by anyone other than Alec—yet I forced myself to not let thoughts of him continue.

People passed by, staring at us as we faced one another in the street.

"The best thing for me would be finding my mother," I said, forcing my thoughts back to something I could control. "I have to talk to her, to understand who I am and where I came from."

"I am not taking you to a brothel, Keira. We don't even know which brothel she might own."

"How can we find out?"

He let out a sigh. "Somerset House is not far from here, perhaps a five-minute walk down the Strand. I went there last time I was in London on business. It's a general register office for the City of London and they might have information about your mother and her whereabouts."

"Will you take me?"

Alec smiled. "I have a feeling if I say no, you will find a way to get there on your own."

I returned his smile.

"Come." He continued to hold my hand as we began walking farther from Buckingham Gate. "We need to be mindful of the time. Aunt Maude would never forgive me if I didn't have you back before the Duke of Severton came to call."

"I do not anticipate that the duke will call."

"He'll call. I saw the way he was looking at you last night."

His words made me feel uncomfortable, but whether it was because it was Alec saying them about another man, or because I didn't want the duke to pursue me, I wasn't sure.

It didn't take long to reach the register office, but they had not opened for the day, so Alec took me to a café across the road, and we had eggs, toast, and coffee. We didn't talk about the ball the night before, or the plans Aunt Maude had for the upcoming season. Instead, we talked about our childhoods. I told him what it was like growing up in Five Points and he told me about his life in Boston.

"My father was a minister," he said. "I always felt I was being scrutinized by his congregation, but I didn't mind too much. There were some good people who surrounded our family and loved both my parents and me. They provided clothes and food when we were running short and made me feel like they valued my father."

"Clothes and food?" I frowned. "Wasn't your mother from a wealthy family?"

He nodded as he held his mug of coffee in hand. "My grandfather disapproved of my father and his profession. He warned my mother that if she married him, he would cut her off and that's exactly what he did. Uncle Edmund inherited everything. But he and Aunt Maude had no children, so he began to sponsor my education and left his business to me."

"I didn't realize—"

"That I also grew up poor?" He smiled, though it was sad. "Perhaps not in the same way as you, but we often went without food or heat until someone stepped forward and provided for us. Father wasn't a proud man, but he didn't like begging for charity, either. God was—and is—a faithful provider. We never suffered long and now I ensure that my parents have a monthly stipend that guarantees they are never cold or hungry again."

"They're both still alive?"

"Yes. I haven't seen them in some time, but I write to them often."

I wanted to meet the people who raised Alec into such a fine young man, but I kept those thoughts to myself and noticed someone entering the records office.

"It looks like it's open."

Neither of us moved right away, and I suspected he didn't want our unexpected breakfast to end any more than I did. But we were running out of time and needed to get back to 7 Buckingham Gate before we were missed.

Alec paid for our meal and then held the door open for me as we stepped onto the Strand and crossed the street.

The General Register Office was large and already busy as we entered. A secretary pointed us in the right direction, and we were soon standing near a desk as we waited for a clerk to gather information for a woman named Nellie O'Day, born approximately 1840.

It took longer than I hoped or expected, but eventually he returned. He was a young man with a mustache and an eager expression.

"I think I may have found who you are looking for," he said. "We have no birth records for Nellie O'Day, but I found one marriage record for someone by that name. Thankfully, the marriage record has a lot of other helpful information. She was married on June 30, 1865, right here in the register office, to a man named Daniel Farmington.

Her full legal name on the record is Nellie Elizabeth O'Day. She was born on May 18, 1837, in Dublin, Ireland, and her occupation at the time of her marriage is listed as actress."

My pulse escalated. "She was married?"

"That's how it appears."

The record said nothing about her being a brothel owner. Perhaps Bernard had been wrong. He'd said it was only hearsay, after all.

"Do you have an address for Mr. and Mrs. Daniel Farmington?" Alec asked.

"I knew that would be your next inquiry, so I took it upon myself to find it for you." He passed a piece of paper across the desk. "They live in Islington, a suburb of London."

"She's still alive, then?" I asked, my mind spinning with so many questions. At least I wouldn't have to visit a brothel.

"I believe so. I did not find a death record, but that could be registered at a different location."

"Thank you." Alec took the piece of paper and slipped it into his pocket.

"My pleasure," the clerk said. "Come again if you need more assistance."

Alec offered his arm, and we left the register office.

"May I please see the paper he gave you?"

"No." He smiled at me as we turned toward Trafalgar Square. "I know you too well. If I give it to you, you'll try to sneak out again and go by yourself. I will take you there at the first opportunity."

"Today?"

He gave me a look. "You will be far too busy today."

"Then when?"

"We'll go as soon as we have a free moment and can get away. I promise, Keira."

I let out a sigh, knowing I could trust him, but not wanting to wait any longer than necessary.

"Promise me you won't go alone," he said.

"I won't go alone. I promise." I wanted his support as I faced my mother, because I wasn't sure how I would be received.

She'd abandoned me and probably never expected to see me again.

But it was a chance I had to take.

17

We returned to 7 Buckingham Gate before anyone noticed our absence and I snuck back into my room before Gallagher came to help me dress. Aunt Maude joined us for luncheon, but neither Alec nor I told her that we had left.

I was wearing the locket again, still worried I might lose it, but confident that the work Alec had done on it would keep it safer this time.

As we rose from the lunch table, Alec said, "I have a meeting scheduled for this afternoon, so I will take my leave."

"You're not staying for morning calls?" Disappointment weighed me down more than it should.

He studied me for a moment, his gaze slipping down to the locket. "I'm afraid you're on your own."

"Not on her own," Aunt Maude said, lifting her chin as she moved toward the door, her back to us. "Never on her own. I will be with her."

Alec smiled at his aunt's retreating form and then his face grew serious as he regarded me. "I wish you all the best today. No doubt you'll be as charming and gracious as ever. You won't need me."

I would have protested, but he was right. I didn't need him. I wanted him. And that was why he shouldn't stay.

With a slight nod, he left the dining room, and I followed Aunt Maude to the front drawing room, where we would have a view of Buckingham Palace Road.

"Last night was a magnificent beginning," Aunt Maude said as she took a seat in a mauve-colored wingback chair near the fireplace. "But we will not know if you were truly successful until your callers appear."

I closed the drawing room door behind me and walked to the window, wondering if anyone would even come. My hand went to my locket, both for reassurance that it was still there and comfort, knowing my mother had thought enough about me to send it with my aunt and uncle.

"What is the history of that lock—" Aunt Maude's words were cut short when the drawing room door opened and the butler, Rodgers, appeared. He presented a calling card to Aunt Maude on a silver salver.

My pulse escalated as I turned toward Rodgers and then Aunt Maude.

She did not look pleased as she read the name, but she nodded. "You may show him in."

I wanted to ask who had come, but I refrained. I would know soon enough.

As Rodgers left the drawing room, I became so nervous, I wasn't sure what to do with myself. I touched my hair, but every strand was in place, thanks to Gallagher. I looked down at my day dress, but there wasn't a wrinkle in sight.

"You look beautiful, Clara," Aunt Maude said with a regal air. "That's why I chose you, remember?"

I did remember, and while I wished I had been chosen for reasons other than my beauty, it was the thing that had drawn Aunt Maude and given me this opportunity.

Footsteps echoed outside the room and then the door opened again, and Rodgers entered with a familiar man in his wake.

"George!" I was so relieved and pleased to see him, my voice rose higher than I anticipated. "How lovely to see you."

George grinned, clearly pleased with my response. But before he formally greeted me, he walked over to Aunt Maude and gave her a slight bow. "Good afternoon, Mrs. Hill."

Aunt Maude did not look pleased. "Hello, Mr. Vanderbilt."

I walked away from the window and extended my hand to him. "It's so good of you to come."

He accepted my hand and bowed over it, his eyes shining. "I just arrived in London last night, but I couldn't wait to call." He shook his head with appreciation. "You look lovelier than I remember, Miss Hill."

"Thank you, Mr. Vanderbilt."

"Won't you have a seat?" Aunt Maude asked him, though I suspected she would have preferred if he left.

"Thank you." He waited until I sat on one of the sofas and then he sat across from me, his gaze never leaving my face. "How have you found London? I wish I could have been here to see your first glimpse of it."

"It's—" I paused as Rodgers opened the door again and presented Mrs. Hill with another calling card.

This time, her face lit up with excitement and triumph, and I knew exactly who had arrived.

"You may tell His Grace he is more than welcome to come in," she said, nodding at Rodgers as she stood.

George and I also stood as George's curious, and a little disappointed, gaze slipped to the drawing room door.

My heart beat so hard, I was afraid George might hear it.

It only took a few moments for the Duke of Severton to appear. His handsome looks took my breath away all over again, and my cheeks were so warm, I was certain they were bright pink. I tried to pretend like his arrival hadn't had such an impact on me, but it was almost impossible.

Did he realize what his presence did to people?

His expression was just as hard to read this morning as it had been the night before while he scanned the room, his gaze falling on me.

"Your Grace," Aunt Maude said, "how good of you to come. We were just saying our goodbyes to Mr. Vanderbilt."

George blinked in surprise and then his jaw tightened as he tipped his head in my direction. "It was lovely to see you again, Miss Hill. I hope our paths will cross again while we're in London."

Disappointment and embarrassment tightened in my chest as I tried to apologize with my eyes. "I, too, hope we'll see each other again. Thank you for coming, Mr. Vanderbilt."

George nodded at Aunt Maude and then walked past the duke, no introduction being offered by Aunt Maude, who would have been the person to do it.

How could she be so unkind to George, especially after using him to further her own cause in New York? My gut burned with anger and disillusionment. If this was how I was supposed to behave once I married and joined the upper echelons of society, I didn't want any part of it.

The duke didn't appear to be insulted that the two men were not introduced. On the contrary, he seemed a little relieved.

He stepped forward and Aunt Maude extended her hand. He took it, bowing slightly. "Thank you for receiving me, Mrs. Hill."

"Of course."

The duke then turned to me. I also extended my hand. Last night I was wearing gloves, but this morning I was not, and neither was he. When his hand touched mine, a shiver ran up my spine. He bowed a little deeper. "It is good to see you again, Miss Hill."

"And you, as well, Your Grace."

When he stood straight, he didn't let his gaze waver.

Of all the women he'd met at the ball last night, what had made him choose to come here? Would he be visiting others this morning? Or focusing his sole attention on pursuing me? Because that was the only reason he would be here.

How much money had Lady Mandeville told him was in my dowry? Surely others could offer him more.

"Won't you sit down, Your Grace?" Aunt Maude asked, indicating the sofa where George had been sitting a few minutes ago.

The duke released my hand and took a seat on the edge of the sofa after I sat across from him.

"Could we offer you some tea?" Aunt Maude asked.

Tea wasn't often served for a gentleman caller, unless the hostess was eager for him to stay longer than the fifteen-to-twenty minutes usually allotted for a call such as this one.

"That won't be necessary," the duke said. "I have come to inquire if Miss Hill would like to accompany me to the opera on Tuesday evening. Lady Mandeville has invited me to her box at Her Majesty's Theatre and told me there are several empty seats. Of course, you would be invited to attend with us, as well, Mrs. Hill."

"How lovely," Aunt Maude said with a gentle smile, as if this hadn't been the plan all along. Though she was acting calm, I knew she was eager to accept. Being seen at the opera with the duke so soon after meeting him would send a clear signal to the other debutantes this season. The duke was staking his claim quickly and decisively. "We would love to accept."

"Then it is settled." The duke nodded, though his facial expression didn't change and I couldn't tell if he was pleased or resigned. "I will arrive at seven to take you to the theater."

"Wonderful." Aunt Maude nodded and then said, "It was so nice to meet you last night, Your Grace. How fortuitous that you would choose this season to come to London when our dear Clara is just debuting into society."

I offered a small smile, but he didn't take the bait to engage in conversation, or pay me a compliment, as most gentlemen would.

His aloofness irritated me in ways I couldn't understand, and I wanted to draw something out of him, even if it was negative.

"Why don't you like London society?" I asked him.

"I don't like any society."

"Not even in Ravenscar?"

"No."

"You live alone? Doesn't that get boring and tedious?"

"I don't live alone."

"Who do you live with?"

"Clara," Aunt Maude said, chastisement in her voice. "The duke hasn't come here to be interrogated."

"If I may be so bold," I said to the duke, ignoring Aunt Maude, "you've come here to court me, is that correct?"

Aunt Maude's eyes grew wide, and she opened her mouth to protest, but the duke's gaze didn't waver.

"Yes," he said. "That is the only reason I've come to London. It doesn't pay to pretend. I need a wealthy wife, and you are looking for a title."

"Really, Your Grace," Aunt Maude protested, her voice feeble.

"It's true," I agreed. "And if you find me pleasant and amiable, I assume a proposal will be forthcoming."

"Clara!" Aunt Maude fluttered her hand.

"That is the plan," the duke said.

"Then I must know more about you. You have given me so little information. I cannot make a lifetime decision without all the necessary questions answered."

Aunt Maude appeared to have given up.

The duke's eyes sparkled with the challenge. "Ask me anything you'd like. I will not withhold the truth. But—" he hesitated for only a moment—"I assume you cannot get all the answers you need in one short visit. I believe that is what the courting ritual is all about. We will get to know each other over the season."

"And if we don't like what we find, I don't want to waste your time," I told him. "It's better to know sooner than later so you could court someone else."

"Clara!" Aunt Maude said again, and I imagined she saw her well-laid plans evaporating before her eyes.

"I don't want to waste my time, either," he agreed. "What do you need to know before we proceed to the opera on Tuesday?"

What *did* I need to know?

"Are you always so cool and distant?" I inquired, feeling no hesitation or qualms about asking him straightforward questions. "Even with those who are closest to you?"

Aunt Maude looked like she was going to faint.

The duke regarded me for a moment and then the edge of his mouth came up in a smile. "I am not always cool and distant with those I trust, but it takes a long time for people to gain my trust, and once lost, it's almost impossible to restore it."

I nodded, appreciating his candor. "Are you kind?"

"Always."

"You said you don't live alone?"

"I live with my younger brothers at Pickering Castle."

"And how old are they?"

"They are all in their twenties."

"Are they kind?"

A full smile filled his handsome face, making my heart pound. "Not always to each other, but always to a lady."

I studied him for a moment and then I slowly smiled. "Is there anything you'd like to know about me?"

His face was serious again. "Are your thoughts and feelings always so unguarded?"

"To my detriment, yes."

His smile returned. "Then I believe I would like to court you, Miss Hill, if you are agreeable to my pursuit."

Aunt Maude held her breath as she stared at me.

I did not want to marry the Duke of Severton or live in Ravenscar, but this was the course set before me. I had agreed to it and there was no going back, no matter how much I loved Alec.

"I am agreeable, Your Grace."

"Good." He nodded, and I could see the matter was settled in his mind.

I was the one he wanted, for better or worse.

On Tuesday, I was allowed to sleep late and take my time preparing for that evening. Alec had kept himself scarce since the duke's visit three days before, making one excuse after the other to leave the house.

George had not returned, nor had he sent a note. I didn't know where he was staying or how to send my apologies, but I was certain I would tell him I was sorry for Aunt Maude's behavior when I saw him next.

Aunt Maude and I had spent the past few days attending social events, riding in Hyde Park, and visiting sites of interest. She and Lady Mandeville felt it necessary to get my name on everyone's lips. After I attended the opera with the duke tonight, that was exactly what would happen. And I would soon have more enemies than just Louise Garfield. Not only had the American women I'd met been cool with me—all but Annabelle and Lily Parker—many of the unmarried British women had been, as well. It was evident that they saw the American heiresses as a serious threat, as well they should.

By the time I was pressed and primped for the opera, I was exhausted from my nerves. Although the duke had been forthright with me on his last visit, there were still a lot of things I didn't know about him. Lady Mandeville had hinted that there was a scandal surrounding the duke's family, but no one really knew what it was. I wanted to ask someone who might know, but I was always with Aunt Maude when I was in the company of others, and she would not approve of me talking behind the duke's back.

None of it really mattered. If the duke asked me to be his wife, Aunt Maude would expect my consent. There was little else to do but accept my situation and make the best of it.

And try to forget about Alec, which was almost impossible while living in the same house.

"There," Gallagher said as she stepped back from pinning my hair. "You look beautiful, miss."

She paid me so few compliments, my eyebrows came up. "Thank you."

Without another word, she began to clean up the mess we'd made during my toilette. But I wasn't quite done. I had a favor to ask her.

"Gallagher, do you think you could do a little investigation for me?"

She paused, a frown on her face. "What kind of an investigation?"

"I know very little about the Duke of Severton, and I have no one to ask, without my aunt hearing me. Could you perhaps ask the servants if they know anything about the duke or his family history? I don't want to be surprised later, if there is something he is trying to hide."

Gallagher and I were not close, but she had been a loyal servant and, as far as I knew, wasn't prone to gossip. At least, with me. Would she help me with this?

"I can see what I can do, miss."

"Thank you." I smiled at her and then left my bedchamber to join Aunt Maude in the drawing room as we waited for the duke's arrival.

Alec was just coming down the steps from the next floor up, where his room was located. He paused on the last step and took in my appearance.

I was wearing one of my Worth gowns. It was cream-colored with swaths of silk draped around the skirt and a garland of pink silk roses trailing down one side and along the hem. It was short-sleeved with ruffles along the collar, and I was wearing matching cream-colored gloves, which went up to my elbows.

Alec continued toward me, a sad smile on his face. "I will miss these chance encounters with you, Keira."

I would miss them, too, but I had decided to set my mind against thoughts of Alec. Instead of dwelling on what could not be, I smiled, noticing that he was not dressed to go out. "Are you not joining us at the opera?"

"I was not invited, and even if I had been, I would decline. The duke needs no help from me to win you over."

I needed to turn my thoughts to something else. "I have no plans in the morning," I told him. "I will not be expected to join Aunt Maude until luncheon. Could we go to Islington tomorrow morning? It's all I've been thinking about since we visited the register."

"You have not been thinking about Severton?"

I stared at him for a moment, wondering why he still wanted to talk about the duke.

"I want to find my mother, Alec." My voice was steady and serious. I did not want to discuss the duke with him. "Will you take me, or must I go back to the register and get her address and go on my own?"

He let out a sigh. "I will take you in the morning. Be ready to leave at eight."

"Thank you." A whole different set of nerves assailed me at the thought of finally meeting Nellie O'Day.

I was about to excuse myself when I remembered the other thing I wanted to ask him, though it wouldn't be easy. He was the only person I knew who might be able to help me.

"What?" he asked. "I can see you want something else."

"It's about George," I said, hesitant. "He called the other morning, but Aunt Maude forced him to leave when the duke appeared. I would like to apologize, but I don't know how to find him. Could you ask around and see where he is staying?"

"I didn't know that he was in town."

"Only just. He called the morning after he arrived in London. I feel horrible about how he was treated, especially after—" I was going to say *especially after he had proposed to me*, but I paused.

Alec didn't meet my gaze for a moment, but then he finally nodded. "I will see what I can do."

I laid my hand on his arm. "Thank you."

His muscles tensed, but he nodded.

A maid appeared at the top of the steps and paused. "The duke has arrived, miss."

"I'll be right down."

She turned and went back the way she had come.

"I hope you have a good time tonight," Alec said. "You deserve to be happy."

Emotion caught in my throat, but I nodded. "Thank you."

I wasn't sure if the duke could make me happy, but I would try to enjoy my time with him.

When I arrived in the drawing room, the duke was already there with Aunt Maude.

He turned at my arrival, and for the first time, I saw a spark of interest in his eyes. His gaze traveled over my gown with appreciation, though he tried to hide it.

"Good evening, Your Grace," I said, offering a slight curtsey.

He was dressed in a handsome evening coat and when he bowed, my pulse sped. In moments like this, I still couldn't believe I was Keira O'Day, from Five Points. What duke in his right mind would want me, if he knew? It was all a façade, gold gilding covering the unpleasant truth beneath the surface. But wasn't the entire aristocracy a sort of gilding? A thin veneer of people who only represented a small portion of society. Perhaps I fit in perfectly.

The duke straightened, his mask of indifference returning to his face as he offered me his arm. "Are you ready to leave for the opera?"

I nodded, accepting his arm, and soon found myself in his carriage with an opera cape covering my gown, sitting next to Aunt Maude as Severton sat across from us.

It was dark in his carriage, and despite Aunt Maude's best attempts to make conversation, the duke was silent. As we passed the gaslit lamps, and light entered from time to time, I caught him stealing glances at me, the scar on his face highlighted in the shadows.

A shiver ran up my back at the thought of driving away in this carriage, alone, as his wife. Could I possibly get to know him well enough to be comfortable with that idea? And what about after the wedding, when I was expected to be his wife in every sense of the word? What then?

I didn't want to think about the intimate details of a marriage. Every time I thought about kissing him, memories of the stolen moment on Christmas Day with Alec filled my mind.

Warmth crept up my neck, and I had to look away from the duke.

Her Majesty's Theatre was not far from Buckingham Gate, and it didn't take long to get there. The street was clogged with other expensive carriages, and we had to wait our turn to leave the conveyance and enter the beautiful six-story building.

When the door finally opened, and I stepped out, Severton offered me his elbow as Aunt Maude followed.

It didn't take long for people to start noticing us, and the whispers began.

The theater wasn't as large as the Metropolitan in New York, but it was still grand and elegant. There were a couple dozen private boxes distributed on two tiers of the house. Lady Mandeville was in the hallway outside one of them, waiting for us. She wore a sparkling tiara and was draped with expensive-looking diamonds.

"There you are," she said as she greeted us, offering the duke a curtsey. "Welcome, Your Grace." She then kissed Aunt Maude and me on the cheeks. "Do come in and make yourselves comfortable."

Severton pulled aside a red curtain and allowed me to enter first.

There were six chairs within, three in front and three in the back. I walked to the front row, and the duke followed me as Aunt Maude and Lady Mandeville stayed near the door, speaking in low tones.

Across the way, in another box, I noticed a familiar woman with blond hair. It was Lily Parker. She was seated with an older gentleman to her left as her mother and two older ladies sat behind her. When she caught my eye, she smiled and I returned the smile. We had seen each other at several events, though we had little time to get to know one another. I'd heard that her father had made a fortune selling shovels and pick axes during the California Gold Rush. After his death, her mother had remarried a man with two daughters, not much younger than Lily. Now, she and her mother had come to London with the same goal as everyone else. To marry into the aristocracy to gain social prominence in New York.

Was the man beside her an aristocrat? He was speaking to Lily and took her attention away.

In another box was Annabelle Wellington. She was sitting with a gentleman closer to her age. She seemed quite smitten with him and was not scanning the theater like I was. Instead, she leaned close to him, whispered into his ear, and then they both laughed.

Perhaps she had forgotten about Alec.

Even though I could not have Alec, something inside of me felt relieved that Annabelle would not have him either.

Severton seemed sullen and was probably wishing he was anywhere else but the theater, so I decided to make the best of things and break the silence.

"Do you attend the opera often, Your Grace?"

"I have never been to the opera." He was sitting close to me, his presence dominating in every way. His height, his breadth, his title, his mood—it was all intimidating. "And please, when we're alone, call me Severton—or Ames."

I had almost forgotten his first name.

"And may I call you Clara?" he asked, his gaze now on me.

"Of course." I swallowed the nerves that suddenly bubbled up. Things had just become very personal. I wanted to change the subject. "What do you do for entertainment in Ravenscar?"

"We hunt."

"Oh? Do you host hunting parties?"

"No. Just my brothers and I."

"Are your brothers married?"

"No."

"And what else do you do to occupy your time?" I smiled at him. "Besides read maps."

"I'm quite busy overseeing the property and managing the tenant farmers."

"What do you do for pleasure? Is there no other form of entertainment in Ravenscar?"

"I read a lot of books. The library at Pickering Castle is unmatched in all of England."

The thought of a library was tempting. I pictured the library at Aunt Maude's home in New York, and memories of Alec surfaced. Why did almost everything turn my thoughts back to him?

"Are there instruments?" I asked, determined not to think about Alec. "A piano, perhaps?"

Something lit up in his gaze—excitement? "Do you play?"

"I do not play, but I like to sing."

"I would like to hear you sometime."

People had begun to gather in their boxes and in the chairs on the house floor. They were turning our way, continuing to talk as they craned their necks to see us.

"I do believe London will have us engaged by morning, Your Gra—"

"Ames." He did not look at the others but kept his focus on me. "And let them. I'd rather it be done as soon as possible."

It almost sounded like a proposal, so I chose to ignore the comment, not ready to discuss such an important topic.

"And what about you?" he asked. "What sort of entertainment would you desire, besides singing?"

"I enjoy books, as well," I said. "But I wouldn't mind entertaining—"

He scoffed. "Pickering Castle is no place for guests."

"No guests? Why not?"

"People do not like staying at the castle," he said, probably hoping to clarify, but it only made me more curious.

"Why?"

"It's an old, drafty monstrosity of a house. Outdated, and—" He paused. "The locals claim it's haunted."

"Is it?"

For the first time, he turned his gaze away from me, his face becoming like stone. "With memories of the past, perhaps."

I wanted to ask him about the scandal that Lady Mandeville had whispered about, but I wasn't sure how to broach the topic. Were those the difficult memories he was thinking about?

"Why do they think it's haunted?" I asked instead.

"Because someone was murdered there."

I blinked several times, waiting for him to elaborate, but he did not, and the music began to play.

18

Early the next morning, Alec helped me into a hansom cab he had hired to take us to Islington. Aunt Maude would not expect to see me before lunch, which would be another four hours from now, so we would have plenty of time to get to Islington and back before she realized we were gone.

Alec stepped into the enclosed cab and sat next to me. It was a small conveyance with room enough for the two of us. His leg pressed against mine as he rapped the ceiling to let the driver know we were ready to leave.

A steady rain fell outside, creating a sort of cocoon for us in the vehicle. I had taken great pains with my appearance that morning, though it wasn't easy to get ready without Gallagher's assistance. I was used to dressing myself, but the gowns I wore now were much more complicated than the ones I wore in Five Points. And the hairstyles I had mastered on my own were nothing compared to my maid's abilities, but I was pleased with my efforts.

I wanted to look nice when I met my mother.

"You look beautiful," Alec said as the cab rattled along the cobblestone street, past Buckingham Palace. He was always quick to compliment me, but I never tired of hearing it, and he always seemed to know when to say something nice.

"Thank you."

"I see you're wearing your locket."

I touched the gold necklace with my gloved hand and ran my thumb over the initials. "Do you think she'll tell me who my father is?"

"I don't know—but everyone deserves to know their parents." His voice was soft and sincere.

We turned right onto The Mall. The park looked gloomy in the rain this morning, though it was still lovely with Buckingham Palace on one side and St. James's Palace on the other. They looked formidable in the mist. I'd been told Buckingham Palace was all but empty. I couldn't imagine how much money the monarchy spent on their properties, while other people suffered greatly just beyond the bounds of the park. People like my family.

"Alec?"

"Yes."

"Do you think God makes mistakes?"

"Never."

"What about me?"

"What do you mean?"

"I was a mistake."

He turned so he was looking at me, and I met his intense gaze. "How could you think such a thing?"

"How could I not? Neither of my parents wanted me and I was discarded the moment my mother was able to give me away. My aunt and uncle didn't want me, either."

"That doesn't make you a mistake." He was quiet for a moment and then said, "The Bible tells us that we are fearfully and wonderfully made in His image. Humans can make mistakes, but God cannot. Every person in the world was deliberately and beautifully designed by their Creator. God knew exactly what He was doing when He made you." His voice became tender. "And I think He did an exceptionally good job."

My cheeks warmed and I smiled. I liked to believe that I wasn't a mistake, that God had created me with intention and purpose. That there was meaning for my life and I wasn't simply something to discard. But my early life had proven different.

"God has a plan for each of us," Alec continued. "One that is filled with hope. Perhaps your parents didn't intend to have a baby, and you were abandoned at a young age, but God still has a wonderful purpose for your life, if you are willing to submit to His plan. Nothing in His kingdom is wasted, Keira."

"Do you truly believe that?"

"I do, very much. I've seen it repeatedly in my life." He took my gloved hand into his and held it gently. "From the moment you were born, God knew that you would end up here. Perhaps you will marry a duke and with the substantial dowry Aunt Maude wants to settle upon your future husband, you could do great things. You could help people, educate them, provide love and care. As a duchess, your voice will carry above the crowd, and you can bring awareness and change for people living in places like Five Points. That might be why God sent you there as a child, so you would know firsthand what it's like. You, Keira, were created to do great things. I believe that with all my heart."

Tears welled up in my eyes and fell down my cheeks. "Thank you."

He wiped away each tear with his gloved hand.

We were sitting so close, and we were completely alone for the first time in a long time. The rain continued to tap against the ceiling of the cab, and it felt as if no one else existed in all the world.

Alec's breathing grew deep, his chest rising and falling with each breath.

I waited, an ache for him tightening inside me—but he blinked and then turned away, looking out the window. He let go of my hand and clasped his together on his lap.

I slowly looked out my own window at the dreary scene. More tears threatened, but I forced myself not to give in to them. It seemed that whenever Alec and I were alone, or even close, the tension and yearning built up inside of me until I was afraid I would burst from the intensity of it. Did he feel the same?

Neither of us spoke for a long time, but then Alec broke the silence. "I meant to tell you sooner, but I asked around about George."

I tore my gaze from the sodden street. "Where is he?"

"He left London the morning after he called on you."

"What do you mean? I thought he was staying in London for the season."

"I believe that was his original plan, but . . ." He let the statement fade.

"But after he was treated so poorly—"

"After he saw you with the Duke of Severton, George knew he had lost and he decided to leave London, his dignity intact." He let out a sigh. "I'm thinking about following suit."

Alarm filled my heart. "You can't leave, too."

"I cannot stay."

"Why not?"

"I have no purpose here. I've met with everyone I needed to and there is nothing left for me to do"—he turned away, and I almost didn't catch his last words—"but watch you fall in love with Severton."

Pain pressed against my chest as I let his comment go unanswered. What else could either of us do?

"Please," I whispered. "Don't leave me here alone with Aunt Maude and all these strangers. Will you at least stay until I find my mother?"

He was silent for a long time, but finally, he nodded.

Relief washed over me. "Thank you."

He didn't let his gaze leave the window as rain washed the dusty streets and turned everything to mud.

I held my locket as we pulled up to a two-story brown-brick home in Islington an hour later. The house was substantial and well-built, with arches over the windows on the main floor and white cornices at the top. The shrubs in front were trimmed and white curtains hung at the windows. It was a beautiful home.

Not at all where I had pictured my mother living while I was growing up in the slums of New York City. I'd assumed she couldn't afford to care for me and that was why she'd given me away.

"Would you like me to wait here?" Alec asked.

I shook my head, not wanting to do this alone. "Do you mind coming with me?"

"Of course not. I would prefer not to send you into a strange house by yourself."

He stepped out of the carriage and then offered his hand for me to get out.

It had stopped raining, but everything was still wet as my foot sank into the mud.

Alec helped me around a puddle as I lifted the hem of my pink day dress and then he escorted me up the front walk.

Nerves bubbled in my stomach as I stared at the door, wondering what I might encounter.

Alec waited patiently as I pulled my courage together.

Finally, I lifted the knocker and rapped it three times before lowering my hand to my side.

Alec laid his hand on my lower back, offering me a gentle smile of encouragement before removing it.

The door opened and a young maid stood before us. She was pleasant as she said, "Good morning. What can I do for you?"

"I'm here to call on Mrs. Farmington," I said, my voice shaking with my nerves as I handed her a calling card. It was white with my name, *Clara Day Hill*, embossed in gold.

The maid took the card and said, "Won't you come in? I'll see if my mistress is at home to receive you."

We stepped over the threshold, and I was struck by the simple elegance of the foyer. The two-story room had a table in the center with a vase of fresh-cut flowers and two beautiful paintings on the wall going up the stairs. As the maid showed us into the front parlor, souvenirs from around the world decorated the space in a tasteful manner. There were ivory statues of animals that looked like they were from India, postcards on a table from Africa, a Chinese lantern hanging from the ceiling, and—I paused in surprise as I noticed a painting of New York City hanging on the wall, like those I once saw for sale near Central Park.

Had my mother been to New York and not tried to find me or Uncle Charlie?

It couldn't be true. Perhaps someone else had traveled to New York and brought the souvenir home.

The room was chilly as we waited for the maid to return, but neither of us spoke.

After several minutes, the maid stepped into the drawing room. "I'm sorry, but Mrs. Farmington is not at home to receive you."

Of course. Why would she receive a stranger known as Clara Day Hill?

"Can you please tell your mistress that my real name is Keira O'Day and I've come all the way from New York City to meet with her?"

The maid frowned but nodded and curtseyed before she left the room again.

If my mother refused to see me now, then I would have my answer. She did not want anything to do with me.

The thought terrified me more than anything else.

Alec was quiet as he looked at the souvenirs. I had the opportunity to observe him, without Aunt Maude or anyone else watching me. He was handsome and refined, a gentleman in every sense of the word. But it was more than his good looks that drew me to him. I had rarely met a man so loving and selfless as Alexander Paxton-Hill. He'd given up his dreams and his parents to go to New York to continue his uncle's legacy, so he could care for Aunt Maude and his mother and father. The longer I knew him, the more I respected and admired him.

He looked up and caught me watching him, and a tender smile lifted his lips.

I wanted him to know how much I appreciated him, and I was about to say so, when the door opened again and a woman appeared.

She stared at me as I stared at her, dumbfounded at how much we looked alike.

"Keira?" she whispered.

I swallowed the nerves climbing my throat and nodded. "Are you Nellie?"

It was her turn to nod. So many emotions played across her face as she studied me. Surprise, delight, sadness—and fear.

"You're—" She paused and shook her head. "You're breathtaking. Absolutely beautiful. And look at that charming gown. How—" She noticed Alec and paused again.

"This is Mr. Alexander Paxton-Hill," I told my mother. "My—friend." How in the world did I explain who Alec was?

He bowed. "It's a pleasure to meet you, Mrs. Farmington."

"And you, Mr. Paxton-Hill." She closed the drawing room door, blinking with confusion. "How did you find me? Why are you here?" Her gaze slipped to my locket, and she looked stunned. "My locket."

I didn't move or breathe as she walked across the drawing room, her eyes never leaving the piece of jewelry. Uncertainty shadowed her face as she slowly reached for it and opened it.

Relief made her shoulders sag as she briefly closed her eyes. "It's empty."

Frowning, I stared at her. "Were there pictures in it at one time?"

"A long, long time ago." She closed it and let it fall on my chest as she took a step back. "I was certain I removed them before I gave this to Charlie, but for a moment, I was afraid I had forgotten."

"Pictures of you . . . and my father?"

Her brown-eyed gaze lifted to mine. "What do you know of your father?"

"Nothing." I swallowed again. "That's part of the reason I'm here today."

She crossed her arms and shook her head. "I'm afraid you won't get what you came for, then. I have nothing to tell you. About anything. It is best if you leave before my husband returns. He—he doesn't know about you, or that sordid part of my life."

"Please." I stepped forward. "I've waited my whole life to meet you. I have so many questions."

"And I don't have the answers." She didn't seem angry—more apologetic. "No one knows the identity of your father, and they must never know. I swore a promise on my life that I would never tell a soul, including you."

"Why can't anyone know? What would it hurt if *I* knew?"

"It would hurt him and his family. They didn't know about you."

"Did he?"

She let out a sigh. "Yes."

"And he didn't want me, either?"

"He wanted you, very much. But we were not married and his family had plans for his life that did not include a young Irish actress. The whole affair was devastating for his family, even without knowing about the baby. The only way I could make things better was to send you away and disappear."

"You didn't go far."

"I returned to Ireland, but by that time, I already had an admirer, Mr. Farmington, my husband. He persuaded me to return several years later, after the scandal died down, and he married me and gave me a new name, so no one had to know who I was." She frowned and I could see that her next words pained her. "I didn't want to let you go, Keira, but I had little choice. When my brother Charlie decided to move to America, and he was willing to take you with him, I saw no other option. I didn't want to send you to an orphanage, and I couldn't care for you on my own. I hoped it was a good life for you in America—and looking at you today, I can see it was."

I thought of the poverty we had lived in, and I shook my head. But what good would it do to tell her how horrible my life had been before meeting Alec and Aunt Maude?

She turned to Alec. "How do you know Keira?"

He looked at me, a question in his eyes. How much did I want her to know?

"Alec's aunt adopted me," I said, drawing her attention back to me. "Just this year. And she's brought me here to make an advantageous match."

My mother studied me for a moment, a slight frown on her face. "How odd to be adopted as an adult."

"I'm her heir—one of them. Mr. Paxton-Hill is the other."

"Then you're planning to stay in England?"

"If all goes as Aunt Maude hopes."

"And she wants you to marry into the nobility?"

I nodded.

Concern deepened her brow. "Be very careful, Keira. There are secrets among the nobility that could hurt you."

Frowning, I took a step closer to her. "What secrets?"

"It's best if you don't know."

"How can I protect myself if I don't know what to look for?"

"Perhaps you should leave." She walked toward the door. "I cannot afford to have anyone asking questions about you or telling my husband you visited."

"Is that why you didn't try to find me when you were in New York?"

She paused. "How did you know I was in New York?"

I motioned toward the painting on her wall. "They sell those near Central Park."

"I had no idea where to even look for you, Keira—and how would I have explained it to Freddie if I had found you?"

"Freddie?"

"My husband. For all intents and purposes, you became Charlie and Orla's child the moment they took you out of my arms. I didn't want to disrupt the life you were living. It wouldn't have been fair to you."

I frowned. "I don't think you were worried about me. I think you were more worried about yourself."

"That's not fair, Keira."

I wasn't sure what I had hoped for, but it was clear she would not tell me what I wanted to know. Perhaps I should be content that she agreed to even meet me.

But I had to try one more time.

"Can you tell me about the locket, at least? It's the only link I've ever had to you and my father."

Her face softened and she approached me again, touching the locket with a tenderness that relayed a thousand memories.

"He gave it to me, after I told him I was expecting you. He said he wanted to marry me, but I knew it would never come to be. It was the last time I saw him."

"And the initials?"

"His and mine."

"His name starts with a B?"

She moved her hand away and wrapped her arms around herself. "I cannot tell you what you want to know, Keira. Please know that we both loved you, but circumstances kept us from the life we wanted to live. That is all I will ever say."

I tried to put the puzzle together in my mind, but there were too many missing pieces. My father was from England, his family would not allow him and my mother to marry, and the locket was given to my mother *after* my father knew about me. He hadn't turned her away when she needed him most. *She* had been the one to walk away.

"Did you love him?"

"With all my heart. I still do."

"He is still alive?"

"I think it's best if you leave now."

Alec stepped forward and offered me his arm. "Shall we?"

I wrapped my hand around his elbow, not wanting to leave the woman I had always dreamed of meeting, but there was little else to do. We needed to get back to 7 Buckingham Gate before our absence was noticed.

"Perhaps it's best if you don't seek me out again," my mother said as I started to walk toward the door. "It might be too hard to explain you to my husband."

I paused and nodded. "If you ever need to find me, we're staying at 7 Buckingham Gate."

She walked over to me and put her hand on my arm. "I'm very proud of the woman you have become."

Emotions clogged my throat, so all I could do was nod as Alec escorted me out of the house.

19

There was more traffic as we made our way back to 7 Buckingham Gate. The rain was gone, and the puddles were drying, but the clouds were still lying low in the sky and everything looked gray.

"I'm sorry you didn't get more answers," Alec said as our cab neared St. James's Palace.

"I am, too." I hadn't spoken much since we'd left my mother. There were too many thoughts and questions circling through my head. But I was ready to talk now. "What did she mean by secrets in the nobility that could hurt me? Is my father an aristocrat? Was that why they couldn't have a life together?"

"I don't know."

"The nobility isn't very large," I continued. "According to Lady Mandeville there are only 580 titled peers in England. And how many of them are in their forties or fifties? Could I possibly find my father through deduction?"

"Even if you did, what would you do with the information? Your mother made it quite clear that it would hurt his family if they learned about you. Perhaps you should trust her and not look for answers."

"I could use the information to protect myself. If I knew who he was, I could avoid his family. What if—" I paused, a thought coming to me. "What if the Duke of Severton's family scandal has something to do with my mother? What if—what if his father and my mother had an affair? My mother said that she and my father weren't married—but that doesn't mean he wasn't married to someone else."

"Your mother said that your father is still alive. The duke's father is dead. You have nothing to worry about on that account."

"No, she said that she still loves him, and when I asked if he was still alive, she avoided the question. Perhaps he did die."

"You are making trouble where there is no trouble. The odds of Severton being your half-brother are very slim." He sighed. "But if it makes you feel better, I will see what I can learn about his family scandal."

"Thank you, Alec." I almost touched his arm in appreciation, but I couldn't risk a moment of intimacy between us again. I had to keep my distance.

As 7 Buckingham Gate came into view, I took a deep breath. I needed to put all this aside for now. We had plans to ride in Hyde Park that afternoon with Lady Mandeville to discuss the party Aunt Maude was hosting for the Prince of Wales in three days. Already, word had spread that the prince would be at our home. That news, along with being seen with the duke at the opera the night before, was exactly what Aunt Maude and Lady Mandeville had hoped for. Our social standing was on the rise, and invitations had started to arrive from the best families in the city.

The cab pulled up to the front of the house and Alec got out before helping me exit the vehicle. He offered me his arm as we walked up to the front door and opened it, allowing me to enter before him.

Aunt Maude paced in the entry hall, the train of her dove gray day dress trailing behind her.

I paused, my heart in my throat, as she stopped and turned her steely gaze on us.

"Where have you been?" she demanded, her voice shaking with fury.

Neither of us spoke. What could I possibly say, but the truth?

I opened my mouth to speak, but she began to walk toward the drawing room. "Come with me."

Alec closed the front door and gave me a look that was full of empathy and concern.

"I'll tell her the truth," I whispered. "It's better than concocting a story that will only make her more upset."

We followed her into the drawing room and found her pacing. Alec closed this door for privacy, too.

"Well?" she demanded, crossing her arms and tapping a foot. "How often do you leave like this? Is it a daily ritual?" She paused, her face going pale. "Are you having a—tryst?"

"Good heavens, no," Alec said.

"We went to visit my mother," I told her.

She lowered her hands, staring at me. "Your mother?"

"I learned that she is living in Islington. We went there today so I could meet her."

"For what purpose?"

"She's her mother, Aunt Maude," Alec said. "Does she need any other reason?"

"Why didn't you tell me?" Aunt Maude crossed her arms again as her gaze bore into me. "Why sneak about?"

"I didn't think you'd let me go."

"I'm not a monster."

"I know—I just wasn't sure—"

"You cannot make assumptions about me without asking me first."

"I'm sorry. I won't do it again."

"And you." She turned to Alec. "What do you have to say for yourself?"

"I wanted to help Clara. It's as simple as that. We went to Mrs. Farmington's home in Islington and then came straight back here. Nothing more. No one saw us."

Aunt Maude briefly closed her eyes and then lowered herself into the wingback chair, placing her forehead in her hand. "It doesn't matter if anyone saw you—they're already spreading rumors about Clara as it is."

"What?" I frowned as I took a seat on one of the sofas. "What are they saying?"

Aunt Maude motioned to the table between the sofas. There were three newspapers lying there.

"It's all over the newspapers. A copy of *Town Topics* just arrived from New York this morning, but it must have arrived at the London offices of *The Morning Post* and *The World* yesterday, because they covered it in their editions this morning."

I picked up the copy of *Town Topics.* It was a salacious New York newspaper Aunt Maude subscribed to that was notorious for sharing gossip about the wealthy social class without directly naming the parties involved.

There, on the front page, was a headline that made me feel weak.

Hotel Widow Adopts Tenement Girl to Pass Her Off as a Niece to Capture a Duke.

Below the headline were all the sordid details about how I had grown up in Five Points. They didn't mention Aunt Maude's name, nor mine, but they didn't need to. Everyone would know who we were.

"How?" I asked, looking at the other two newspapers that shared all the same information. "Who would have told *Town Topics*?"

Aunt Maude's lips were grim as she stared at me. "Your dear old Uncle Charlie and Aunt Orla."

"What?" I frowned. "How do you know?"

"They tried to blackmail me right before we left New York, but I ignored their threat." She rose and paced again. "I should have just paid them what they asked for."

"They wanted money for their silence?" Betrayal sliced through me. How could my uncle and aunt hurt me this way? Did they want to remove everything good from my life? Was that it?

"I'm sure *Town Topics* paid them well for their story." Aunt Maude shook her head. "And just when everything was going as we planned. What will we do now? Will the prince even want to come for a dinner party? And what of the duke? When he hears that you are not my niece, will he continue to pursue you?"

I caught Alec's eye, and he looked just as disappointed as I felt. Even though I suspected it was hard for him to watch me with the duke, he truly wanted me to be happy.

"What will we do?" I asked.

Aunt Maude stopped pacing and set her shoulders. "We will continue as we have been. As soon as Lady Mandeville arrives in her carriage, we will go riding in Hyde Park. If she does not come, then we will rent a carriage and go on our own. I will not kowtow to anyone. We all have a right to be here. My money is just as good as anyone else's. If the Duke of Severton doesn't want it, then we'll find another aristocrat that does. And if the Prince of Wales doesn't want to come for supper, we'll get along without his approval." She nodded once, as if the matter were settled.

I'd learned that once Aunt Maude set her mind to something, she was almost guaranteed success.

I hoped this time was no exception.

At the appointed hour, Aunt Maude, Alec, and I were back in the front drawing room, ready and waiting for Lady Mandeville to arrive. Gallagher had helped me into a white day dress with a black belt and a black, wide-brimmed hat with white ostrich feathers tucked into the crown. I held a white parasol, closed at the moment, and white kid gloves, which I would put on before we left the house.

None of us spoke as the clock ticked by. Lady Mandeville was ten minutes late.

Alec stood near the window, looking out onto Buckingham Palace Road. He was wearing a black riding suit, with a cutaway jacket and a green waistcoat underneath. His hat was beneath his arm as he stared out the window.

"How long will we wait before we accept that Lady Mandeville isn't coming?" he asked the room at large.

Aunt Maude sat in her wingback chair in a beautiful gown, staring at the door. "We will wait one hour."

The next fifty minutes would be excruciating.

I stood from the sofa and paced to the window to join Alec.

Lady Mandeville's carriage rounded the corner and came to a stop in front of the house.

"She's here!" I said to Aunt Maude.

"I knew she would come." Aunt Maude slowly rose from her chair. "She has too much at stake if we're not successful. I told her I would only pay her once an engagement was announced."

"Really, Aunt," Alec said as he moved away from the window. "Please don't discuss the financial implications of all of this with Clara around. It only causes her undue stress."

"She'll benefit the most from it," Aunt Maude said with no regret.

"Still." Alec glanced at me with an apologetic smile.

I shook my head, not wanting him to worry about me. This affected him as much as it did me and Aunt Maude, perhaps even more so. If things didn't go as we hoped, his hotels would suffer, and their financial situation would be grim.

We met Lady Mandeville in the foyer. She did not greet us with her usual enthusiasm but sighed. "Is it true?"

"Is it true that I adopted this beautiful young woman and she is my heiress, just as I claimed?" Aunt Maude nodded. "Yes. Shall we go to Hyde Park as planned?"

"Is Clara your niece?" Lady Mandeville asked.

"Does that matter? She's an accomplished, intelligent, *wealthy* young woman who would make any duke proud. She, like the rest of us with new money, is just as deserving of a place in society. Now. Shall we proceed with our plans, or must I find someone else who will help us achieve what we want?"

Lady Mandeville stood for a moment, as if weighing her options, but eventually she, like Aunt Maude, squared her shoulders. "I do believe my carriage is ready for our ride in Hyde Park."

"Good. Rodgers," Aunt Maude called to the butler. "We are leaving."

He must have been standing just out of sight, though not out of hearing, because he stepped into the foyer and opened the front door.

The sky was still overcast as we left 7 Buckingham Gate. Lady Mandeville's carriage top was down, allowing us to see and be seen as we traveled the short distance to the park. Aunt Maude and I sat together on one seat and Alec and Lady Mandeville on the other.

"Keep your chin up, Clara," Lady Mandeville said. "This isn't the biggest scandal of the season, I can assure you. But we will have to weather the storm."

It wasn't bright enough for me to use my parasol to hide under, so I kept it closed at my side as we entered Rotten Row, where all the fashionable members of society would be riding today. It was a long, dusty avenue that cut through the park. Spectators stood along the fence to watch the wealthy parade by.

"Have you heard from the prince?" Aunt Maude asked Lady Mandeville. "Will he still come for the dinner party?"

"If he doesn't, you will probably not get anyone else to come, either," she warned. "But I will speak to him personally. He tends to enjoy American drama and often walks toward it, instead of away from it, preferring it to other forms of entertainment. If he is still planning to come to your party, you can be assured that the rest of society will continue to embrace you. But we will have to see."

"And in the meantime, our adversaries will use this information against us," Aunt Maude said as we approached a carriage with familiar occupants.

The Garfields.

Mrs. Garfield caught sight of us and then a supercilious smile lifted her thin lips before she tilted her nose in the air and purposely turned away without acknowledging us. Louise did the same, giving us the cut direct, a social rejection that was meant to send a message to anyone watching that they did not know us or were not willing to acknowledge us.

It meant nothing to me, but I looked at Aunt Maude to see how it affected her.

Her eyes narrowed and she, too, lifted her nose, as if to tell the Garfields, and anyone else, that she didn't care what they thought of her.

"The only people you need to worry about right now are the Prince of Wales," Lady Mandeville said, "and the Duke of Severton. His family scandal has kept him locked away at Pickering Castle for so long, he might either want to avoid another scandal, or he might relate to Clara, if she comes with a substantial dowry, that is."

Yes. The dowry. Anyone could put up with me and my past for the right price.

The cynical thought was not like me, but I'd found myself having more of them the longer I stayed in society.

"When might you know if the prince will still come?" Aunt Maude asked Lady Mandeville.

"I'll send him a note as soon as I get home. If he is not too busy to reply, I might know by tonight or tomorrow."

"Then we'll continue on as we have until then," Aunt Maude said. "We will still plan to attend the ball at Lady Randolph Churchill's home."

Jennie Jerome, now Lady Randolph Churchill, had been one of the first heiresses to marry into the aristocracy, not long before Lady Mandeville. She was a leader in London society, and the mother to two little boys, Winston and Jack. I'd met her on several occasions since our arrival and she seemed quite eager to help my cause, though now that she knew the truth about me, I wasn't so sure.

"Jennie has endured enough scandals to stand up under this one," Lady Mandeville said. "I believe she will still welcome you into her ball, though we must be prepared for anything. If you're cut by enough society leaders, there is little you can do to recover."

"Then we will not allow ourselves to be cut." Aunt Maude nodded as another carriage approached.

This one contained Lily Parker, the young woman who had been presented to the queen before me. Her mother was inside the carriage with her.

I held my breath. Would they cut us?

Instead of lifting her nose and looking away, Lily offered me an encouraging smile.

Either she hadn't seen the newspapers, which would be unlikely, or she was simply kind.

I decided to believe the latter.

At least I had one friend in London. Perhaps two, if Annabelle would still acknowledge me.

As we continued down Rotten Row, we passed several carriages, some with English society and some with Americans. For the most part, we were given curious looks and hesitant greetings, though some people overlooked us entirely.

"Once we have the prince's approval, the rest will follow," Lady Mandeville assured us.

I hoped she was right and that we would learn soon if he still planned to come to our dinner party. Tomorrow night, the Duke of Severton would be at Lady Randolph Churchill's ball. If we didn't know by then, I was afraid he would cut us and move on to another heiress.

Even though I didn't want to marry him, the truth was, I needed to.

We couldn't let everything we had accomplished—and all the money Aunt Maude had spent—be for naught.

20

The following evening, Gallagher helped me prepare for Lady Randolph Churchill's ball. Aunt Maude had selected a beautiful pale green gown with a generous bustle and a flattering bodice that had silver ivy threaded into the fabric. I sat at the vanity as Gallagher finished styling my hair and looked at my reflection. I really did look a great deal like a younger version of my mother. It was remarkable.

"Gallagher," I said as I glanced at her in the mirror. "Did you get a chance to inquire about the Duke of Severton's family?"

"I did, miss, and it's all very mysterious."

"How so?"

"Some say his home is the most haunted castle in all of England."

"He mentioned that people think it's haunted." I frowned. "Do you know why?"

Gallagher paused and glanced toward the door, as if someone might be listening. She lowered her voice. "They say that each duke is cursed, and the three before this one have all been murdered."

"Three of them?" The duke had mentioned something about murder—but could it be true that there was more than one?

"And each one was murdered by his wife," Gallagher continued, her voice still low. "That's why they've all been cursed and why the Duke of Severton hasn't wanted to look for a wife until he became desperate. He didn't want to be murdered."

"That's preposterous."

Gallagher shrugged. "That's what they say."

I frowned. If it was true that the last three dukes had been murdered by their wives, did the current duke truly think it would happen to him, too?

"They say that the castle drives each duchess mad," Gallagher continued. "That the first person murdered was the first Duchess of Severton, two hundred years ago or so, and her ghost walks the moors at night, pleading for revenge, and only the current duchess can hear it. Eventually, she goes mad and is convinced to seek revenge for the Wailing Duchess."

I turned fully in my chair and stared at Gallagher. "Who told you this?"

"Several of the staff, miss."

"I've never heard of anything so absurd."

"There has to be some truth to it, or why would the current duke hide away and avoid society for all these years?"

I nibbled my bottom lip for a moment and then turned back to the mirror so Gallagher could finish. "There has to be a different reason."

Yet as I finished my preparations, then made my way down the stairs to wait for Aunt Maude and Alec, I couldn't shake the foreboding feeling that wrapped around me. I didn't believe in ghosts, but I had no wish to live in a scary castle on the moors, either.

Alec was in the front drawing room, standing near the fireplace, lost in thought when I entered the room. He was wearing a well-tailored evening coat with his face freshly shaved and his hair styled.

He glanced up and his eyes told me everything, even before he uttered, "You look beautiful, Keira."

"Thank you."

He continued to admire me as I entered the room and stood before him. He was wearing the silk flower he'd purchased from me outside the Metropolitan Opera House in his button hole.

"You brought it with?" I asked, a smile warming my face.

"I always have it with me." He shook his head. "It feels like just yesterday that we met, yet I can't seem to remember a time when you weren't part of my life."

My smile widened as I realized I felt the same way. Learning about Alec's childhood over breakfast last week made me feel as if I had known him my whole life.

"I hope tonight is a splendid success for you, Keira. You've worked so hard for this moment. I hope it won't be ruined by a gossip column."

I let out a breath. "Even if things turn around in our favor, I'm not sure if I still want to marry the duke."

He frowned. "Why not?"

"It's silly, but Gallagher heard some rumors about the duke's home and family, and to be frank, I don't want to find out if they are true."

"I inquired about the duke down at White's gentlemen's club."

"Did you learn anything valuable?"

"Rumors and speculations, though there was one thing I did discover that is verifiable."

"What is it?"

"His mother killed his father."

My eyes widened. "That was one of the rumors Gallagher heard—but that she was the third duchess in a row who killed her husband."

Alec frowned. "I hadn't heard that. What I did learn was that the duke's mother died shortly after entering prison."

"How horrible for all of them."

"Apparently, and this is the part that you need to understand—" He studied me as he spoke. "It was the duchess who had been having an affair, and when her husband learned about it, there was an altercation. This happened fifteen years ago, well after you were born. I do not believe the Duke of Severton's family has anything to do with yours."

I nodded. "But there is still much to consider. I cannot let the duke's past hinder my decision, just as I hope my past won't hinder his, but do I want to live in a castle that is so shrouded in rumors and mysteries?"

"You would be a fool to turn him down," Aunt Maude said as she entered the room.

We both turned at her arrival.

"It doesn't matter what rumors surround His Grace," she continued. "He has a title. That's all we need."

"We're talking about Clara's life," Alec said. "She must take into consideration more than the title."

"Why?" Aunt Maude lifted her chin. "That was what she agreed to when I adopted her. Are you getting picky now that you've realized you could have any of the single men in London?" she asked me.

I shook my head, feeling guilty that she would even think such a thing.

"Very well." She tightened her jaw for a moment. "I want to hear no more of this talk. We should leave for Lady Randolph Churchill's ball. There is much at stake tonight and we need to be a unified front."

Alec straightened and I readjusted my gloves.

Ready or not, it was time to face society head-on.

While in London, Lord and Lady Randolph Churchill lived at 2 Connaught Place on the north side of Hyde Park, near the Marble Arch. Their home was an impressive display of wealth, since Jennie had been an American heiress and brought a significant dowry into their marriage.

As Lady Mandeville's carriage pulled up to the Churchill townhome, my nerves were so frayed, I was afraid I might be sick. It was one thing to be cut in Hyde Park, but another to be cut in a ballroom with everyone watching.

The Duke of Severton had not called on me that morning or sent any messages. Soon, I would know if he had passed me over.

"Have you heard from the prince yet, about my dinner party?" Aunt Maude asked.

"Not yet," Lady Mandeville said. "But that doesn't mean we should give up hope. I will let you know as soon as possible."

When the carriage stopped, a footman opened the door and Alec exited, then he helped each of us alight. As I laid my hand in his, he gave it an encouraging squeeze.

My heart squeezed with it. If he felt the same way for me that I felt for him, how much harder was it to watch me go through this difficulty? And to try to encourage me?

I offered him a sad smile.

Lady Randolph Churchill stood just inside the front door, next to her husband. As each guest arrived, she greeted them in turn, commenting on one thing or another until they moved into the house.

When it was our turn, her gaze fell on me and for a heartbeat, I was afraid she would turn us away.

Instead, her face beamed and she said, "My darling Miss Hill, how lovely to see you." She leaned forward and placed a kiss on both of my cheeks, then said, close to my ear, "Keep your head up, my dear. You've just as much right to be here as anyone else."

When she pulled back, she greeted Lady Mandeville, then Aunt Maude, and finally Alec.

We arrived later than most and the house was full of people, many of whom I'd already met, though there were others who were strangers.

The first familiar face was Lily Parker. She saw me from the other side of the foyer. She was standing with her mother and an older, portly man with gray hair and watery eyes. She crossed the foyer to greet me.

"Hello, Miss Hill. I'm so happy you've come."

"Thank you." My gratitude carried far deeper than pleasantries. "You've been so kind to me."

"Us Americans need to stick together." She glanced over her shoulder, and I caught sight of Louise Garfield—standing next to the Duke of Severton. As Louise spoke, she was laughing, and she put her hand on his arm in a playful, flirtatious manner. His serious expression didn't change as he watched her, but that meant nothing when it came to the duke.

"I'm sorry," Lily said. "I suspect that you liked him."

"It's—complicated."

"Aren't all relationships?" She sighed. "My mother is set on me marrying the Earl of Cranford." This time she looked over her other shoulder to the man she'd been standing with, the one who had been at the opera with her. "He is twice my age and has a daughter even older than me. And he has no country estate but lives full time in London." Her brow furrowed. "I've resigned myself to making a good match here so my younger sisters can marry well in America, but I do not care for city life and would prefer to be as far away from London as possible. With a man more suited to my age and tastes," she added.

"I've always imagined a little cottage by a stream would be ideal."

Her blue eyes lit with pleasure. "That sounds delightful. I don't mind a ball, and enjoy the company of close friends, but this crush of people is almost unbearable."

"I believe you and I will be good friends, Miss Parker."

She smiled. "Please call me Lily."

"And I'm Keir—Clara." It had been several months since I'd almost slipped and given the wrong name.

"We'll storm the castle together, shall we?" Lily asked with a sparkle in her eyes.

I nodded.

"Lily, dear." Her mother called for her, a new man, even older than Lord Cranford, at her side. "Lord Parkhurst would like to meet you."

"Perhaps *he* has a cottage by the stream," she said with a bright smile. "Ever onward."

As Lily walked away, my gaze returned to Louise and the duke. She was still monopolizing his attention. She spoke incessantly, laughing at her own jokes and giving the duke as many flirtatious looks as she could manage.

"There you are, Clara." Annabelle appeared out of a small group of people and came to my side. "I've been meaning to visit with you since we arrived in London, but it's been such a rush of activities."

"Hello, Annabelle."

She took my hands and leveled a look at me. "How are you holding up? I read the ghastly articles in the newspaper today. How small of the people who broke the news."

"You—you aren't appalled?" I asked, worried that she would turn on me.

"Goodness, no." She laughed. "Why would I be? Aren't all of us here because we weren't good enough for America? Until we had money, we were nobody, and now that we do, we're trying to become somebody. Mrs. Astor might disagree, but one day, her opinion won't matter. You're no different than the rest of us."

"But you're not upset that I hid the truth?"

She leaned forward. "We're all hiding something, Clara. Don't let anyone tell you differently." She nodded to the duke. "Some more than others."

A shiver ran up my spine at her words.

Alec was speaking to Lady Randolph Churchill. I glanced in his direction and Annabelle's gaze followed mine.

"How is Alec?" she asked me.

I took a deep breath. How *was* Alec? How were either of us?

"I haven't spoken to him since we arrived in London." She sighed. "Mother has warned me not to, and to be honest, it's been good for me. I have decided to leave Alec in the past." She smiled. "Lord Devan is quite charming. I do believe he'll propose at the end of the season, and I've made up my mind to accept."

"Is he the man I saw you with at the opera?"

Her face glowed. "He is."

"I'm happy for you."

She leaned forward. "And what of the duke? Will you accept if he proposes?"

I looked in his direction again and he glanced up, noticing me in the middle of the foyer. He did not lower his gaze, but openly studied me.

It was maddening how difficult it was to read his emotions. Was he pleased to see me? Angry? Disappointed? Happy?

"I'm uncertain," I finally said to Annabelle, though I knew I would accept, having no other option.

Several maids appeared with stacks of dance cards, which they distributed to the ladies.

"It's been lovely speaking to you, Clara," Annabelle said as Alec started toward us. "I'll see you later."

She left before Alec joined me. He glanced in Annabelle's direction but made no move to call her back, nor did he look upset that she was gone. Instead, without a word, he took my dance card and wrote his name by the first dance.

"Finally," he said with a tender smile, "I'll get the first dance."

"Thank you, Alec."

As a maid handed Louise a dance card, distracting her attention, the duke used the opportunity to walk away from her.

My heart pounded hard as he approached and Alec stepped away.

"Miss Hill," he said, offering me a slight bow.

"Your Grace." I curtseyed, my legs wobbly with the effort.

"May I have the first dance?" he asked.

My lips parted in surprise, and then disappointment warred in my divided heart. I'd promised the dance to Alec, and I wanted to dance with him more than anything else, but it was imperative that I dance with the duke. Not only to show him that I was still eager to pursue a possible marriage, but to demonstrate to the rest of society that I wasn't being cast aside.

Yet I couldn't do to Alec what Aunt Maude had done to George.

Swallowing, I said, "I'm afraid—"

"I think I wrote my name on the wrong line, Clara," Alec said, stepping forward and reaching for my dance card. "Ah, yes." He put a line through his name and took the second dance of the night. "There we are. I do apologize." He gave me a slight bow and then walked away without a glance back.

My heart tore in two as I knew what it had cost him to give up that dance. For me. For Aunt Maude. For his uncle's business.

What did Alec ever get?

The duke was watching me closely, so I mustered my wits and offered him a shaky smile. "I would be honored to dance the first dance with you."

"And the last, if you please." His voice was even, unemotional, but his eyes continued to study me as if he was searching for something. Was he trying to ascertain if I would one day murder him? The thought was ludicrous, but then, so were the rumors Gallagher had told me.

"Of course." I wrote his name on the first and last lines.

Aunt Maude and Lady Mandeville joined us, each curtseying before the duke.

"Your Grace," Aunt Maude said, "I do hope you'll join us for the dinner party we're hosting two nights from now."

He had already been invited and accepted, but this was the reassurance Aunt Maude needed. We still didn't know if the prince would come, but if the duke would be there, surely that had to count for something.

He gave Aunt Maude a slight bow. "I will be there."

Her face filled with relief, but she hid it well. "We will be honored to have you."

The orchestra began to tune their instruments, so the duke offered me his arm. "Shall we?"

I accepted and allowed him to escort me into the ballroom.

Louise Garfield stood in the same spot where the duke had left her. She lifted her nose, just enough to tell me that she didn't care if the duke had come to me, but I knew the truth. I could see it in her angry eyes.

The duke did not hesitate but brought me to the dance floor as the strains of the first dance of the evening filled the room. With elegant ease, he began to twirl me around the ballroom.

Somewhere, at some time, someone had taught him to dance, and he was good at it.

There were so many things I wanted to ask him about the rumors I'd heard. Alec said it was true his mother had murdered his father—but what about the other dukes before him?

"What do you want to ask me?" he said.

I lifted my eyebrows, shocked at how astute he was.

"Don't feign innocence." His voice was steady. "I'm certain you've been asking around about me, and you've learned shocking things that are bothering you. Come right out and ask me, and let's get it over with."

I took a deep breath. If he was going to be straightforward with me, I would be straightforward with him. "Is it true that your mother murdered your father?"

I got right to the heart of the scandal, and I could see it pierced his soul to hear the question. But he squared his shoulders and nodded. "She did." He clenched his jaw, and it caused the scar on his face to tighten. "Come out with the rest of it, or would you like me to just tell you all the sordid details?"

"You told me to ask, so I am asking."

"Then ask."

"Is it true that the two previous dukes before him, and the duchess before that, were all murdered?"

He looked away from me, storm clouds in his eyes. "Some of them came to questionable ends, but there is no proof they were all murdered."

My eyebrows rose high. "They all met untimely deaths?"

"Yes."

I stared at him as my feet faltered.

He continued to dance, overlooking my missteps.

"Is that why people say the castle is haunted?" I asked, just above a whisper.

"Yes."

"And because the first duchess roams the moors at night, crying out for vengeance?"

He gave me a look. "I've never heard her."

"Because you're not one of the duchesses. Only the duchesses hear her wailing. Did your mother ever hear her?"

The duke was silent as he stared at me.

My eyes opened wide. "She did?"

"I do not speak of my mother." His jaw clenched again.

We circled the room, and I gathered my courage to ask him another question. "Did you see the newspapers today?"

"I did."

"And does it bother you that I'm not Mrs. Hill's niece?"

"You are her heir, correct?"

"Yes."

"That's all that matters."

His words pierced my heart this time. All he cared about was the money. Of course.

But before the dance ended, I decided to ask the last burning question on my mind. "What makes you think your story will be any different from the previous dukes'?"

As the music ended and we came to a stop, he stared down at me. "I've accepted my fate. I am the 5th Duke of Severton, chosen by God to bear the title and all that comes with it."

"And what of my fate?"

"That is in your own hands."

A shiver ran up my spine as he gave me a bow and turned away.

Alec approached as I stared at the back of the duke.

Was my fate in my own hands?

21

The two days following Lady Randolph Churchill's ball were chaotic at 7 Buckingham Gate. Aunt Maude insisted that she and I oversee every detail of the dinner, and she had changed her mind several times, which always meant more work for everyone.

Lady Mandeville had sent word the morning after the Churchills' ball that the prince still intended to dine with us, and word of that had quickly spread throughout town. We had not received any notes of regret from the others who had previously responded that they were coming, and Aunt Maude was confident that all would continue as we hoped.

I wasn't so sure. I couldn't shake the unsettled feeling in my stomach about the duke.

And worse, no matter how much I tried not to think about Alec, he was always on my mind. He was the first thought I had each morning and the last thought I had before I fell asleep. I searched for him whenever I entered a room and was disappointed if he wasn't there.

Even when I slept, my dreams had been full of him.

What would I do when he left?

I'd accepted that it would be better to just get married to the duke and be done with it. The sooner it was over, the sooner I could put Alec behind me and face the inevitable future at Pickering Castle, ghosts and all.

Yet the very thought filled me with such sadness, I wanted to weep.

"Mrs. Hill has saved the very best dress for tonight," Gallagher said as she walked out of my dressing room with a beautiful white gown that had sparkling rhinestones sewn into the design. It was a stunning dress, and I was certain Aunt Maude had spent a fortune on it.

I was once again reminded that if this scheme didn't work, Alec's business would suffer. I couldn't live with myself if all his hard work and sacrifice were for nothing.

Gallagher had styled my hair high on my head and placed a narrow diamond tiara of flowers and ivy around it.

After the gown was on, Gallagher stood back and admired me. "You look like a duchess, miss."

I took a deep breath at the thought.

After putting on my long white gloves, I left my room. The dinner would start soon, and our guests were set to arrive. Lady Mandeville would be the first, and she'd warned us the prince would probably be the last.

As I walked down the final set of stairs, I found Alec, Aunt Maude, and Lady Mandeville standing in the foyer.

All three looked up at me at the same moment, but it was only Alec I watched.

Placing my hand on the railing, I walked gracefully down the stairs, my feelings all mixed up inside me. I wanted to throw myself into Alec's arms and feel his love. At the same time, I wanted to run back to my room and weep.

The longing in his eyes was so keen and palpable, I wondered how I had ever convinced myself it wasn't there. Tears threatened and I had to blink them back.

Alec stepped forward, as if he wasn't aware of Aunt Maude or Lady Mandeville, and offered me his arm. He didn't need to speak. Neither of us did. His eyes conveyed everything.

"You look stunning, my dear," Lady Mandeville said as Alec escorted me to her side. "The prince will be so taken with you."

"I've heard he has quite the reputation," Aunt Maude warned, "so don't let him take too much."

"Aunt Maude," Alec protested.

Embarrassment made my skin crawl. I'd heard the prince was a philanderer and had several mistresses. His wife knew of his indiscretions and turned a blind eye. Would he really proposition me?

The house smelled of fresh-cut flowers, and a small orchestra ensemble had been brought in from Paris to play dinner music. Aunt Maude and Lady Mandeville had thought of everything. There were two menus, one in French for the prince and his retinue, and the other in English for everyone else. A French chef had been hired, and he'd prepared all the prince's favorite foods, including *tartelettes aux fraises*, a delicious strawberry dessert.

Lady Mandeville handed me a bouquet of lilies of the valley and whispered, "The prince loves how they smell."

I hadn't had time to be nervous before now, but I was suddenly overwhelmed with anxiety. Of all the events I'd attended thus far, this was the pinnacle moment, even more important than meeting the queen. I needed to impress the prince and entertain him for several hours.

"And remember," Lady Mandeville said to Aunt Maude. "If you see the prince drumming his fingers on the table, that means he's bored, and that is every hostesses nightmare."

Aunt Maude nodded gravely.

The doorbell chimed and Rodgers went to answer it.

Aunt Maude and Lady Mandeville stepped into place, and Alec and I followed suit.

Over the next hour, we greeted our guests, including the Duke of Severton. There would be thirty people in all, including four who would come with the prince. Princess Alexandra had sent her regrets, but Lady Mandeville said that it was common and nothing to worry about. It was the prince we needed to win over.

Finally, after the rest of the dinner party was assembled, Rodgers opened the front door and the prince stood on the stoop, his retinue behind him.

He wasn't a handsome man, but he exuded confidence and importance.

Everyone in the large foyer bowed or curtseyed as he stepped over the threshold.

I held my breath as I offered a deep curtsey, wondering if he remembered me from the drawing room presentation.

"Thank you for inviting me to your home, Mrs. Hill," the prince said as he stopped in front of her. "I'm always keen to meet Lady Mandeville's American friends."

"It is our honor, Your Royal Highness," Aunt Maude said as she rose. "I don't believe you've met my nephew, Mr. Alexander Paxton-Hill."

Alec bowed before the prince. "How do you do?"

"How do you do."

"And, of course," Aunt Maude continued, "you must remember my niece, Miss Clara Hill."

When I slowly rose from my curtsey, the prince was watching me as he had done in the drawing room presentation.

"I believe my mother called her breathtaking," he said, curiosity shining from his gaze. "And I quite agree."

"Thank you, Your Royal Highness."

The atmosphere in the foyer shifted as everyone began to look at me with renewed interest.

All because the prince had complimented me.

I slowly let out the breath I'd been holding all evening.

It seemed my aunt and uncle's attempt to foil our plans had not succeeded.

As I stood there, with everyone looking at me in a new light, I realized the truth had finally been revealed. They knew I came from an impoverished background, and yet, because of the prince's approval, and the duke's continued interest, none of it seemed to matter to them.

When Lady Mandeville and Aunt Maude motioned for the prince to meet some of the guests in attendance, Alec turned to me, a smile in his eyes.

"No matter what any of these people think of you," he whispered. "Your identity is not in the circumstances of your birth, or where you were raised, or even in the prince's acceptance of you. It's in who God says you are. He sees you, values you, and calls you His own. I hope you'll start to believe that in God's eyes, you're more than a duchess. You are the daughter of a King."

Tears gathered in my eyes, and I had to blink them away.

The duke approached and Alec stepped back. I didn't want him to go. He filled my heart with peace and joy. From the moment I'd met him, he'd seen me for who I was—in the best possible way, even if I had doubted it at times. The duke would never visit Five Points or meet my aunt and uncle and cousins. He would never truly know me like Alec knew me. Because the truth was, my past, for better or worse, was a part of who I was today. And Alec was right; it didn't matter what anyone thought. Only God's opinion mattered, and I was no less worthy of His love than anyone else.

"May I escort you into dinner?" the duke asked, offering me his arm.

Alec glanced in our direction but then pointedly looked away. I didn't blame him—if the roles were reversed, it would tear my heart out to see him with another woman.

I took the duke's arm. My lot had been cast, and this was the life I had promised Aunt Maude I would seek when we came to England. I would have to make the best of it, come what may.

The dining room had been transformed into a floral garden. Richly scented rose bouquets filled each corner, while white orchids spilled from satin bags hung on the corners of the table. In the center of the long table, low-lying bouquets of a variety of flowers covered the vast expanse. The orchestra played softly as the dinner guests entered the room and found their place cards.

"You have the seat of honor, Your Royal Highness," Aunt Maude said to the prince. "At the head of the table."

He acknowledged her comment and found his seat.

Since Lady Mandeville was the highest-ranking woman in the room, her place card was positioned to his right, and the second-highest-ranked woman in the room was to the prince's left.

I was seated farther down the table from him.

"Miss Hill?" the prince said. "Would you sit next to me?"

Everyone turned to look at me as embarrassment warmed my cheeks. "Of course, Your Royal Highness."

"You don't mind, do you, Lady Fitzgerald?" he asked the woman to his left.

She looked like she did mind, but who could argue with the prince?

Lady Fitzgerald and I switched seats, placing me between the prince and the Duke of Severton.

"Ah," the prince said to me, squinting as if he was trying to get a closer look. "That's better."

The duke held out my chair and then took the spot next to me as all the other men found their seats.

"I'm honored, Your Royal Highness." I was also leery, given his reputation. Why had he asked me to sit next to him when protocol dictated the seating arrangements?

Fifteen footmen appeared from the butler's pantry door, steaming bowls of soup in their white gloved hands. One of them placed a bowl in front of the prince first, and then the rest of us were served.

"I'm very curious about you, Miss Hill," the prince said, lifting his spoon from the table. "You seem to have taken the London season by storm in such a short amount of time. Where are you from?"

With all pretense gone, I could tell him the truth. "New York City. I was raised in a neighborhood called Five Points."

He frowned as he dipped his spoon into the soup, signaling for the rest of us to begin eating. "I've never heard of the place."

"Not many have. It's quite unpleasant and most people choose to avoid it."

"Quite so." He took a sip of the tomato bisque and raised his eyebrows in delight. "Delicious."

Aunt Maude was at the other end of the table, but I saw her watching closely. Not only did the meal need to go off without a hitch, but we could not bore him, with the food or the conversation.

"I learned from the newspapers that you were adopted by Mrs. Hill," he continued. "Is that true?"

"Yes, just recently."

"Fascinating. I rarely hear of an adult being adopted. Is that an American thing?"

"I couldn't say."

"And your parents?" he asked, his gaze filled with avid interest.

How did I explain my parents?

"I was given to my aunt and uncle as an infant, Your Highness. I'm afraid I know very little about my parents."

"How unfortunate." He frowned. "Were you born in New York?"

"No." This, at least, was easy to explain. "I was born right here in London but left soon after. I've come home, in a way."

He no longer seemed merely interested, his curiosity going deeper. "And your aunt and uncle took you to New York?"

"Yes." I tasted my soup, and it was warm and tangy on my tongue. I was about to include the duke in the conversation when the prince posed another question.

"What does your uncle do for a living?"

Question after question kept his attention on me for most of the meal. Lady Mandeville had said he enjoyed American women, and it was apparent that she was right. He asked me about America, about my childhood growing up in tenement housing, and how I had come to live with Aunt Maude. Not once did he drum his fingers on the table.

The meal lasted for two hours, and rarely did I have the opportunity to talk to the duke. He sat quietly to my left, eating his meal. He did not engage in conversation with the woman to his left, though she made several attempts.

"I very much enjoyed my visit to America in 1860," the prince said. "I was only eighteen years old, but it made a lasting impression. I do believe I was the first British monarch to visit North America. I'm thankful I went before the War Between the States, or I might never have gone."

He recounted his trip, arriving in Newfoundland, touring Canada, and then visiting the United States, including a tour of President George Washington's home at Mount Vernon. I had never been to any of the places he mentioned, except New York City. But I listened with rapt attention. He was a great orator and he loved it when I asked him questions.

"You really must see Chicago," he said to me. "That's in Illinois."

I nodded, though I didn't tell him I was aware of where Chicago was located.

"You really are remarkably beautiful," he said, abruptly changing the subject and leaning on the armrest to get a good look at me.

My neck grew warm under his scrutiny, but I tried not to squirm and look uncomfortable. All the rumors about his infidelity filled my mind.

He glanced at the Duke of Severton for the first time. "Is this the young man you plan to marry?"

Surprised at the bold comment, I shared a look with the duke, but neither of us spoke.

"You would make a strikingly handsome couple." The prince put his napkin on his plate. "I approve, wholeheartedly, of making her a duchess. But, Severton, you mustn't take this jewel to your drafty castle until we've all had the opportunity to enjoy her company. Do you hear me?"

The duke looked bewildered for a moment. It was the first time I'd seen his well-built façade crack. "But I must return home as soon as possible," he said. "There is ledger work to be done, crops to manage, tenant farmers to oversee. Not to mention the work that needs to be done on the castle."

The prince waved his hand. "Go back to Ravenscar and do what needs to be done but leave Miss Hill here. We've only just begun to know each other, and I will not let her go easily."

"Your Royal Highness," I protested. "The duke and I have only just met. He has not proposed and I have not accepted."

"He will," the prince said. "I'll see it's done before the end of the month—or even the end of this week. At a ball he hosts, no less. You must become a duchess, my dear. But I will not let him take you away."

I glanced at the duke and then caught Alec's eye. He was sitting on the other side of the table, close enough that he could hear our conversation. I think *everyone* heard our conversation, as the noise in the room quieted.

It was hard to read Alec's expression, but I sensed that he wanted to be anywhere else but here.

And I wanted to join him.

The prince left after the meal ended and the guests slowly took their leave, as well. The whole event was a magnificent success, with the prince asking when we would receive him again.

Finally, it was just the duke left. He had silently waited, and when the others were gone, Aunt Maude and Lady Mandeville made an excuse to go into the front drawing room and Alec said good night and went upstairs.

For the first time, the duke and I were completely alone together.

"Thank you for the evening," the duke said to me as we stood near the door.

"I want to apologize for the prince's comments—"

"There's no need." He interrupted me. "He was not wrong. I am in need of a duchess, and I would like to return to Pickering Castle as soon as possible. I can't abide playing games or wasting time. I intend to ask for your hand in marriage and there is no use pretending otherwise. But now that the prince is involved, I will be forced to host a ball, though I loathe and despise such things."

"I'm so sorry."

"It isn't your fault." He gave a slight bow. "Please be on the lookout for an invitation soon."

"Of course."

"Good night, Miss Hill."

"Good night, Your Grace."

With those final words, he left 7 Buckingham Gate.

Aunt Maude and Lady Mandeville rushed out of the drawing room, their faces aglow with success.

"Did I just hear the duke make his intentions known?" Lady Mandeville asked.

"I believe he did."

For the first time since I'd met her, Aunt Maude cheered. It was undignified and unladylike, but it was raw and honest and full of victory.

And it made me angrier than it should have.

"*And* he's hosting a ball!" Aunt Maude said. "Oh, how Mrs. Garfield will fume!"

As Aunt Maude and Lady Mandeville reentered the drawing room to celebrate their victory, I slowly walked up the stairs, my heart so heavy, I was afraid it might stop beating altogether.

There was a small sitting room on the second level, and it had been empty each time I'd passed it, but tonight, a light burned bright under the door.

I paused on my way to the second set of stairs that would take me to my room, almost certain I knew who I would find inside. I wanted to be with Alec, to have his reassurance, even if he had none to give. Though I knew it was incredibly foolish.

Slowly, I opened the door to the sitting room.

Alec stood by the window, looking out on to Buckingham Palace Road.

"Is he gone?" he asked.

"Yes."

"Did he propose?"

"No." I took a deep breath. "But he plans to."

I closed the door behind me and took a tentative step toward him. "I'm sorry, Alec."

"Why?" He let the curtain fall back into place and then turned to face me. "You've done nothing wrong, Keira. I'm the one who should apologize. I know you don't want to marry him and live on the coastal moors. In an old castle with nothing but the ghosts of the past for companions. I'm the one to blame. I should have stopped Aunt Maude on the very first day."

"You couldn't, even if you had wanted to. And I didn't know better."

"I should have tried harder." He paused. "If you are truly unhappy, I will live with the guilt of it all my days."

"I won't be unhappy," I tried to promise him as tears stung my eyes, because it wasn't true. "I'll be far away from the city, living a solitary life like I always dreamed." My voice caught. "Even if it's not quite how I imagined. I'll find a way to survive. I always have." I couldn't stop the tears, and they fell unashamedly down my cheeks.

He stepped toward me and drew me into his arms. "Please don't cry."

I clung to him as more tears fell. “I love you, Alec,” I whispered, unable to hold it in any longer, knowing I couldn’t utter the truth once I was engaged to the duke.

He held me tighter but didn’t speak.

I pulled back, but when I did, my heart tore in two.

Alec’s eyes were red from the tears he had not shed, and when he met my gaze, his hands came up and gently cradled my face.

My tears fell harder as I shook my head.

“I love you, too,” he whispered. “With all my heart and soul.”

And then Alec kissed me. It was nothing like the chaste kiss on Christmas evening. This kiss was months in the making. Passion and pain mingled with love as he deepened the kiss, until I was breathless.

He kissed my lips and then my cheeks, and my nose, and finished with a kiss so achingly tender on my forehead, I was afraid I would never breathe again.

When he pulled me into an embrace, he said, "What will we do?”

I held the lapels of his jacket, my cheek pressed against his chest and simply wept.

22

For the first time in a long time, Aunt Maude let me rest. The success of the previous week had put her in a good mood, and she had not demanded that we go riding, or pay calls, or visit one of the many museums in London.

It could not have come at a better time, because after last night's kiss, and the words I'd longed to give and receive had passed between Alec and me, I felt more wretched than ever. To know such love and passion existed between us and not be able to bask in the glow of God's greatest gift, was torture.

Gallagher had helped me dress in a simple pink day gown, and I sat on the window seat in my room, looking out at the back side of Buckingham Palace. The street was congested with carriages and people. Overhead, the sky was a brilliant blue, and sunshine bathed the city in a golden hue.

If things had been different, and my parents had been able to marry, it was strange to think I might have grown up in London. This place that seemed so foreign would feel like home and I wouldn't be thinking about New York as much. More importantly, I would probably never have met Alec, and this gaping hole inside me would not exist.

Tears fell down my cheeks, and I had to wipe them away again. Would I ever stop crying?

Gallagher had come in with a lunch tray when I had not gone down to eat, and with it, she had brought a white envelope with the duke's seal. He had scheduled a ball for Thursday evening, just six days away. Six days until I would be bound to him, his family, and his history, forever. Because once an engagement was agreed upon, there was no way to break it without a scandal and, perhaps, a lawsuit.

I had put the envelope inside the desk, not wanting to see it and be reminded of all I was about to lose.

With a sigh, I moved away from the window and paced, restlessly, across the room. Somewhere in the house, Alec was probably just as miserable. Part of me wanted to find him, to enjoy each stolen moment while we could, before I was engaged. But the other part knew it was foolish and disingenuous to the duke. I owed it to him and our future attempt at happiness to stay away from Alec.

Gallagher returned for the lunch tray, though I had hardly touched a thing. Just before she stepped out of the room, she paused.

"Mr. Paxton-Hill has booked tickets home to America," she said to me, her voice low and sympathetic. "The tickets were purchased this morning. His valet told me they were going to leave as early as tomorrow, but Mrs. Hill caught wind of it and made him postpone until the day after the duke's ball."

I sank onto the trunk at the foot of my imposing bed. I didn't blame Alec for wanting to leave immediately, but I also couldn't imagine him going away and never seeing him again. How would I survive all that was to come without him? He'd seen me through the worst of my journey with Aunt Maude so far.

"I'm not one to gossip," Gallagher assured me, "but I also know—" She paused. "I also know he's special to you."

"Thank you, Gallagher."

She nodded and then left the room.

I closed my eyes, knowing I needed to face the reality of Alec leaving, but I didn't have the strength. Everything had happened so quickly once we arrived in England. I was still trying to make sense of it all.

I thought I would have more time.

A book tried to beckon me, though I had no ability to concentrate. I'd written to Imogen and Patrick, but those letters were already posted. My only consolation was that once I was married to the duke, I would have my own allowance, and I could send help back to my younger cousins.

My bedchamber door burst open, and I jumped.

Gallagher appeared, her eyes wide. "The prince is here, and he's asked to speak to you, privately."

"What?" I hadn't heard her correctly. What would the prince be doing back so soon?

"The Prince of Wales—he's here. In the front drawing room. Mrs. Hill received him, but when she called me to come and get you, she said: 'His Royal Highness would like to speak to Miss Hill privately.' That's what she said."

"The prince?" I could hardly believe it. I wanted to ask her why he had come, but Gallagher would have less insight than me.

"Would you like to change?" she asked me.

"I don't think I should keep the prince waiting." I glanced in the mirror and made sure I didn't look like a blubbering mess. My eyes were a little red and puffy, but nothing too appalling.

I pinched my cheeks and blinked a few times, though there was nothing to be done about it.

My heart was pounding as I left my room and walked down the two flights of stairs to the main floor. Why in the world would the prince want to see me? According to Lady Mandeville, it was rare that he would make an unannounced call, unless he was very close friends with the person he was visiting.

I paused as my foot stopped on the bottom step.

Had the prince come to proposition me, as I had feared? How would I tactfully refuse him? *Could* someone refuse him?

I was more nervous than ever before as I walked across the wide foyer and stopped at the drawing room door. It had been left open, and I saw Aunt Maude and the prince sitting on the sofas, across from one another.

The Prince of Wales was dressed in a simple suit, nothing fancy or out of the ordinary. His side whiskers had been trimmed and he was freshly shaved.

They turned to look at me when I arrived, and they both rose to their feet.

"Your Royal Highness," I said, dropping into a curtsey. "To what do I owe this pleasure?"

Except, it wasn't a pleasure to have him there. It felt somewhat like a nightmare.

"Good morning, Miss Hill. I've come to have a word with you, if I may."

"I'll step out," Aunt Maude said, nodding in his direction as she moved toward the door.

I moved out of her way, but she gave me a warning look, as if cautioning me not to ruin anything.

Without another word, she closed the drawing room door, leaving me alone with the prince.

He watched me as I crossed the room to take a seat. My legs were so weak, I wasn't sure I would reach the sofa. I tried not to cower under the weight of his stare, but it was more intense than last night.

"Pardon me," he said, "but ever since I saw you at the drawing room presentation, there is something about you that is so familiar. It startled me when I saw you for the first time, and then last night it intrigued me. But this morning, I'm at a loss."

We were facing each other, with the tea table between us.

"Won't you have a seat?" I asked in a feeble voice.

He sat on the sofa, seeming almost unaware of it as he continued to regard me.

I also lowered myself, thankful for something solid to anchor myself to.

"You are probably wondering why I asked you so many questions last night," he said.

"I thought—" I paused, my lips and mouth suddenly dry. "You were friendly," I finished in a lame voice.

He scooted forward to the edge of the sofa. "You remind me of someone, Miss Hill, and at first, I thought it was a mere coincidence at the drawing room presentation, and then last night, I began to suspect it was more than coincidence with the answers you gave me."

I frowned.

He took a deep breath. "I'm almost afraid to ask, worried that the answer will confirm what I suspect—and terrified it won't."

I shook my head, at a loss.

"Does the name—" He paused and swallowed. "Does the name Nellie O'Day bear any meaning to you?"

The world felt like it tipped on its side for a moment as I stared at him. I'd never told anyone the name of my mother, except Aunt Maude and Alec.

"How? How do you know about her?" I whispered.

Something shifted in his eyes. Shock, then vulnerability, and then joy. "Is she your mother, Miss Hill?"

I nodded, unable to find my voice again.

He smiled and shook his head as wonder filled his face. "You look just like her."

"You—you know my mother?"

"I loved your mother, once upon a time." He took a deep breath. "I still love your mother."

"But how do you know her?" Had he really come all this way to simply inquire about her? Why hadn't he asked me last night? He could have done it in a way that would not have drawn too much attention. He'd asked me so many other questions.

He stood and paced to the fireplace.

For a moment, I wasn't sure what to do. If he rose, did I have to rise? I wasn't certain my legs would even hold me up at the moment.

"I met her in Ireland, when I was nineteen. After I returned home from my trip to America, I was sent to Curragh Camp in County Kildare for military training. A group of friends and I went to a play that was traveling through town, and it was there that I first saw Nellie on stage. It was love at first sight."

The Prince of Wales had been in love with my mother? I could hardly believe it.

"I returned the next night, and then the next. Finally, one of my comrades told Nellie that I was in attendance and would like to meet her." His face brightened with the look of a young man in love. "She was even more beautiful off the stage than on. We spent several days together, and they were the happiest of my life. When her acting troupe planned to leave County Kildare, I begged her to stay, and she did."

He continued to pace as he spoke, but I remained motionless.

"The scandal made its way back to England," he said, stopping at the fireplace and leaning his arm against the mantel, lost in his memories. "My father came to Curragh Camp to speak to me. We spent hours walking around the parade ground, in the rain. He impressed upon me the great magnitude of responsibilities on my shoulders and my need to be morally astute." He scoffed. "I could never live up to my parents' expectations, so I had long stopped trying."

He turned to look at me. "That night, after walking with my father, I returned to my quarters and Nellie told me she was with child." His voice was low and serious. "With you, I suspect."

My heart stopped beating as I stared at him. I opened my mouth to ask him to repeat himself, but nothing came out.

"I have never been happier in my life than in that moment," he said. "Your mother was beside herself, knowing that nothing could come of our love, but I wanted to convince her otherwise. I went out the next day and found a gold locket, which I had engraved with our initials. N for Nellie and B for Bertie. I gave it to her and told her I would abdicate the throne for her and for you. I was never more serious in my life."

He paused as emotions overcame him, and he looked away for a moment.

"When I woke up the next morning, she was gone, and I've never spoken to her since." He shook his head. "I had someone locate her just after you were born. She'd come to England to live with her brother, Charlie, and give birth to her daughter—our daughter. But after that, both of you disappeared and I've never heard a word about you since. You can imagine my great surprise to see you walk into the drawing room, almost identical to the woman I knew as a younger person, so long ago."

I was still staring at him, dumbfounded by his confession.

I was the daughter of the Prince of Wales—the *granddaughter* of the Queen of England? Me? Keira O'Day from Five Points?

He studied me for a moment, swallowing. "Say something, Miss Hill, please."

My mouth cracked open, but I could think of nothing to say that would make sense.

"I know this is quite a shock," he said. "But I had to know for certain."

"I—I have the locket," I whispered.

He blinked, surprised. "You do?"

"In my room. My mother gave it to my uncle to give to me." I frowned. "But I thought your name was Albert."

"It is." He smiled. "But my friends and family call me Bertie."

I finally rose, unsure what else to do. I felt stronger than I anticipated. "What does all of this mean?"

"To me, it means the world. To everyone else? Nothing." He walked over to me. "No one must ever know the truth. This will be a secret between you, me, and your mother. One we will need to take to the grave, I'm afraid. The scandal it would cause, especially now that you've created quite a stir in London society, would be detrimental to the health of the monarchy—and my mother." He sighed. "I'm afraid she already holds me accountable for my father's death. You see, after he visited me and returned to England, he became very ill and died not long after. My mother believes it was from the strain caused by the scandal, and all the time we walked together in the rain. If that scandal came back to haunt her, it would be catastrophic."

I nodded. "I understand."

"Good." He lowered his eyes. "Do you—do you know where your mother might be?"

I wanted to tell him, but it would not be wise. Both of them were married now. Nothing good would come of them seeing each other again. So, I decided to keep another secret, to protect the people I loved.

"I'm sorry."

He nodded. "Just as well." He lifted his gaze again. "Thank you, Miss Hill—"

"It's Clara—or, at least, that's what Aunt Maude calls me. My mother named me Keira."

"Keira." He smiled. "That's beautiful."

"Thank you."

He stood for a moment, smiling at me. And then he said, "I should probably take my leave. I wouldn't want Mrs. Hill, or anyone else, asking too many questions about my visit." He grew very serious. "I must beg your promise that you won't speak about any of this to anyone."

"I promise." Though it would be excruciating not to tell Alec. "What should I say about your visit?"

"Tell them that I am quite taken with you and that I wanted to further our friendship." He grinned. "I'm the prince. No one can ask me why."

I smiled at him.

He started to walk toward the door but paused. "May I call on you again, Keira?"

I nodded. "I would like that."

"Very good." He smiled and then bowed, in a gesture that was reserved only for royalty. "It was a pleasure, my dear."

I was speechless again as he left the drawing room, and when Aunt Maude entered a few moments later, I was still standing where he'd left me.

"Well?" she asked. "What was that all about?"

Blinking, I only shook my head. "He said he was taken with me and wanted to further our friendship."

Aunt Maude frowned, but then her face softened. "And what the prince wants, the prince gets."

Except he had wanted Nellie, and he had wanted me, and he got neither.

23

Over the following week, grief filled me every time I thought about Alec's inevitable departure, and my engagement to the duke, but joy took me by surprise when I thought about the prince's visit—my father's visit. It had changed everything to know who he was, and who my family members were.

For the first time since I'd agreed to Aunt Maude's wild plans, I realized that I was more than qualified to become a real duchess. And I spent a lot of time thinking through my childhood, wondering if there had been some part of me that always knew the truth. Uncle Charlie and Aunt Orla had called me Duchess growing up, but it had been a derogatory term, meant to shame me. I was certain they had no idea who my father was, but had there been a part of my bearing or mannerisms that had reflected the truth?

I would never know, so I tried not to dwell on it. The world would never know the truth, but it was enough that I knew. For the first time in my life, I had a sense of belonging, of understanding who I was and where I came from. Both of my parents had told me they wanted to keep me. My father had even said he would have abdicated the throne for me and my mother. But Nellie had chosen the wisest course for the sake of England, even if it had been a great sacrifice for the three of us to bear.

As I stood in the front drawing room at 7 Buckingham Gate, dressed in the gown I would wear to the Duke of Severton's ball, I looked out the window at Buckingham Palace and marveled that God had returned me home. The puzzle pieces of my life were all together now, and I could see the picture in its entirety.

"There you are," Aunt Maude said as she entered the drawing room, resplendent in a Worth gown fit for the mother of a duchess. "Lady Mandeville's carriage will be here shortly. Are you ready?"

I gave her a brief nod but looked behind her to see if Alec had joined us.

He hadn't.

"You look lovely, Clara," Aunt Maude said as she pulled on her long white gloves. "I like what Gallagher did with your hair."

"Thank you." I touched the coiffure, my own gloves making it impossible to feel the strands of hair. I was wearing a new silver and diamond tiara that Aunt Maude had purchased from Garrard & Company, the royal jeweler. It was a simple tiara, but it was beautiful, and, I was certain, expensive. What would Alec think when he saw the extravagant purchase?

Aunt Maude and I had done a lot of shopping that week. She was convinced that once the duke and I were engaged, the revenue boost from their hotels would more than compensate for her expenditures.

I wasn't so sure, but then again, I didn't understand how those things worked.

"Are you ready, my dear?" she asked me.

"Is Alec not coming?"

She pursed her lips and lifted her chin. "I do not believe so."

I had not seen him since the kiss in the sitting room. He had spent all his time at White's, leaving in the morning before I woke up and coming in late at night, after I was in bed. His avoidance was almost worse than anything else.

"Why did he stay in London if he wasn't going to attend the ball tonight?" I asked, trying not to let my disappointment show.

She briefly closed her eyes in irritation. "I asked him to stay until the morning after the ball, assuming he would *attend* the ball, but when I spoke to him this morning, he told me, in no uncertain terms, that he would not." She sighed. "And because I did not want to argue with him, I chose to let it go. We really don't need him anymore."

Her words stung. Aunt Maude had used both Alec and me to get what she wanted. The way she so easily threw people aside when she was done with them was alarming and heartless. The longer I knew her, the less I wanted to be like her.

Through the window, I saw Lady Mandeville's carriage arrive out front.

My insides were twisted in knots as I took a deep breath. When I returned to the house tonight, I would be engaged to the Duke of Severton—to Ames Welby. I had seen him on two occasions that week, both at social events we'd attended. Just like before, he and I had shared witty banter, but there was no spark of romance between us. At least, not on my part. He had shared nothing more about his family's scandalous past, or his home at Pickering Castle. I'd resigned myself to the fact that I would learn everything I needed to know about him *after* we were married. A dubious prospect, since I'd be legally and morally bound to him at that point and would have no recourse if the truth was too difficult to bear.

With no time left and nothing else to be done, I followed Aunt Maude out of the drawing room and toward the front door, where Rodgers stood waiting. My gaze went up the stairs, hoping and praying Alec had changed his mind and would join us. Would I even see him before he left in the morning? Would our final parting be that impassioned kiss in the sitting room last week?

Tears threatened, but I forced them back. I couldn't arrive at the duke's ball with red, puffy eyes.

Lady Mandeville was in her carriage, waiting for us.

"Clara, how lovely you look," she said, approval in her gaze as I stepped into the vehicle. "You are meant to be a duchess."

"Thank you," I managed to say, though my throat was dry.

Aunt Maude stepped in next and settled on the seat beside the countess.

"Is Mr. Paxton-Hill not joining us?" Lady Mandeville asked.

"I'm afraid not," Aunt Maude answered, but that was all she would say.

Lady Mandeville raised her eyebrows and looked at me, as if to ask whether I knew anything about Alec's decision.

I offered her a weak smile and shook my head.

The duke's family home was in Belgrave Square, almost too close to Buckingham Palace Road to take the carriage, but it wouldn't be fashionable to walk.

As the carriage clattered over the cobblestones, I looked out the window, admiring the front of Buckingham Palace as we drove by. It was strange and wonderful to think that if my father had been able to marry the woman he loved, I might have grown up there. That I might have stood next to the queen during the drawing room presentations, and that I could have one day inherited the throne.

It was all too much to consider.

"There's something different about you, Clara," Lady Mandeville said as she studied me. "I do believe that the thought of becoming a duchess has caused your shoulders to lift and your bearing to become more regal."

She and Aunt Maude shared a knowing smile, but if they saw a difference in me, it was because I finally understood who I was. It began the night of Aunt Maude's dinner party, when Alec had whispered, *"I hope you'll start to believe that in God's eyes, you're more than a duchess. You are the daughter of a King."* Alec hadn't known and still didn't know the truth. He had meant that I was the daughter of God, the King of Kings. But he had seen me, understood me better than anyone else, and he valued and loved me as Keira O'Day *and* as Clara Day Hill.

If my shoulders had lifted, it wasn't because I was about to become a duchess, or I had learned that my father was the prince. It was because Alec had fallen in love with me, the real me.

The duke's home was not as impressive as some I'd seen, but it was still beautiful and in the heart of one of the most exclusive neighborhoods in London. The sun had just set and the first of the evening stars sparkled in the night sky. A footman appeared to help us out of the carriage, and when the house's front door opened, the butler stood there to greet us.

My heart was pounding hard as I stepped into the duke's townhome, noting the absence of flowers that had graced all the other homes I'd attended parties in this season.

The décor was dated, but the walls looked like they had been freshly painted, and everything was clean. When was the last time this house had been occupied or held a party?

There were several dozen people already in attendance and more carriages had pulled up behind ours. Many people suspected the duke's intentions with this party, and no doubt they wanted to be present as a new duchess was selected. We hadn't known each other long, but Lady Mandeville had assured me that a quick engagement wasn't unusual, especially with American heiresses who were not necessarily marrying for love.

The duke stood near the doorway, his face a mask of disinterest. I couldn't imagine how much he hated this ball, especially since he was so used to the quiet of life at Pickering Castle. How desperate must he be to marry for money? He probably hated himself for giving in to the need. He looked to be in his late twenties or early thirties, so he had put it off for as long as possible, no doubt.

When he caught sight of me, something seemed to relax in him for a moment—probably relieved I'd come—and then he stiffened again.

"Your Grace," I said as I gave him a slight curtsey.

He dipped his head. "Miss Hill, I'm relieved you're here and I didn't go to all this trouble for nothing."

I wanted to tell him I had little choice, but there was no point. "I wouldn't have missed it."

"Good." He nodded toward the drawing room. "The ball will take place in there. I will join you shortly."

"Thank you."

He greeted Aunt Maude and Lady Mandeville as I waited and then the three of us walked into the drawing room.

A dividing wall between the front and back drawing rooms had been removed, as had all the furniture, allowing for an adequate space to dance. A three-piece orchestra was tucked into one corner and here, there were a few bouquets to brighten the room and add a nice scent.

People were chatting as we entered, but many people glanced in my direction, their conversation quieting for a moment. Neither the Garfields nor Lily Parker were in attendance, but Annabelle was there with Lord Devan, her arm wrapped through his, her attention focused solely on him. I only recognized a few people, and most of them were aristocrats.

"The prince is here," Lady Mandeville said in an excited tone. "And he's early!" She smiled at me. "He seems very eager to see you and the duke engaged."

Despite the fact that I knew the prince was my father, or perhaps because of it, I was more nervous around him than ever before. I hadn't seen him since he'd visited to share the truth with me, and I had wondered how I would behave when I saw him again.

He scanned the drawing room, and when his gaze landed on me, he smiled.

I returned the smile, joining the others as I curtseyed.

He approached and stopped in front of me. "I know the duke will want the first dance tonight," he said to me, "but I am asking if you will honor me instead. I have a previous royal engagement to attend and I cannot stay long, I'm afraid."

"Of course." I nodded, wondering what everyone was thinking of his behavior.

Aunt Maude didn't seem curious as she basked in the interest it brought to her from the rest of the room.

The prince offered me his hand and then walked me into the center of the room, though the orchestra had not started to play, and others were forced to move out of the way.

Quickly, the orchestra lifted their instruments and fumbled to begin. Soon they were playing a beautiful waltz, and the prince took me into his arms, dancing me around the ballroom as the guests watched.

"I had hoped to stop by to see you again this week," he said to me.

Thankfully, with the sound of the music drowning out his words, none of the onlookers could hear our conversation.

"I would have liked that."

He turned me a few more times and then said, "You look lovely tonight, Clara. The duke is a lucky man."

I couldn't hide the pain his words caused, though I tried.

"What's wrong?" He frowned. "Don't you want to marry the duke?"

I pressed my lips together and tried to remember to breathe.

"Are you in love with someone else?" he prodded.

Without looking at him, I nodded, trying to keep the tears at bay.

"Tell me about him."

"It doesn't matter." I forced myself to rally. "Aunt Maude needs me to marry the duke."

"Why?"

I found myself telling him all about the hotel situation and Louise Garfield and all the reasons that Aunt Maude had adopted me.

"None of it makes sense to me," I said as I finished, and the music was coming to an end. "But it matters to her and to Alec." My voice caught and I had to look away from him.

"It's Alec, then?" the prince asked.

I could only nod.

The song ended and we came to a stop on the dance floor.

"I'm very sorry," he told me. "I understand more than anyone, for the reasons you might guess."

"I know." I tried to smile. "Thank you."

He returned my smile as I curtseyed to him.

"Whatever you decide," he said, "I hope you will be very happy, Clara."

"Thank you," I said again, knowing that the choice had already been made, and I doubted that I would be happy.

The ball proceeded with few diversions. I danced with the duke, and he asked if he could have the pre-supper dance, as well as the final dance, which would tell the rest of society that we were either engaged or would be soon.

"I would like an opportunity to talk to you during supper," he had said, when he handed me back my dance card. "Alone."

I had nodded, though it was hard to find my voice, knowing why he wanted to talk to me.

The small ballroom had become overly warm, despite the cool evening. My head had started to hurt and the noise from the orchestra, the guests, and the shuffling of feet over the parquet floor were grating on my nerves. The one bright spot had been the prince's dance, but that could not carry me through the rest of the evening.

After dancing with the Earl of Hartford, I glanced at my dance card and saw that there were only two more dances until the duke would have his turn and then we would talk.

Aunt Maude and Lady Mandeville were visiting with a group of women on the edge of the room, and the duke was nowhere to be seen. After our first dance, he had disappeared, and I'd only glimpsed him here and there as the night progressed.

He had danced with no one else.

I glanced around the ballroom to locate Sir Huntington, my next dance partner, when I saw Alec enter.

He had come, and he looked handsome in his formal evening wear.

Butterflies filled my stomach at the sight of him, and I wanted to rush across the room to throw myself into his arms. But I stayed on the dance floor, watching as he searched the room for me.

When he finally saw me, his brown eyes lit up with so many emotions. But overriding them all was pure joy. He looked so happy to see me, it brought tears to my eyes. And the way he openly admired me in my gown sent heat into my cheeks.

"Miss Hill?" Sir Huntington asked as he approached and bowed. "I believe I have this next dance."

I hardly looked at him as I said, "I beg your forgiveness, but I am going to sit this dance out."

Good manners dictated that he bow out gracefully, which he did.

I left him and crossed the ballroom, where Alec was still standing, a smile on his face.

"You came," I said, blinking back my tears.

"I'm sorry I wasn't here earlier." His smile fell and worry suddenly replaced his joy. "Am I too late? Did the duke announce your engagement yet?"

I shook my head. "No, he hasn't."

"May I speak to you? Alone?"

Curiosity made me frown, but I nodded. "Yes, of course." Doors let out to a garden behind the house, and I could see that there were torches lighting a path. "Will the garden do?"

"Anywhere would do," he said, his gaze never leaving my face.

The music started for the next dance, so Alec and I moved around the edge of the room toward the doors. People might see us leaving, but they thought of Alec as my cousin and would think nothing of us being alone together.

Aunt Maude and Lady Mandeville were on the other side of the room, and hopefully they wouldn't see us through the crush of people.

Alec opened the door, and I stepped through, then he closed the door behind us.

The coolness and fresh air were a godsend. Thankfully, the small garden was unoccupied as Alec took my hand and led me away from the door. He walked me to a corner, where a bench awaited, but neither of us sat. The light from a nearby torch didn't quite reach the space, offering us some privacy.

"What is it?" I asked him, breathless.

He turned to me, the happiness returning to his eyes. "I love you, Keira."

I frowned and smiled in quick succession.

"And I don't want you to marry the duke," he continued.

"I don't want to marry him, either," I whispered, my heart beating so hard, I was certain he could hear it. "But—"

"Shh." He put his finger over my lips, his gaze following the motion of his hands. "I want you to marry me, Keira O'Day."

My lips parted under his finger, surprise and confusion warring in my mind. "I don't understand."

He lowered his hand. "The Prince of Wales came to the house this evening and told me I must marry you."

Again, I frowned and then smiled. "What? Why did he do that?"

"He told me that you were in love with me and that it was a royal order to propose to you." He drew me into his arms. "But I told him, not only am I an American and he cannot dictate what I do—but there was no need to force me, because if you would have me, I would marry you tonight."

"Alec," I laughed, still confused, but not fighting him as he wrapped his arms around me. "I don't understand. I thought I didn't have a choice—that you needed me to marry the duke. The hotel—"

"The Prince of Wales made me an offer I can't refuse." He smiled, his gaze slipping down to my lips again. "He said that he wants an invitation to our wedding, and he insists we hold it in Newport, at our hotel, where he intends to stay. After that, he said he will go to New York and stay in one of our hotels there."

"He told you that?" Excitement started to race through me.

"He did, indeed." Alec smiled. "You charmed him, just like you've charmed me and everyone else, and he would do anything for you. Keira, you can't imagine what that will do for our hotels. Everyone will want to stay where the Prince of Wales stayed." He chuckled. "And he's insisting that we rename our Newport hotel The Prince of Wales, in his honor, to remind people for years to come that he graced it with his presence."

My grin could not be contained. My father was giving me the greatest gift of my life. He was giving me the opportunity to marry the person I loved, something that had been denied to him. And Alec wasn't even questioning why.

"So," Alec said, lowering his forehead to mine, "what do you say, Miss Keira O'Day? Will you marry me?"

I wrapped my arms around him, unable to hold back my love any longer. "I will marry you, Mr. Paxton, and love you with every breath God gives me."

He kissed me then, his arms around me, and this time, he held nothing back.

I was going to become Alec's bride, a thought that made me happier than I'd ever been before.

The only thing hindering my joy was the knowledge that I would need to tell the duke...and then Aunt Maude.

24

When Alec and I reentered the ballroom, the duke was standing near the wall, scanning the room. The moment he saw me, relief briefly filled his face, and then his mask of indifference appeared again.

Dread filled my heart at the thought of turning down his proposal. He'd gone to all the trouble and expense to have the ball, and he fully expected my agreement. My only consolation was that there were several other American heiresses in London, looking for a duke, and he would have no trouble finding one who would be his wife.

The duke approached and I glanced at Alec. He offered me an encouraging smile, and I was certain that if he could be there to help me through the difficult conversation, he would be. Unfortunately, I would need to speak to the duke alone. I owed him that much.

"I believe I have this next dance, Miss Hill," he said, hardly looking in Alec's direction.

The Duke of Severton was single-minded. I would give him credit for that. He knew what he wanted, and he was willing to risk everything to get it. Did he really want to marry me, or was he simply set on taking any wife who would give him financial freedom?

I smiled and nodded, though my nerves were making me shake.

When the orchestra ended their current song, the duke offered me his hand. "Shall we?"

Taking the hand he offered, he led me onto the dance floor as we waited for the orchestra to begin.

It felt like an interminable amount of time passed as we waited. Finally, the strains of the next song filled the room, and he took me into his arms.

He was stiff and unyielding, though he was a good dancer. We waltzed around the dance floor, passing others, who watched us with keen interest—Aunt Maude and Lady Mandeville included.

What would they say when they learned I turned down the duke after all their hard work? It was yet another difficult situation Alec and I would have to maneuver through, though we would do it together.

For now, the duke was my problem alone.

"What is bothering you, Miss Hill?" he asked. "Beyond the obvious issue of our impending betrothal."

He was also straightforward and unafraid to address issues, another quality in his favor.

"Would you like to talk about it here, Your Grace? Or wait until we are alone?"

After a moment, he said, "Let's discuss it now. I do not like to wait."

Just as before, the noise from the music and shuffling of feet drowned out the words of the dancers. I could not hear what others were saying, so it was safe to believe they couldn't hear us, either.

I took a deep breath and plunged ahead, knowing there would be no easy way to start. "About the betrothal. I do not want to presume you are going to ask me—"

"It's obvious I am. I would not have gone to the trouble of having this ball if I weren't." The scar across his cheek tightened as he spoke and his dark eyes focused. "What about the betrothal?"

I swallowed my nerves. "I am so sorry, but I cannot accept."

His expression did not change, but he was quiet for a moment, and then he finally said, "I will not beg you to become my wife, Miss Hill. And I'm certain you have your reasons, but it is very inconvenient that you waited until now to give me this answer. Could it not have come sooner, before I was forced to have this ball?"

"I do apologize," I said, feeling horrible. "I was given new information just now that has solidified my decision."

"New information?" He frowned. "About me?"

"No." I quickly shook my head. "About my . . . options." How much was I required to tell him? "I—I am in love with someone else, and until now, there was no opportunity for us to move forward. But he has told me a way, and we are going to take it."

The duke looked toward Alec, still standing by the door. "Mr. Paxton-Hill?"

My heart filled with love, and I said, "Yes."

Again, the duke was silent as we continued our dance. Finally, he said, "I would not want a wife who was in love with another man, and for that reason, I will not ask you to marry me, Miss Hill."

He was saving his pride. There had been no proposal offered and none accepted—or rejected. He might be disappointed or even angry, but a gentleman would act with grace.

Even a brooding, secretive duke from the coastal moors.

"I am very sorry for the inconvenience," I said. "Had we known of this path before, we would have spared you the expense and time, Your Grace."

"No need to say anything more, Miss Hill."

"Perhaps—" I paused. "May I suggest you inquire after Miss Lily Parker? She is eager to get away from London, and..." I let the words trail away. Under his gruff exterior and brooding good looks, the duke and Lily were after the same thing. A quiet life in the country.

He did not respond, but I could see that my suggestion was being considered.

We remained quiet for the rest of the dance, and when it was almost over, he said, "I think it best that Mr. Paxton-Hill take my place on your dance card for the final waltz of the evening."

"Thank you."

"No need to thank me. And I believe I will go into supper alone, if you please."

"Yes, of course."

When the dance ended, he gave me a slight bow and then left me on the dance floor, his head held high.

Almost every eye in the ballroom was on me as he walked away and I could see questioning glances thrown between the guests. Why hadn't the duke escorted me into supper? What had he been talking to me about? Why did I look so wretched?

Aunt Maude and Lady Mandeville approached, concern etched into their brows.

If I was going to create as little scandal as possible, I would need to remain at the ball until the bitter end. To leave now would only cause tongues to wag all over London. But to stay, I needed to keep Aunt Maude and Lady Mandeville questioning.

"Well?" Aunt Maude asked, her one question summing up a dozen others.

"Nothing," I told her.

"Perhaps he is waiting until the end of the ball," Lady Mandeville said, eyeing the duke's retreating back.

"Alec," Aunt Maude said with surprise as he joined us, "when did you get here?"

"Not long ago," he said, his gaze finding mine, a question in his eyes.

I gave him a faint nod, to let him know all was well.

At least, for the moment.

Soon we would have to break our news to Aunt Maude, and she would not be as easy on me as the duke had been.

After the duke and I did not speak during supper, the others began to whisper among themselves. And when he did not return to the ballroom, even Aunt Maude and Lady Mandeville started to look worried.

Finally, the last dance of the evening arrived, and Alec approached me for his turn.

Those in attendance no longer looked confused, but outright shocked. Not to see Alec and me dancing together, but that the duke was nowhere to be seen. And because he had not reappeared for his own ball, I was the one to take the full brunt of their stares and whispers.

A just punishment for putting him through the ordeal.

When the final dance ended, I had Alec help me get my wraps. We did not wait to thank the duke, who had still not appeared, but simply walked out of the front of his townhome and into the wee hours of the morning.

Carriages were lined up on the street outside and it was easy to find Lady Mandeville's with her family coat of arms painted on the door.

A footman appeared and opened the door for us as Alec helped me inside.

"Now," he said, joining me, "we wait for Aunt Maude and the fight of our lives." He took my hand as he sat next to me, his voice gentle. "It will be a fight I will not give up."

"Nor I." I had come so close to being betrothed to a man I did not love. I would do anything to marry Alec, even if that meant standing up to the woman who had dictated my every move for the past seven months.

It did not take long for her to arrive.

As she and Lady Mandeville stepped into the carriage a few minutes later, Alec let go of my hand. Both women were breathless and confused.

"What in the world happened, Clara?" Aunt Maude demanded even before she was fully seated. "What did you say to the duke?"

I took a deep breath, ready to go to battle. "I simply told him I could not accept his marriage proposal."

Her eyes widened as she stared at me. "Why in heaven's name did you do that?"

"Because I do not love him."

"Did he actually propose?" Lady Mandeville asked, her face filled with just as much shock.

"No, because I told him before he had the chance to ask. I wanted to save his dignity."

"What? Why?" Aunt Maude sputtered. "You knew your role, Clara. You had one job. Why would you throw away all our hard work? You ungrateful—"

"Stop," Alec said, his voice filled with warning. "Keira is not ungrateful. But she could not throw her life away on a man she did not want to marry."

"Keira?" Aunt Maude turned a venomous glare on Alec. "Her name is *Clara*."

"No. Her name is Keira," he said, "and I hope it will soon become Keira Paxton." He took my hand in his again and gave me a smile.

"What?" Aunt Maude almost rose out of her seat, and though it was dark in the carriage, I was certain her face had turned a shade of crimson. "You're both ungrateful! This will be the ruination of us all. How could you do such a thing to me? I've given you everything—"

"You've given me only that which suited your own desires," he said, his voice calm and collected. "And the same with Keira. You've done nothing out of the kindness of your heart, but only what you knew would give you something in return. And you've hurt a lot of people in your wake, Aunt Maude."

She tried to speak, but she was so upset, no words came out.

For her part, Lady Mandeville lowered her eyes and seemed to retreat into the cushions of the carriage seat, probably wishing she was anywhere but here. Anger brimmed in her eyes, too, but it was probably because she was wondering if she would get paid.

"This will ruin us," Aunt Maude finally said in a tight voice. "How could you be so selfish? Both of you? And for what? *Love?*" She said the last word as if it was dirty and undesirable.

"Yes, for love," Alec said, his hand tightening around mine. "But it will not ruin us." He glanced at me. "Keira has so charmed the Prince of Wales that he was the one who demanded that we marry." His smile directed at me was tender. "When he heard that we were in love, and what was at stake, he volunteered to aid us."

"How did he know what was at stake?" Aunt Maude's voice had evened out, though she was still stiff with anger. "And what do you mean he wants to aid us?"

Alec turned back to her. "The Prince of Wales wants us to get married in Newport, and he plans to attend and stay in our hotel. From there, he will travel to New York, where he will stay in one of our hotels in the city. Thereby raising our status and elevating our business. He also wants us to rename our Newport hotel 'The Prince of Wales' in his honor, so people remember his visit for years."

Aunt Maude and Lady Mandeville simply stared at Alec.

Finally, Aunt Maude turned to Lady Mandeville and asked, "Is this normal behavior for the prince?"

"I've never heard of such a thing," she confessed. "It's quite irregular. But—"

"But what?" Aunt Maude demanded.

"The prince loves grand gestures that bring him attention, and he is quite loyal to his friends, so it does not truly surprise me. He often talks of his visit to America and how he'd like to go back one day. It appears he is making plans as we speak."

Aunt Maude no longer looked outraged, but she still seemed doubtful. "Are you telling me the truth, Alec?"

"I have never lied to you before," he said, "and I am not lying now."

"Well"—she gave a pointed look to our hands—"perhaps you haven't lied, but you've clearly kept something a secret from me."

I looked at Alec, and he smiled at me.

"There are some things that cannot stay hidden forever," I told her. "And this is one of them."

He lifted my gloved hand to his lips and placed a kiss there.

"I love Keira," Alec said, turning back to Aunt Maude. "And I would like to marry her, as soon as the prince is able to join us." He took a deep breath. "Do we have your blessing?"

I wasn't sure what we would do if she didn't give it, but there was little that could keep me from marrying Alec.

She looked from me to him, and then back to me.

"I don't know what you did to convince the prince to help you," she said to me, "but it's quite evident that he's fallen under your spell. I am disappointed that you betrayed me this way—however, having the

Prince of Wales as a guest at my niece's wedding will make Mrs. Astor squirm to get invited and will do more for my social status than having you marry the Duke of Severton. So, I will give you my blessing."

Though I was relieved we would not need to fight her any longer, I had determined then and there that I was done bowing to her dictates.

Being adopted was supposed to be an unconditional gift, and I now knew I was worthy of that gift. Not because the Prince of Wales was my father, but because I was the daughter of the King of Kings.

Alec moved a little closer to me on the seat, and I knew that from this day forward, nothing could drive us from one another's side.

25

AUGUST 9, 1883
NEWPORT, RI

Three months after the night of the duke's ball, I stood in one of the drawing rooms at The Prince of Wales Hotel overlooking the Atlantic Ocean in Newport. My heart was so full of wonder, I had to place my hand on my chest to contain it, touching the locket I'd chosen to wear on my wedding day.

"You want to walk me down the aisle?" I asked the prince as I faced him. "What will people say?"

Light streamed into the room through the windows, illuminating his bearded face as he smiled at me. "If I cared what people said about me, I would have no fun at all, my dear."

I returned his smile and recalled what Aunt Maude had said in London. What the prince wanted, the prince would get.

He stood before me in impeccable clothing, a watch chain hanging from his pocket, highlighting his expanding middle. He was the height of fashion.

"I would be proud to have you walk me down the aisle," I said to him.

"Very good." He offered me his arm, about to speak, when he noticed the locket. Pausing, he lifted it and held it tenderly in his large hand. "I never thought I would see this again."

"I wanted to wear it today, to feel close to my mother."

He slowly lowered the locket and met my gaze. "I still cannot believe how much you look like her."

I smiled. It was the greatest compliment.

"Are you ready?" he asked me.

I was wearing a magnificent white silk gown, ordered from the House of Worth in Paris. A stunning train descended from a generous bustle, and long sleeves came down to my wrists. Alec had purchased a beautiful diamond engagement ring for me before we had left London, and it sparkled now in the daytime sun. I had not wanted to wear gloves and cover it, so Aunt Maude had insisted on the long sleeves.

When the prince had first stepped into the room where I waited, he had uttered the same thing his mother, the queen, had said to me in her drawing room presentation. "You are breathtaking, my dear."

I felt lovely today, but the feeling came from within, where Alec had touched my heart. How could I be anything but beautiful when he loved me so well?

A magnificent carriage waited outside for us, with the top down. Aunt Maude was already seated inside, looking very proud and regal as the crowds watched. Dozens of people had been gathering in front of the hotel since morning, hoping to catch a glimpse of the prince. They cheered as we exited the large, yellow building. It was a grand hotel, much larger than I had imagined, with 125 guest suites. A central tower reached eight stories tall, offering panoramic views of the Atlantic Ocean and Newport, and a beautiful covered porch wrapped around the building.

The prince smiled and waved to the people watching as he helped me into the carriage.

"It's so good of you to have come," Aunt Maude said to the prince, though he'd been at the hotel for several days and she'd uttered the sentiment many times.

"I would not have missed this for anything," he said as we settled into the carriage, his loving gaze on me.

As we drove down Bellevue Avenue to the Channing Memorial Church, where Alec would meet us, the crowds continued to line the street, cheering and waving, calling out for the prince to notice them.

I glanced at him, but he didn't seem to mind the attention, and Aunt Maude drank it all in. How odd it felt to be the center of so much interest. I'd spent most of my life trying to blend in to stay safe. But here I was, sitting next to the Prince of Wales, in a fancy carriage, in a parade, on my wedding day.

Ever since our wedding had been announced, and word had spread that the prince was planning to attend, the hotel had been at full capacity. Reservations were booked throughout the next year, as well, and the revenue from all the Hill Hotels had increased. Things were better than we ever hoped or anticipated.

As much as I loved having my father at the wedding, and as excited as I was about marrying Alec, I couldn't wait for the moment when Alec and I were finally alone together. When the cheering crowds had faded and the chaos of the day had died down. He had a surprise planned for our wedding trip and I was eager to see where he would take me.

Two whole weeks to be alone.

I sighed with pleasure just thinking about it.

Several young people waved energetically at me, and I smiled and waved back, and then I caught the prince watching me.

"You could have been a princess," he said, his voice wistful. "And what a princess you would have made."

Aunt Maude smiled indulgently at him, but she had no idea that he spoke the truth.

I could have been a princess, but I was much happier being Keira O'Day from Five Points, then recently of Newport and New York City. Before I'd met Aunt Maude, I had thought God had forgotten about me or never knew I existed. Yet looking over the course of my life, I could see His hand at work, even in the difficult times. Everything had happened for a reason, and He had been gracious and faithful to reveal it to me.

And now here I sat, about to become Alec's bride. If my story had played out differently, I might never have met him and what a great loss that would have been.

"I almost forgot to tell you," the prince said as he continued to watch me. "The Duke of Severton took a bride not long after you left London."

"Oh?" I wasn't surprised. "Who did he marry?"

"Miss Lily Parker."

My eyes widened, because this *was* surprising. Had my suggestion been enough to persuade him? There were no two people less alike. He was dark and brooding, full of secrets. She was bright and vivacious, with not an ounce of guile. Even their looks were opposite. She was like daytime and he the night.

But, they both wanted the same thing, and I prayed they would be very happy together.

"He's much younger than the other men her mother was parading in front of her," Aunt Maude said. "Good for her."

I smiled at Aunt Maude, knowing that if the prince had not agreed to come to our wedding, she would not have been happy for Lily.

There were more crowds when we reached the church, perhaps five hundred people standing outside, and a great cheer erupted when we pulled up to the front doors.

The prince waved at them, his royal upbringing evident in the way he lazily lifted his arm in greeting. I had not asked him what his mother or wife thought about his trip to America, or what they would say when they learned he had walked me down the aisle. Those would be his troubles to bear, and I had a feeling he bore them often.

I, on the other hand, was not used to the crowds of people, and felt out of place as I waved back at them.

After the prince stepped out of the carriage, he helped Aunt Maude down and then it was my turn. I carried a bouquet of simple white roses, with white satin ribbons trailing from the stems. I held them in one hand as he took my other and helped me step down.

Aunt Maude assisted me with my train, allowing it to sweep behind me as I faced the large, granite church, with its impossibly tall steeple and beautiful stained-glass windows.

"I'll go inside and get seated," Aunt Maude said as she came around the front and placed a kiss on my cheek. "You look lovely."

"Thank you."

Ever since the night of the duke's ball, things had shifted between us. Any time she started to demand or dictate how things should be done, Alec or I had to remind her that she was no longer in control. If Alec was going to run the business, and I was going to be his wife, he would become the head of the family. Not Aunt Maude.

She had slowly accepted her position, though she still pushed back from time to time. Thankfully, she'd been so busy with her social life since returning to New York, she'd had little time to try to manipulate or cajole us.

Mrs. Caroline Schermerhorn Astor had paid a call on Aunt Maude within days of our arrival home from England. Word had quickly spread that the Prince of Wales would attend our wedding, and Mrs. Astor did not want to be left out. She had accepted an invitation for a dinner party thrown in our honor at Aunt Maude's home shortly thereafter and when it was time for the wedding invitations to go out, one had proudly arrived at Mrs. Astor's home. She was waiting inside with all the other wealthy and influential people Aunt Maude had invited.

Alec and I had also invited Uncle Charlie and Aunt Orla, hoping to mend hurt feelings, but they had sent their regrets, written in Uncle Charlie's handwriting. I suspected that it was Aunt Orla, and not Uncle Charlie, who had sold our story to *Town Topics*, but I held no ill will toward either of them. They'd raised me as best as they could, even if there had been pain along the way.

What surprised me the most in Uncle Charlie's letter was his note of thanks to Alec for sending them a monthly stipend. They had moved away from Mulberry Street and were living in a nicer home close to Fiona. Imogen and Patrick were attending school and only the adults were doing piecework.

I thought I couldn't love Alec more until that moment.

As I prepared to enter the church, the invitation foremost in my mind was the one I'd sent to my mother. I very much doubted she would attend. But, perhaps, it was better that way.

The prince offered me his arm, and I took it with ease. It had been nice to have a few days in his company before the wedding. He still felt like a stranger, and intimidated me because he was the prince, but I was starting to grow more comfortable in his presence. I wasn't sure when I would see him again after today, but he'd told me he was great at correspondence and expected long, newsy letters from me as often as I could write them. In return, I should expect the same from him.

I took his arm, and we stepped into the narthex. The double doors into the nave were closed, but upon our entry, two footmen opened them, and we moved into place.

The "Bridal Chorus" began on the organ as the congregants rose to their feet.

My heart beat a quick, joyful pace as the prince patted my hand, laying on his arm.

"I'm very happy for you, Keira," he said. "And I'm honored to be here today. I wish things could have been different, but I'm glad they've ended this way."

"Thank you, for everything." I smiled at him, my eyes awash in tears. "This is all because of you."

"I think you had something to do with it." He laughed and let out a contented sigh. "I'm only thankful I could be here to witness it. Shall we?"

With a nod, he began to lead me down the aisle.

Pleasant smiles greeted me as we walked toward the altar. I knew some of those in attendance, but many of them were strangers from Mrs. Astor's Four Hundred. Alec's parents were in attendance, and I had instantly loved them, quickly understanding from whom Alec had inherited his kindness. They'd been at the hotel all week and we'd spent many happy hours together.

As I was about to turn my gaze to the front, where Alec would be waiting, one face caught my attention, and I paused in surprise.

My mother had come.

I quickly regained my footing, but it was enough for the prince to look at me and then follow my line of sight.

I knew the moment he saw her, because he, too, faltered.

Nellie O'Day.

The three of us were in the same place together for the first time.

We continued toward the altar. There would be an opportunity for them to reunite later, if they so chose. But it was not my place to be there, or to even know if they did.

For now, all I wanted to think about was Alec.

He stood at the front of the church, attired in a beautifully tailored black suit, his face shining with love.

I broke into a smile as all other thoughts faded away.

The top was down as Alec and I sat side by side in the small buggy, a trunk strapped to the back. He managed the single horse with ease. My arm was wrapped around his and my head was on his shoulder.

Our wedding breakfast was held at The Prince of Wales Hotel dining room, and the prince had given a speech to a round of cheers. My mother sat in the back of the room, alone, watching us with pride. I had wanted to go to her, but there were so many things pressing for my attention, and when I finally had the opportunity, she and the prince were no longer in the dining room.

I smiled to myself now, as the sun warmed my face and the clip-clop of the horse's hooves pressed against the dirt road hugging the edge of the cliff. To my right, the Atlantic Ocean spread out in all its glory, a gateway to both my past and future. Someday, I would return to England with Alec and perhaps I could get to know both my mother and father better.

For now, I was quite content to focus on my husband.

"Where are you taking me?" I asked Alec in a lazy sort of voice, not eager to be anywhere in particular, except by his side.

"You'll know the moment we arrive," he said with a smile in his voice.

We'd only been married for six hours, but it felt as if I'd known him my whole life. Being Alec's wife was the most natural thing I'd ever done. And our journey had only just begun.

"Do you think Aunt Maude is angry that we've decided to use your family name?" I asked him.

"Perhaps," he sighed. "But she'll have to get used to it." He kissed the top of my head. "I like being Mr. and Mrs. Paxton. And I am especially fond of the name Keira Paxton."

I snuggled closer to him, thankful I'd taken the time to have Gallagher help me change into a traveling gown, though I still wore my locket and I'd attached the flower broach Alec had given me for Christmas. He'd also changed clothes with the help of his valet, and he was wearing the silk flower he'd purchased from me outside the Metropolitan Opera House. We'd left the breakfast before anyone was the wiser. No doubt Aunt Maude and the prince would do a fabulous job entertaining people for as long as they wanted to stay. And since many of them were renting rooms at the hotel, the party might continue all day.

Seagulls dipped and glided over the ocean as a gentle breeze tossed the tendrils of hair around my face. I'd quickly fallen in love with Newport and had decided that whenever Alec needed to travel there for work, I would come with him. We had our own suite of rooms in the hotel, and they would very much feel like home.

We were only five miles north of Newport when he turned off the road and onto a tree-covered lane. The sunlight dappled the horse as we plodded forward, and I looked up at Alec with anticipation.

"Soon," he said, kissing me gently on the lips.

A small stone bridge appeared up ahead, and I sat straight, delighted by a bubbling brook that ran beneath it. He paused on the bridge to give me the opportunity to watch it for a moment and then tapped the reins against the horse's back to continue.

We hadn't gone far when the path turned to the right and the trees opened to reveal a little stone cottage, tucked into the woods. The stream meandered around it, disappearing into the trees. Just behind the cottage was a stone foot bridge and beyond that was an orchard.

Alec pulled the reins and the horse stopped. But he wasn't looking at the enchanting scene before us. He was watching me.

"What do you think?" he asked me. "It's almost as far as you can get from the Mississippi River, and it's not really a cabin, but it's near a stream and it's all yours, Keira."

I tore my gaze away from the cottage and studied him. "All mine?"

"Every last square inch. It's my wedding gift to you, and whenever we come to Newport for business, we won't need to stay at the noisy hotel, if you don't want. We can get away here, just the two of us, and enjoy a little solitude. There are no neighbors for miles—and even if someone wanted to build a house here, they couldn't, because I've purchased several hundred acres around the cottage."

"Alec." I shook my head in amazement and disbelief.

He grinned. "You don't need to say anything. Your face is telling me everything I need to know." He kissed me, tenderly and thoroughly, leaving me breathless.

"Let's go inside," he said. "I have another surprise for you."

"How did you manage all of this?" I asked.

"I've had my eye on this cottage for a long time, even before I met you. And when you described your dream to me, long ago in Aunt Maude's library, I began to picture this moment." He chuckled. "I still can't believe God orchestrated all of this, but I will spend the rest of my life thanking Him."

He tethered the horse to a hitching post with a mounting block nearby, and after securing the reins, he helped me use the mounting block to step down from the buggy.

The cottage appeared bigger up close, with large windows on either side of the front door and a second floor under the eaves above. A small porch covered the front of the house and Alec held my hand as we stepped onto it.

Two rocking chairs graced the porch, with a view of the stream nearby. I smiled, picturing us there in the evenings, Alec reading aloud as I spent my time sewing. I'd already laid plans for an organization to provide clothing for children in the tenements. In my spare time, I hoped to sew dresses for little girls who grew up like me, and I'd already found others who wanted to help. I couldn't wait to return to New York and set our plans into action—but first, our honeymoon.

After he opened the front door, he surprised me by lifting me into his arms to carry me over the threshold.

I laughed in delight and wrapped my arms around his shoulders. He kissed me again, using any opportunity he could, and I relished it.

The main room of the cottage was just as charming as the rest, with rustic timber and a stone fireplace. But it was the far wall that made me inhale with pleasure.

"A library!" I told him.

He grinned and set me on my feet. "Everywhere we live, I want us to be surrounded by books."

"Alec." I shook my head as I walked across the wide-plank floor to the shelves that covered the wall. "There are so many of them."

"Not quite as many as in Aunt Maude's home, but these are my personal books. I had my parents bring them from Boston when they came, and Mother helped me organize them."

"Your parents have been here?"

"Many times this week. Mother helped to decorate, just enough for us to be comfortable these next two weeks, but I told her that you would want to put the finishing touches on everything."

I turned to look at the main room, noting the crisp white curtains hanging at the windows and the fresh bouquet of wildflowers on the table. There were pictures of Alec as a child on the mantel and comfortable rugs on the floors.

"It's perfect," I said, turning back to look at him. "I wouldn't change a thing. Thank you, Alec."

He wrapped his arms around me, his tenderness and love making me feel cherished. "I'm the one who should be thankful. I've never known such happiness in my life, Keira, and it's all because of you."

"Then it seems we're a good pair, because I feel the same way about you, my love."

It was so quiet and peaceful in our little cottage, and there was no one and nothing to bother us.

So this time, when Alec kissed me, nothing stopped him.

To Dance with a Duke

The Dollar Princesses Series Continues...

One determined heiress. Five stubborn brothers. A crumbling castle—and a house party that could change everything. For those who love *Seven Brides for Seven Brothers.*

In 1883, Ames Welby, the Duke of Severton, is desperate. His ancestral home is falling apart, his tenant farmers are starving, and his family name is tainted by a mysterious scandal that keeps people away. With no fortune and no time, he does the unthinkable—marries for money. But Lily Parker, the American heiress he weds in haste, is no pampered socialite. She's practical, passionate, and has a plan to restore Pickering Castle—and the reputation of the five reclusive Welby brothers.

Inspired by her love of matchmaking and her longing for connection, Lily invites four eligible young women to a summer house party, hoping to spark romance and rebuild the family's future. What follows is a whirlwind of mischief, mismatched couples, and unexpected love. But when Lily's belief in true love clashes with Ames's fear of family curses and social ruin, their fragile marriage is put to the ultimate test.

As storms rage and secrets unravel, Ames must decide: will he fight for his legacy—or for the woman who's taught him that love is the most daring risk of all?

Historical Note

If you've read some of my other books, you've probably realized that I love the Gilded Age (the time period not the show by Julian Fellowes—although, I'm a fan of that, as well). The term was coined by Mark Twain who wrote a book in 1873 titled *The Gilded Age: A Tale of Today*. It implied that the worst parts of American society were covered by a thin veneer of wealthy individuals who made the whole country appear successful. Though, underneath, things weren't pretty. This period started around the end of the American Civil War in the late 1860s, during Reconstruction, and ended around 1900, when the Progressive Era began.

In England, this time period is often referred to as the Victorian Era, so named for Queen Victoria who reigned from 1837 to 1901.

It was a time of great change around the world, when a vast divide was created between the rich and the poor. In 1848, there were only about 50 households that were worth over 1 million dollars (about $40 million today), but by the end of the Gilded Age, there were over 4,000 households that boasted that wealth. People like the Vanderbilts, the Rockefellers, Andrew Carnegie, and J.P. Morgan skyrocketed to fame because of their fortunes, and many of the new money, or *nouveaux riches,* moved to New York City to show off their wealth and gain social status. They came from all over the country, and even as far away as the gold fields of California.

Upon arrival in New York, they quickly learned that, even though they were richer than most of the "old money" families, they were not welcome in society.

Caroline Schermerhorn Astor was one of the scions of New York society, her ancestry reaching back to some of the original Dutch settlers to the city. She had inherited money from her father, but it was her husband, William Backhouse Astor, Jr., whose family provided their great wealth. She had a fashionable home built at 350 5th Avenue, where the Empire State Building now sits, and she became the arbiter of society when new money was moving in.

According to Mrs. Astor and her friend, Mr. Ward McAllister, to be "included" in society, a person's wealth had to be inherited and not earned. Because of this, hundreds of wealthy families were left "out."

It's hard to imagine, but in that day and age, social standing meant everything. Many people believed that if you were wealthy, it was your duty to show it off to the world. So, while the husbands were busy making the money, their wives were busy spending it. Because of this, New York society was chiefly controlled by the women, and almost everything about it was tailored to their specifications.

Many "new money" women took matters into their own hands. When they were shunned by Mrs. Astor and her Four Hundred, they took their marriageable daughters to Europe, mainly France and England. There, the British aristocracy was desperate for money. With the expansion of the American Midwest after the Civil War, crops were in abundance and flooded the market. Because of this, farmland in Europe was now worth very little, and most of the landowners were aristocrats. With no money, their homes were falling into disrepair, and many were going into serious financial debt, some being forced to sell priceless family heirlooms to cover living expenses.

In walks the heiresses.

With a daughter now married to a duke, earl, marquess, or even a baron, a wealthy woman could return to New York and expect to be included in Mrs. Astor's circle. How could Mrs. Astor *not* invite the mother of a duchess to tea? And, in exchange for this title, the heiress's family would provide a handsome dowry to cover the lord's debts and living expenses.

It's hard to know how many of these marriages occurred, but most sources agree it was over two hundred, and they brought over twenty-five billion dollars in American money with them. A fabulous book about this era is called *The Husband Hunters: American Heiresses Who Married into the British Aristocracy*, by Anne de Courcy. The audiobook is especially engaging!

Like many of my historical novels, I had to make a change or two for ease of reading. One liberty I took with the timeline was when the Metropolitan Opera House opened in New York City, which was October 1883—not October 1882 as I say in the story. Another is that Lady Consuelo Mandeville was Alva Vanderbilt's childhood friend, and Alva threw her fancy dress ball in Consuelo's honor, which meant Lady Mandeville was in New York at the time of my story, not in London, awaiting Keira's arrival.

Another bit of history I used was a well-documented event in the Prince of Wales's life. In 1861, at the age of nineteen, he went to Curragh Camp in County Kildare, for ten weeks of military training. While there, his friends reportedly brought an English actress for him to meet. Her name was Nellie Clifden, and she was close to his age. His appointment book from that time has cryptic notes about being with NC on September 6th, 9th, and 11th.

This information got back to his parents, Queen Victoria and Prince Albert, and they were not pleased. His father traveled to Ireland to address the issue, and just as I state in the book, they walked for hours in the rain. When his father returned to England, he became sick and died a couple months later. The queen blamed her son for the death of his father, claiming the stress of the situation killed him. At the time, it was believed that he had Typhoid, but modern historians think he might have suffered from Crohn's Disease.

When I learned this history about the prince, it made me wonder what would have happened if he and Nellie had produced a child...and thus, *To Love a Lady* was born.

By Gabrielle Meyer

If you've enjoyed *To Love a Lady*, be sure to look for these other books by Gabrielle Meyer

The Ladies of the Wilderness Series

Timeless Series

American Brides Series

GabrielleMeyer.com/books

About the Author

Gabrielle Meyer is a Christy-Award winning, bestselling author of over 45 books, including her popular Timeless Series. For over a decade, she worked for the Minnesota Historical Society, where she became passionate about sharing real history through the art of storytelling. She continues to write fictional stories inspired by real people, places, and events. Gabrielle currently lives in central Minnesota on the banks of the upper Mississippi River with her husband and four children. You can learn more about Gabrielle and her books at www.gabriellemeyer.com.

Connect with Gabrielle on Facebook, Instagram, and Goodreads!

Printed in Dunstable, United Kingdom

76805993R00190